Other Books By
David Michael Slater

Picture Books
Cheese Louise!
The Ring Bear
Jacques & Spock
Ned Loses His Head
Missy Swiss!
The Sharpest Tool In The Shed
Comin' Through
7 Ate 9
Flour Girl
The Bored Book
Ned Breaks His Heart
Ned's Nose Is Running
On The Level
A Wrench In The Works
Milo & The Monster
Battle Of The Books

The Sacred Books Series
The Book Of Nonsense

Adult Fiction
Selfless
The Book Of Letters (Collection)

The Book of Knowledge

SACRED BOOKS

VOLUME II

David Michael Slater

Children's Brains are Yummy Books
Austin, Texas

Children's Brains are Yummy Books
www.childrensbrainsareyummy.com

The Book of Knowledge
Sacred Books, Volume II

ISBN (10): 1-933767-02-2
ISBN (13): 978-1-933767-02-4

Library of Congress CIP data available.

Printed in the United States by Versa Press.
Job # J09-05810
Printed on 60# Husky Recycled

For Heidi,
the apple of my eye.

Contents

Part I: The Infinite

not a bad man 1

food for thought 15

dirty words 24

picker 30

monsters 46

more monsters 65

mixed (up) messages 75

burning desires 98

burning desires (part ii) 112

(not) breaking and entering 119

family matters 136

departures and arrivals 144

tired ideas 161

still not a bad man 180

Part II: The Library

a bit of a situation 201

like father, like son 210

like father, like daughter 224

the good life 234

black spider, brown cow 246

the cleaning party 267

study buddy 285

school daze 300

seventh period .317

major big news 340

a little help 360

news travels fast 380

in the dark 392

not a bad man ii 403

earth-shattering news 421

falling in love 430

another mother 433

the difference a day makes 441

afterword 449

I have always imagined Paradise
to be a kind of library.

— Jorge Luis Borges —

Part I

The Infinite

not a bad man

"Adem Tarik—Adem Tarik—I—I—"

"Here we go again," Dexter groaned, turning away from the early morning TV talk show he'd been half watching. He shot an irritated look at his sleeping father.

"But it sounded like he was going to say something else that time," said Daphna. She hauled herself off the couch where she'd been slumped next to her twin brother and approached Milton's bedside. A glimmer of hope had surfaced in her speckled green eyes, but it faded when he failed to say anything further. Daphna huffed and spun around.

"We need to do something, Dex," she said. "I think we should wake Dad and tell him everything we know."

Dexter's own speckled green eyes were skeptical. "But what if that makes him worse?"

"How could it?" Daphna said. "Besides, Latty will be here with his stuff from home soon. You've seen how paranoid she's getting again. Who knows when we'll get another chance."

Dex closed his eyes. Up until a second ago, everything had been going fine. The trip from the hospital to the Multnomah Village Rest and Rehabilitation Home had gone off without a hitch, and more importantly without a single mention of the name Adem Tarik.

Milton, worn out by the transfer, passed out the second he'd been settled into bed, so the twins had seized the opportunity to plop onto the room's guest couch and veg out in front of the TV. For nearly five minutes, they'd been able to relax. But now that exasperating name was on their father's lips again.

The surgeon who'd operated on Milton's broken hip said he'd been raving the name when the ambulance attendants wheeled him into the emergency room. He'd stopped when they'd administered the anesthetic before surgery but then started again as soon as it wore off. Back in his hospital room, groggy on pain medication, Milton had kept it up, repeating the name over and over for almost two days.

"Adem—Tarik," Milton mumbled once again. Dex rolled his eyes, but Daphna put a finger to her lips. "I—I am—" their father continued, "I am not a bad man—I—Adem—"

"Hey!" Dex exclaimed, "that's what I told you he said in his sleep at home!"

Daphna thought a moment. "He's been blaming himself for being a bad father," she said, "for neglecting us all the time to scout books, like Latty told us. Or maybe he feels badly for not catching Mom before she fell in the caves."

"Or maybe there's something else going on," Dex protested. "We still have no idea why his mattress is stuffed with all that money. What if he did something illegal and feels bad about it?"

Daphna sighed. No matter how much they learned there was always something left to baffle them. But the suggestion that their father did something criminal was unacceptable.

"If you think that, Dexter," Daphna snapped, "then you should want to tell him what we know so we can get to the bottom of it!"

Dex rubbed his temples, which hurt. His whole face still hurt: black eye, split lip and all.

"Oh, all right," he said. "But he's probably going to have us committed."

Daphna shrugged, then turned back to her father, eager to ease his mind. She touched his shoulder with a gentle hand. "Dad?"

Milton stirred, opened his brown speckled eyes partway under their bristly gray brows and murmured, "Um?"

"Dad, Dex and I want to talk to you. We want to tell you something."

"Hmrm," Milton murmured, drifting away already.

"We know the truth about Mom," Dex declared, now standing behind his sister.

At this, Milton seemed to rouse himself. His eyes weren't exactly lucid, but they were all the way open now. "What's that?" he asked.

Daphna felt sure they were doing the right thing. "Well—" she said, suddenly at a loss where to begin. "First we need to tell you about that book you were trying to get back from the ABC, the new shop in the Village that burned down. Where that disgusting boy knocked you—"

"Daphna," Milton said, "there are no new bookshops anywhere in Portland." Then he fell straight back to sleep.

Daphna's face fell. He still didn't remember, and he wasn't pretending. A psychologist who'd come to talk with Milton in the hospital confirmed that. Her first theory was that he was suffering from an "adjustment disorder," which meant he was having trouble dealing with a recent traumatic event. Being thrown to the ground by a giant, demented red-eyed boy certainly qualified, especially since he wound up with a broken hip and a concussion.

But when she learned that Milton had forgotten not only the incident, but also the events leading up to it, she said something more significant was involved. Given the endless repeating, it was more than likely something connected to Adem Tarik.

Latty seemed to confirm this by sharing the history of the name. Dex and Daphna were there for the whole conversation.

"For many years," Latty told the psychologist, "the twins' mother, Shimona, had a rare book business in Israel. I was her manager and best friend." Latty stopped a moment, struggling to maintain her composure, but then she went on.

. "Just a few months after the kids were born," she said, "someone calling himself 'Adem Tarik' phoned me with a tip. He said some caves had been discovered in Eastern Turkey containing books far older than the oldest ever found before. He even gave directions. We didn't know what to make of it, of course, but we also didn't see the harm in investigating.

"Shimona, Milton and I dropped the kids off with a friend and flew right there. We followed the instructions to a small opening in the side of some craggy hills not too far from a town called Malatya. We'd been inside for less than fifteen minutes when the caves started collapsing. There was an earthquake. Apparently, they're quite common in that area."

Latty acknowledged that going into those caves so unprepared, even going into that region of Turkey, was foolish and irresponsible, but she said bookscouts often did foolish and irresponsible things in pursuit of rare finds.

Of course, since becoming Milton's business manager and taking over as caretaker for the twins—and turning into the biggest worry-wart of all time—Latty never did anything remotely like that again. She told the psychologist it was a miracle any of them survived.

"Milton escaped with a blow to the head," she said, "and I collected more nasty bruises and cuts than I could count. But Shimona—she fell into a chasm."

Other than Adem Tarik's involvement, none of this was news to the twins. But there was more.

"We were all together," Latty continued, choking up, "the three of us, making our way along the edge of some sort of crevasse. Milton lit a torch, but he dropped it over the ledge when the earthquake hit."

"Go on," the psychologist gently urged.

"Milton got a hold of Shimona and me, but the cave floor was shifting," Latty said. "We all got thrown in different directions, and the next thing I knew, I was on the ground bleeding and couldn't get up. Some light was coming down from high above, and I could see Shimona. Her arms flailed as she teetered on the edge. It was so loud and chaotic and terrifying with rocks falling everywhere." Latty's voice went almost too low to hear.

"Milton desperately tried to keep Shimona from falling," she whispered. "He grabbed at her. It looked like he got a hold of her again, but then he was knocked out and—she fell."

Dexter and Daphna had both found

themselves staring at the shiny white hospital floor while they absorbed these alarming details, details clearly kept from them all their lives.

Latty, struggling to hold back tears, managed to explain that when Milton came to, he didn't remember anything that had happened.

"Of course he was told that Shimona was lost," she said, "but I didn't tell him how I'd seen him fail to save her. I never told anyone. It was so horrible. I dream about it all the time. Those flailing arms. It was like they were trying to fly."

Since Milton had hit his head on the sidewalk when he'd broken his hip the other day, the psychologist suggested that the blow might've triggered the return of all his dreadful memories, and that he was fighting to fend them off.

But when Daphna mentioned he'd been acting oddly even before he'd hit his head, she proposed that Milton's memories had begun returning on their own, something that eventually happened to a lot of people with traumatic events in their past. The new blow might actually be holding them back.

The psychologist asked Latty if there had been something Milton was planning or looking forward to way back before the accident in the caves, something that happened recently.

Latty nodded. "Well," she sniffed, "in the caves, before the quake, we were talking about time, about how quickly it goes, and about how little time parents have before their children are grown. Milton felt quite strongly that children are really only children for thirteen years. He was telling us how he wasn't going to waste any of them and that he'd have a great celebration for the kids on their thirteenth birthday. And all this recent craziness did seem to have started when he came back just before they turned thirteen."

"That's very likely it, then," the psychologist decided. "The approach of the kids' birthday may well have punctured a hole in the dam blocking this memory. I'd say the second hit on the head is clogging that hole. If I'm right, it'll be a temporary obstruction. It's only a matter of time before the whole dam breaks."

That's when Latty's dam broke. She began sobbing outright. She said she'd do anything to save Milton from having to relive such horrors, but the psychologist said he had to if he was ever going to have a genuinely healthy mental life.

Latty was obviously not convinced, but she didn't press the issue. Instead, she walked unsteadily from the room with a wad of tissues pressed to her streaming green eyes. When she'd gone, the psychologist warned the twins not to pressure their father to see things clearly too soon.

All of this ran back through Daphna's mind as she looked at her sleeping father, but she decided a little pressure wouldn't kill him.

"Dad, think," she said, nudging him until an eye opened to her. "You brought a strange book back from Turkey. It was beaten up and full of all kinds of crazy nonsense words—"

"Daphna," Milton said, producing a patient but wavering smile. "I haven't gone to Turkey yet." His eyes, pools of foggy brown now, closed again.

"Dad," Dexter said, "Mom isn't who you thought she was." Milton didn't reply to this, but he looked at his son.

"You're probably going to think we're a couple of lunatics," Dex said, "but she was old, really old—not like you, I mean." Dexter hesitated, then took the plunge. "She was thousands of years old."

"Listen, Dad," Daphna put in, trying not to give her father a chance to tell them to stop being ridiculous, "I know this is all going to sound very weird. Just promise you won't say anything until we're totally done. Promise?"

"But it sounded like Dex said she was thous—"

"Promise, Dad!"

"Okay, okay, I promise."

"Good," Daphna sighed. "Right. Mom was part of a group, a Council, searching for a book," she said quickly, "a book that could someday show people a dangerous language called the First Tongue." Then she added, almost under her breath, "It's also called The Language of Power. It's sort of magic—or mystical, I guess."

Milton raised an eyebrow, but at least he was listening.

Daphna forged ahead. "See, there's this ancient myth that says God read from a book to create the world. No one knows if that's true," she hastened to add. "Anyway, it doesn't matter. The point is that people got hold of the book, early people. They used it to do good things for a while but then mostly to wipe each other out. But the book kept getting lost, and eventually everyone forgot the language because it's really hard to learn and use."

"But somebody found the book again," said Dex. "And he tried to train a group of thirty-six child geniuses to use the language to bring peace to the world. Mom was one of them! He wanted to make Heaven on Earth. He taught the kids a Word to give themselves super long lives so they could do it."

"But there was a war between the kids," Daphna said, "The War of Words it was—"

Milton's eyes fluttered. They were losing him.

"Anyway," Daphna hurried, "the book wound up getting changed. The words, on the pages, they change. Mom did it to hide the language! So the Words of Power can still show up on the pages, but maybe not for a million years."

The eyes were nearly closed.

"But it got lost again!" Daphna shouted. "That's why Mom was searching for it! To destroy it once and for all!"

"But she finally gave up on the search to marry you!" Dex cried.

"But then she got that call that made you guys go to Turkey!"

"Dad! You found the book on your trip to Turkey this summer! That was it! That was the book everyone was searching for!"

"But you gave it to Asterius Rash at the ABC! He made you! He was the kid who started the war!"

"But we got it back before the store burned down!"

"But Emmet, his assistant, got it from us in the park after all the Councilors were killed! They lived here! He's the one who knocked you—Wait!" Daphna cried, realizing she had some proof of all this. She fumbled her mother's letter out of her pocket.

"Dad!" she nearly screamed, "we found the letter Mom wrote before she went to the caves! Here, read it!"

But Milton didn't take the crumpled paper. He only looked at it trembling in Daphna's hand for a moment. Then he regarded his breathless children with a thoughtful expression.

The twins looked at their father with wide,

anxious eyes, waiting.

"You kids," Milton finally said. He chuckled, and then he fell asleep.

Dex and Daphna tried to shake him awake, but he was beyond reach. "Adem Tarik—" he muttered when they gave up and fell back onto the couch, "I am not a bad man—"

food for thought

The twins slouched back over to the couch, sank into it and stared up dumbly at the TV. But no sooner had they settled in, a voice called out urgently from the hall, "I'm coming! I'm coming!"

Latty.

She swept into the room, a frizzy-haired whirlwind of stress hauling two suitcases, a grocery sack and a shoulder bag with Milton's laptop.

"Oh, thank goodness!" she said after casting a worried look over both the twins and their fitfully sleeping father. "It looks like you two have everything under control—not that I'm surprised, mind you." Without a moment's pause, she began unpacking and toting neat piles of clothes to the various dressers around the room.

"We're fine," Daphna said, trying not to sound as annoyed as she felt. "You said you weren't going to worry about us so much anymore."

"I know," Latty conceded. "But it's not easy."

"He started up again," Dexter said, dejectedly. "And now he keeps trying to say he isn't a 'bad man.'"

Latty looked horrified. "Listen, kids," she said, dropping some shirts into a drawer. "I don't care what that psychologist said. I don't think it would be good for your father to remember. I remember, and I've never put what happened behind me. It was too terrible. What I wouldn't give to forget what I saw! I don't think we should say anything, anything at all, about Adem Tarik, or the accident, or your mother. I'm so afraid of what it'll do to him if it all comes back. Listen, I want you both to promise me something."

"What?" both Dex and Daphna nervously asked.

"I can't be here twenty-four hours a day," Latty said. "When you kids are here, and he starts in on this—this nonsense, I want you to discourage it. Change the subject if he starts to realize what he's talking about. Okay?"

"Ah—" Daphna said.

"Um—" was the best Dex could do.

"Promise me."

"Okay," two sheepish voices agreed.

Latty tried to smile. "Everything will be okay," she said. "I'm sure Milton Adam Wax will be up and at 'em in no time at all." But this was hardly convincing from a world-champion fretter.

"What do you think Dad'll do?" Dexter asked, hoping both to change the subject and get some answers. "I mean, if he gives up scouting?"

"He's gonna need a job, right?" Daphna added.

Latty glanced at Milton, then turned to the twins. "I feel like it's been a million years since we've had a good talk," she whispered. "This feels good. I can see you two are worried about this, and that just proves you really aren't children anymore. I don't think we should have these silly secrets."

The twins snapped to attention. "Secrets?"

"Your father's a fine bookscout," Latty said quietly, "but he never made much money at it, not very often anyway. It never really mattered, though. The truth is, he's rich."

"What?" both twins gasped.

"Your mother left him a great deal more money than you ever knew."

"How much more?" Daphna demanded.

"Much more," Latty admitted. "If he didn't want to, your father wouldn't have to work for the rest of his life. And I'm taken care of too, kids, so don't worry about me either."

In fact, the twins had never wondered how Latty was paid. They just knew she'd loved their mother like a sister and felt partly responsible for her death since she took that phone call and then got off so easy in the caves.

The Waxes lived in a fairly small house with nothing too fancy inside, though they had some expensive antiques. Multnomah Village was a nice neighborhood, but it was hardly the West Hills. There was rarely money for things like fashionable clothes, or techno-gadgets, or summer camps—

"We're rich?" Daphna cried. She felt blindsided.

"Shhh!" Latty warned.

"You mean," Dex demanded, feeling blindsided, too, "that he's been ditching us all these years to search for books when he didn't even have to?"

"Please!" Latty begged. But she could see she had some serious explaining to do.

"Fine," she sighed. "Let's talk. But not here. We'll go to the cafeteria."

The trio sat down at the end of a long table. At the sight of all the food, the twins realized they were famished, but they were even hungrier for the truth.

"Okay," Latty said, sounding rather businesslike, "first, Daphna: since you were a little girl, you've had an amazing will to succeed at everything you do. It's who you are. It's your very identity, and Milton never wanted to sabotage that. Wealth can change a person, honey. It's not uncommon at all."

For once Daphna was not the least bit pleased to be praised. This was completely unsatisfying.

Latty turned to Dexter despite the look on Daphna's face. "Dex," she said, "rest assured, your father never intended to neglect you. He was not wasting his time. The reason he spent the last thirteen years scouting has nothing to do with finding actual books."

"What do you mean?" Dex asked, trying

to ignore the obvious implication that, unlike his stupendous sister, he had no will to succeed. Maybe he didn't, but that made it no less insulting.

"I mean," Latty said, "that what your father has been doing for thirteen years is searching for Adem Tarik."

'But—but, why?" Daphna asked.

"At first he was searching for information," Latty explained. "And I certainly couldn't blame him. In fact, I helped him. There were unanswered questions. No one ever took credit for discovering those caves, and no books were ever found, though I don't know how they could've been after the collapse. The name Adem Tarik was all we had to go on. Your father and I spent months looking for answers when we moved here."

"How come you didn't look while you were still there?" Dex asked.

"That might have been easier," Latty acknowledged, "but I pushed for us all to move right away. Your father was in such a bad state. I wanted him to get started on a new life as quickly as he could, so I flew here to find a house a few days after the accident. Your mom had already sold her shop, so I never even went back to Israel from Turkey. You all came a few weeks later."

"If she sold her shop, why'd she go book hunting in the first place?" said Daphna.

Latty shrugged. "I guess it wasn't completely out of her system. I wasn't surprised she wanted to go. Not at all."

"So, you never found out a single thing about Adem Tarik?" Dex asked, getting back to the point.

"Not one thing," Latty confirmed. "But believe me, we tried. Eventually, I let it go, but I couldn't get your father to do the same. I'm sorry now, but after a year or so, I encouraged him to consider scouting. It seemed like a good idea, even though it meant sometimes being away from you two. I thought the traveling lifestyle would be good for his health."

"His health? Was he sick?" Daphna asked.

"Your father was a picture of health before the accident," Latty said. "He'd never mention it, of course, but he was as strong as an ox. He could've run a marathon, even at his age. I'm not exaggerating."

"Dad?" the twins scoffed.

"Yes," Latty insisted, "but after the accident, he deteriorated. It was like his age caught up with him overnight. It wasn't anything medical, the doctors said. Grief can do that to you."

Latty paused to let a twitch pass over her cheek, and the twins could see plainly how fragile she was becoming. Her normally open, pink face was drawn and anxious. Her hair, usually kept in a neat bunch, was almost as out of whack as Dex's spiky mess.

"They say traveling is the best medicine for mourning," Latty continued. "To tell you the truth, I figured he'd settled into the job for its own sake years ago. He really did develop into a fairly decent scout. I wish I'd seen the signs better."

"What signs?" Daphna asked.

"Well, for example, after scouting for a few months, he set aside a large amount of money—scouts keep a cache just in case a deal comes along that won't wait for banks to open or checks to clear. The silly old-fashioned man stuffed his mattress with it." Latty smiled at the thought.

Dex and Daphna looked at each other, relieved.

"But he wasn't using it for that?" Dexter asked.

"I don't think so. I've always done the financial record-keeping kids, so for that first period of time, I could see he was spending money on side-trips not related to the scouting itineraries I prepared. He was keeping up his search for Adem Tarik. I'm quite sure he really put the money aside so he could continue without having to endure my pestering him to get on with his life."

The twins sat absorbing all of this, certain there was much more to ask. But before either thought of anything, Latty got up.

"Let's go check on your father," she said. "He's been alone for far too long."

dirty words

"It's that time again, everyone! Just say the word!"

"Wacky!" the audience shouted.

Dex and Daphna once again sat on the couch watching TV, or staring at it glumly anyway. The Anne & Anthony Show.

"Righteo!" said Anthony. He was a man with a chiseled jaw and the fakest smile ever.

"Okay, we have a caller on the line," said Anne, the sculpted, bottle-blonde co-host. "Here's your Wacky Word—remember," she said, "if you define it correctly, you win! Anthony, why don't you do the honors?"

"Love to, Anne." Anthony flashed gleaming teeth at the camera and said, "Are you there, caller?"

"*I'M PICKER!*" the caller screamed, a man with the high, whining voice of a petulant child. Anne and Anthony, along with the entire audience, jerked back in their seats a bit.

"Whoa! Okay then, Picker!" Anne said.

"We picked a doozy for you. Ready? It's—'Whackembackemphobia.'"

"Abracadabra! Make me famous!" Picker shouted.

Dex and Daphna looked at each other and smirked.

"Aww," Anthony said, "I'm afraid you only get one chance. 'Whackembackemphobia,' is the fear of broken ribs. Children get it when Mom slams on the brakes and whacks them with her arm to keep them in their seat."

The audience laughed. Lots of nodding heads, especially among the kids.

"Shazam!" the man cried. "*I AM PICKER! MAKE ME FAMOUS!*"

The twins snickered.

"Well, Picker," Anthony said, glancing off-stage. "Best we can do is send you a couple of fine Anne and Anthony mini-statues. They're good luck! Hang on the line—"

"I always tell them," Picker blurted, "you gotta pick through a lot of garbage if you want to find a gem! That's why I work here! I do it on my breaks! Make me fam—!"

There was a click. Picker was disconnected.

Anne and Anthony looked at each other,

momentarily stripped of their grins. Then they shrugged.

"And they say our show is trashy!" Anthony quipped, recovering his face.

"Well, like they also say," Anne added, "you can picker your friends, and you can picker your nose—but you can't picker your friend's nose!"

This joke was rewarded with gales of laughter from the audience.

Dex clicked the TV off.

"What a freak," he said. "Shoulda tried 'Please.' That's the real magic word, right?"

Daphna, who'd been contemplating the stupidity of morning TV, was jolted by Dex's words.

"Um, Latty?" she gulped, barely able to contain her excitement. "Where does the garbage from Multnomah Village go?"

Latty didn't look up from the drawer she was filling. "Metro Central, I think," she said, "over in Northeast. Why do you ask?"

So Latty hadn't been listening. Daphna scanned the room, wracking her brains for an idea.

"Dex and I are supposed to go see it. We're working together on a—summer project. We've been putting it off forever. It's due on the first day of school."

"But, that's eight days away!" said Latty, alarmed. "That's not like you at all, Daphna. And right now is such a bad time to leave your father—Wait a moment, did you say you were doing a project together?" Latty looked at Dexter, unable to hide her wonder at the very idea. Dex hadn't the slightest idea what his sister was talking about.

"Yes," Daphna insisted, signaling to her brother with a significant look that this was important. "We're supposed to take a tour," she said, "and we're supposed to keep a journal of what we see. A *ledger*—" she added as forcefully as she could.

Dexter looked at the TV, then finally caught on.

"Yeah!" he cried. "It's my fault we haven't done it yet. Daphna's just being nice."

"Teal's in our group, too," said Daphna. "Her mom's supposed to take us over there this morning."

"The girl that looks like you?"

Daphna nodded. *But prettier*, she couldn't help thinking.

The twins looked at Latty as she considered the matter, worried she'd consider it all too unlikely a story. Latty seemed terribly anxious, but after a moment, she smiled broadly.

"This is the best news I've heard in who knows how long!" she declared, nodding like she always knew they'd come to like each other. But then a fearful look passed over her features again. "Oh, I guess I better not let my worries get in the way," she said. "Your father will be fine. But, please, kids, please—be careful."

"We will!" the twins promised, already halfway through the door.

In short order, they were scurrying through Multnomah Village, dodging the multitude of ruts, crevices and giant potholes in the roads along the way. It seemed like all they did anymore was tear through these crazy streets. It would be much easier if there were decent sidewalks. Despite the constant threats to their ankles, the twins were home in less than five minutes, trying to catch their breath in the kitchen.

"'Abracadabra' and 'Shazam,'" Daphna panted. "They're probably real Words of Power if you say them right! Someone at the dump must've found Rash's Ledger!"

Dexter nodded, leaning on the table. "Thank God I threw it into a garbage truck!"

The moment Dex said this, Daphna realized why he'd thrown away Rash's collected Words of Power. He'd finally admitted to her that he couldn't read. So what good was the Ledger to him? She was sure he had the syndrome she'd heard about last year, a visual problem like Dyslexia that made words appear all mixed up and moving on their pages. She'd been meaning to look it up, but she hadn't had the time with everything else going on.

"We've got to go out there," Dexter said. "Let's take a taxi."

"Good idea. Do you have any money?"

The twins looked at each other.

Dex ran to his father's room while Daphna called a cab.

When it arrived fifteen minutes later, Dex held out a stack of bills to the driver and said, "How fast can this thing go?"

picker

For the following ten minutes, the twins—
Dex white, Daphna green, both clutching door
handles—watched the streets of Portland fly
by under the wheels of their hurtling cab.
The driver, whose license said his name was
Herman Merk, seemed more than happy to en-
danger the lives of everyone in the vehicle. He
went through five red lights, laughing at every
squeal of tires and scrape of the undercarriage.
But now he was finally slowing down.

It had been the most frightening ride of the
twins' lives, but they'd asked for it. Slowly, their
terror subsided, and they began to look around
at Industrial Northeast Portland.

Despite the fact it wasn't long past nine
o'clock, large, lumbering trucks belching black
fumes turned this way and that around them.
On either side of the straight roads were large,
dilapidated warehouses and dirty silos. A per-
sistent hum seemed to vibrate in the air amid
the sounds of engines and the scrapes and

groans of massive bundles being raised or lowered on forklifts.

The cab bumped over railroad tracks. Then it crossed a bridge and approached a large fence with an open gate. As they passed through, the buzz behind them was drowned out by a tumultuous noise coming from somewhere on the grounds of the facility.

Daphna was just about to let Herman know he could stop when yet another noise reached them, the sound of panicked cries. Seconds later, a mini-tide of white-faced workers, burly men in orange jumpsuits, flooded through the gate and rushed toward them.

Herman jammed on the brakes as the twins recoiled, but the men took no notice of the car. They fled around it as if running for their lives. Dex and Daphna turned to watch them bolting down the road. Just then, a bone-rattling collision rocked the cab, sending the twins crashing to the floor. When the car settled, Herman lunged through his door, bellowing. The twins, dazed but unharmed, followed suit.

An enormous piece of misshapen metal had been driven right through the hood. The engine was smoking.

Suddenly, something slammed and shattered on the gravel directly between the twins. It was, or had been, a stone birdbath. Dex and Daphna gawked at its carcass. Clearly, it would've killed one of them had it landed a foot away in either direction. Without a word, Herman turned and fled.

"What's going on?" Dex asked, unable to look away from the deadly shards scattered at his feet.

"Let's go see," Daphna replied, more prudently peering up into the sky. It was empty but for a large number of pigeons flying furiously away from the area.

Hesitantly, the twins walked in through the gate, past an empty booth and toward an immense warehouse. The riotous noise they'd heard at the gate was coming from within. Devastating crashes, the sounds of breaking glass and tearing metal, were shaking the walls of the building.

As they approached, something shot into view, a black streak, out of a broken window. Garbage bags. Dozens of oversized garbage bags streamed into the air and fell to the ground like fantastically swollen black raindrops.

Dex and Daphna watched the spectacle with nervous fascination as they moved slowly toward the entrance of the warehouse. Once it came into view, their attention turned toward the now nearly earsplitting sounds coming from inside. It was dark and difficult to see, even with the jagged shafts of sunlight slicing in. What they could see, they could scarcely believe.

Objects of every conceivable shape and size careened around the unlit interior of the warehouse in the midst of a newspaper, cardboard and plastic hurricane. With devastating force, the objects were colliding and crashing into the inner walls, most of which had been felled in the tumult. It was as if a giant hand was shaking a snow globe filled with all the world's junk. Complete and total chaos reigned. Entering would surely kill them.

A voice, barely audible through the din, cried out something incomprehensible.

"Someone's in there!" Daphna shouted.

"How could that be?" Dex yelled back.

The twins strained to listen, but just then, the pandemonium ceased. All in one instant, everything fell to the ground. It was as if someone had flipped a switch. Lighter objects, mostly sheets of plastic and newspaper, wafted around. It was the eeriest thing Dex and Daphna had ever seen.

For a moment, all was silent, but then the voice came again. "*I AM PICKER!*" it bellowed. "I will be famous!"

"That's him!" Daphna whispered. "He's got Rash's Ledger!"

"Famous!" the voice wailed. "Famous!"

Without consulting each other about the wisdom of the idea, Dex and Daphna stepped tentatively into the warehouse. The smell was repulsive, but they put it out of their minds and tried to head toward the voice. Between the paper and plastic fluttering all around, and all the other debris now strewn willy-nilly, it was nearly impossible to move anywhere with purpose, but they did the best they could, working toward the cry of, "Famous! Famous! Famous!"

The twins chose different paths, each wending their way over and around stacks of sheet metal, mounds of concrete and piles of paint cans, but neither seemed to get any closer to the source of the voice. At some point, they ran into each other at the foot of a mountain of old tires. By then, both were covered in what looked like sheathes of laundry lint.

"This is impossible," Dex whispered. "I can hear him. He sounds close, but I can't tell—"

"*I AM PICKER!*" the voice roared. It was definitely coming from nearby. "*I WILL BE FAME*—What the—?" Picker's voice suddenly took on an entirely different tone, a terrified one. "Where did you come from?" he shrieked. "It ain't nowhere near Halloween you—Holy God! Is it yours? *NO!* I won't let you take—"

There then came the sounds of a brief struggle, followed by an awful crack, after which Picker screamed, "*AHHH!*"

It sounded as if he took off running. He screamed as he went, though his high-pitched wail was interrupted every few seconds by the sounds of him crashing into or falling over something on the ground and then fumbling back to his feet. "*AHHHHH!*—ooomph! *AHHHH!*—ooomph. *Oooooomph!*"

Picker's last collision was with Dex and Daphna. Standing at the edge of the tire heap, they'd watched helplessly as a reedy orange figure blundered around a blind corner and charged at them with his head down and one arm held awkwardly to his chest.

When the little man neared the twins, he tripped and took a header right into them. They all crashed back into the tires together. Dex and Daphna clambered to their feet, unharmed, but Picker remained where he was, on his back, screaming bloody murder with his eyes closed. Now he was clutching a twisted leg with his good arm.

"Are—are you okay?" Daphna asked, though she wasn't sure she could be heard over Picker's howling.

Picker opened his eyes. The sight of the twins seemed to stun him momentarily because he stopped wailing and blinked at them. Dex and Daphna blinked back. He was smaller than they were, and they were average-sized for thirteen year-olds.

"It's not right!" Picker whined. He tried to get up but couldn't manage it. Instead he sank further into the tire mound and, red in the face, cried, "I found it fair and square! They can't mock me anymore. I am Picker!"

"Who can't mock you anymore?" Daphna asked, though she meant to ask if he was all right again.

"My colleagues," he answered, bitterly.

"Always giving me the heaviest loads just to laugh at me 'cause I'm weak, always teasing me for picking through stuff to salvage for my collections. They've been calling me Picker for years. Well, I showed 'em how I pick 'em today, I did! You should've seen their ugly mugs! Scared to death, down to the very last one!" Picker grinned at his triumph and tried to sit up again, but he grimaced and lay back down.

"It's not fair," he bawled. "That—that—huge *thing* took it!" Then, almost as an afterthought, he added, "It had no skin, and it stank a million times worse than anything around here."

Dex and Daphna looked at each other. They were thrilled to have guessed right about the Ledger, but they knew this Thing. It was Emmet, burned beyond recognition when he dragged his master, Asterius Rash, back into the inferno that had been the ABC. Somehow, he'd survived.

"Who are you anyway?" Picker asked.

The twins didn't get a chance to answer because they heard labored breathing nearby.

"Give me back my book!" Picker screamed toward it. "Give me back my book, you lump of foul deformity! Give me back my book!"

Dex squatted down and put his hand over Picker's mouth, stifling his cries. Crashes now came from the other side of the tires. Emmet was tossing junk out of his way as he came toward them saying something they couldn't hear clearly. Picker tried to bite Dex's hand, causing him to yank it away.

Picker opened his mouth to scream again, but Dex managed to whisper desperately, "He's coming to finish killing you!" This had the intended effect, though the truth was that it would be Dexter and Daphna Emmet finished killing if he found them. Picker paled and remained silent, but Emmet was starting to climb up the back of the pile anyway, repeating whatever it was he was saying as he went.

Dex and Daphna rose, ready to run, but just then the sound of sirens, many sirens, made them freeze. When they turned their attention back to Emmet's voice, it was gone. Dex climbed tentatively up the pile and quickly returned.

"Disappeared, didn't he?" Picker finally moaned.

"But, how?" asked Daphna.

"He just popped out of nowhere," Picker

said. "It must be his book."

The sirens were getting louder, which seemed to please Picker.

"The cops are coming!" he cheered. "That means news crews!" He screamed something that wasn't English, and the tires began to tremble.

Dex and Daphna immediately jumped off.

"Picker don't—!" Daphna yelled, but the little man called out the Word again, and tires started sliding off the top of the pile.

The twins knew they didn't have much time, so they headed quickly into the jungle of junk. Most of the debris had settled, which made it possible for Daphna to retrace her steps. Dex followed on her heels, having learned long ago to trust his sister's sense of direction. But soon enough, objects were beginning to hurtle past their heads and shoulders. Brother and sister dropped to all fours and crawled the last fifty yards to daylight.

Once outside, Dex and Daphna got up and sprinted for the gate, but halfway there, they stopped. A gigantic and ominous creaking had sounded behind them. Turning back, they saw the entire warehouse lift an inch or so off the ground.

It was impossible, of course, but so was everything else happening to them. The building hovered precariously in the air for one long, tense moment, almost as if it were trying to find the energy to fly away. Instead, it dropped to the ground. On impact, the entire structure buckled, then collapsed.

The thunderous sounds of snapping beams rent the air, then the blare of sirens cut through. Three police cars and two news vehicles raced through the gate past the twins, so the pair tore their eyes away from the calamity and hurried forward into the nearby streets. They walked swiftly without talking for ten minutes, until they felt sure they were safe.

Daphna spoke first. "Do you think—?" she asked. "Picker—?"

"No chance," Dex said. "But he's probably going to get his wish."

"What do you mean?"

"He's going to be famous for a while."

Daphna didn't reply to this. The twins walked for a while in silence again. All they could do was, literally, take this new death in stride.

Finally, Dex said, "Where are we anyway?"

He stopped to scrape off plastic and newspapers and the filmy lint still clinging all over him. They were standing in front of a long fence topped with coiled barbed wire.

"Dex, Emmet is alive," was Daphna's response. "And now he has the *Book of Nonsense* and Rash's Ledger. And he can use some Words! That must be how he survived the fire! What should we do?"

"It's obvious," Dex said.

"What's obvious?"

"We have to get the *Book of Nonsense* back and destroy it. The Ledger, too. There's no one left to do it but us."

Daphna didn't respond, but she didn't have to. Dexter was right. The pair fell silent again.

"By the way," Daphna finally said, "I don't have the slightest idea where we are. Let's just walk until we see a cab."

The twins walked on, passing warehouses until they emerged from the industrial section. A taxi sat at a red light.

"Wait!" Dex yelled running to the car. The driver looked at him skeptically through her open window, so Dex pulled a handful of bills out of his pocket. She seemed mollified, if not exactly pleased. The twins jumped in.

"Address?" the cabby asked, still looking unsure about taking them anywhere. The license said her name was Sharon Ferry. Daphna gave it to her, looking nervously at Dex. Fortunately, Sharon turned the car in the direction of the highway.

Relieved, the twins pressed back into the vinyl seats and tried to settle their rattled nerves. It was almost a gift that increasingly incredible things kept happening because each new event prevented them from dwelling on the last.

Sharon turned on the radio. Classical music was on, and Daphna found it soothing. "Lyre," she couldn't help saying. Dex rolled his eyes, but it was comforting for him, too. The twins sat and just listened for a few minutes, until Daphna's thoughts went racing again.

"Dex," she said, "if that letter from Mom was important enough for Dad to keep in his mattress with all that money—I mean, he's been saving it for thirteen years—why wouldn't he read it? He looked at it like it was a prop we made for our crazy story."

"I don't know," Dex replied without much interest. "He doesn't even know what day it is.

He probably just forgot—"

"Quiet," Sharon ordered. "If you kids are running away, or robbing people, I don't want to hear about it. Next thing you know, I'll be on a witness stand."

Dex and Daphna didn't bother to reassure her. They turned back to their own thoughts, which were the same: how do you track down a giant, half-incinerated lunatic who wants to kill you? And more importantly, what do you do if you find him? Also, *Are we really rich?*

A weather report came on as they drove over the river. The forecast was good, finally: sunshine. After that a newscaster said, "When we return, a review of breaking stories, including a disturbance at a rest and rehab home in Multnomah Village."

Blood drained from the twins' faces.

Sheer dread restrained the unthinkable from forming fully in their minds, but it was there anyway. They couldn't even manage to exchange one of their by now routine looks of alarm. Instead, they clutched each other through an endless serious of inane commercials.

Finally, the news returned.

"In Southwest, at the Multnomah Village Rest and Rehabilitation Home, a large man clad in black and wearing a mask and gloves refused to leave when asked to state his business. He fled only when the Director called the police, who are now investigating to determine whether this incident is connected in any way to the recent murders of several residents of the home."

Daphna let go of Dex's arm, leaving two sets of deep fingernail marks. She was indescribably relieved, so much so that she didn't bother wondering if there was still reason for concern. Dex was relieved, too, but he still looked worried.

"What is it?" Daphna asked.

"It was Emmet," Dex whispered. "He was wearing a mask—that's why Picker said something about Halloween. He must have taken it off to scare him."

Daphna, fearful again, sat back up. "What was he doing at the R & R?"

"Looking for one of us," Dex said, trying to keep his voice down. "He probably tried our house first, then went there."

"Those are the only places he knows I go,"

Daphna said, slightly relieved. "Does he know anywhere you—?"

Daphna stopped short because she and Dex knew exactly where they needed to go.

At the same moment, they asked the same question of their driver. "Can you take us to Gabriel Park?"

"If I don't hear another word," Sharon said.

And she didn't.

monsters

Dexter and Daphna stood at the head of the path leading into Gabriel park, wondering what exactly they thought they were doing. The last time they were here, the twins were fairly certain they were being led to their deaths. In that case, they'd had no choice. Rash's old partner-in-crime, Ruby Scharlach, had a gun and the *Book of Nonsense*, and they had no idea Daphna's reading group was actually the seven remaining Councilors.

It was a miracle they came out of there alive, even with the Councilors giving up their lives to protect them. And now it seemed they were voluntarily going to risk their lives here again. They were going to walk right up to the thing that killed Ruby and took the book.

"He's been hiding in the woods—in my Clearing," Dex declared, trying not to focus on his fears.

"But how does he know about it?" Daphna asked. "How'd he find us there with the

Dwarves—I mean, the Councilors. I shouldn't call them that anymore."

A vague memory came to Dex.

"He—decked me, over there by that tree," Dex explained, "and when he left, I went to the Clearing to sleep. It's where I go when I skip school. I thought I heard noises in the woods when I was lying there all day, but I was too messed up to check. It had to have been him. He must've seen me go in."

A wave of hot shame swept over Dexter as he heard himself describe his run-in with Emmet. He hadn't been decked, of course. Emmet had yanked him off his feet by the neck, nearly strangling him. He'd wet his pants—and it seemed like half the neighborhood had witnessed it.

Dex had blocked out the whole incident as best he could, but he knew it was a doomed effort, even with all the insanity going on. And the humiliation wasn't even the worst part.

No, Dex had been forced to face a harsh reality that day: he'd never be the type of boy who did what he wanted—he'd always be the type who did what he could. And learning that Daphna had wet herself when Emmet tried to murder her didn't help in the least. It made him feel even worse.

"What are we going to do?" Dex asked, forcing this all away. "Waltz in there and ask him nicely if we can have the Book and the Ledger? And by the way, please don't kill us?"

Daphna thought about this for a moment. Then she said, "Dex, I think I should go in there alone."

"What? Are you crazy?"

"I'm not crazy," Daphna replied. "It's just that—no offense, Dex—but I think I have a better chance by myself."

"But Daphna," Dex protested, "you lied to him, remember? To get him away from the store so I could take the Ledger. You *flirted* with him."

"Yeah, but I'm the one who made him remember he'd been happy in an orphanage before Rash took him and turned him into a killer. I saw the way he looked into my eyes, Dex, when he stopped strangling me. I think I can reach him again.

"Besides," said Daphna, "if Latty heard about what happened at the Dump, she'll be freaking out. She might even call Teal's mom.

You should run back to the R & R and tell her we're okay."

Dex thought this was a terrible idea, even though Latty probably would be freaking out. He could hardly believe he was considering letting Daphna face that maniac alone.

This was exactly what galled Dex. It wasn't that he was scared of getting hurt. Since the incident in the park, he'd taken Emmet's best shots, but he still felt ineffectual. He still felt that his own life was not his to control. He couldn't even make his own sister give an inch.

"Look, Dex," Daphna said, sensing some of what her brother was thinking, "I'm not going in there to fight him. Obviously, if I thought that was going to happen, I'd want you to go. I'm going in there so there won't be a fight. If Emmet looks even the slightest bit violent, I'll run for it. I'm not stupid, Dex. Let's make a deal. If I'm not at the R & R in an hour, you can call the cops."

Dex struggled with the semi-reasonableness of the plan. It was clearly their best option, but agreeing to it was still going to make him feel like a wimp.

"Dex," Daphna prodded, "we're wasting time."

"Fine," Dex finally agreed. "Half an hour."

"Deal." Half an hour was exactly what Daphna was bargaining for.

Dex regarded Daphna severely for a moment. He wanted to say something angry, but he couldn't find the words. Instead, he took off.

Daphna watched her brother until he was out of sight. After a deep breath, she clenched her fists, gritted her teeth, and strode into the park. Despite the near state of shock she'd been in the last time she walked down this path, she remembered just where Dex had led the group off of it.

Chaotic thoughts swirled in Daphna's head as she entered the woods again. She hadn't found time to think any more about how she'd gotten Emmet away from the ABC that day. There'd been no time to lose, so she'd just charged up to him, hoping to come up with something—and the next thing she knew, she was flirting away like a Pop girl at school.

It wasn't something she'd planned. Daphna had no idea she was even capable of such a thing. She'd never been confident enough even to wonder. But now a cascade of tingles raced down her spine as she stepped lightly over clusters of branches and leaves. Everyone knew that girls who could order boys around earned the right to do the same to other girls.

But this thought nearly crushed Daphna. She'd always been one of those other girls! She'd been used! Wren and Teal, those two-faced Pop phonies. Those snobs. They'd lied about going away to camp for the summer so they wouldn't have to hang out with her. Those back-stabbing liars sat with her at lunch every few days and told her she was their friend.

Oh, she'd been a fool, a stupid, stupid fool. How gullible could she be not to have realized they buddied up to her only when they needed help with their homework? And what was her "help" anyway? Practically doing it for them. No, completely doing it for them. How could she have let that happen to her, especially when it was so obvious the way they manipulated everyone else!

The fury that had overwhelmed Daphna when she first realized she'd been blatantly used returned, though with far less self-pity. She hadn't had a second to think about how she'd fallen apart in her bedroom over all this, either. Daphna had no idea what she was going to say to those two when school started, but she was going to say something, that was for sure. An angry red haze clouded her vision, and she began knocking aside tree branches and kicking at rotten logs. Daphna completely forgot where she was going, but her feet found their way on their own.

By the time she managed to reach the trees ringing the clearing, Daphna was in a blind, stumbling rage. She barged right through a wall of overlapping limbs, stepped on something soft, then tripped on something else that sent her headlong to the ground.

Daphna scrambled to her feet. It was Emmet, or something that used to be Emmet. He'd been curled up on a blanket wearing a black sweatsuit. There were a pair of black gloves, a plain black ski mask and a portable television lying nearby. Everything had tags still attached.

But now he was slowly getting to his feet. And now Daphna got a good look at what remained of his face. It was nothing but peeling crimson parchment. His hands and feet were gnarled, waxy and wet, dripping with something that looked like pus.

Emmet looked at her tentatively, so Daphna tried not to look away, willing herself to focus on his eyes, his red, ruined eyes. They'd shaken her so much before, but now they were the least frightening thing about him.

"It's you," Emmet finally said, looking down at Daphna with what she could plainly see was simple shyness. No amount of damage to his face could conceal it. His voice sounded nervous, just the way it had when she'd lured him away from the store. "I was hoping to talk to you one more time, this time," he added.

"This time?" Daphna asked. Between Emmet's timid expression and his strange comment, she managed to forget her fear for the moment. "What do you mean, 'this time?'"

"This lifetime," Emmet replied. "Who knows if I'll even know you in the next."

"You sound like Rash," Daphna said. "I hardly understood anything he talked about."

"Rash only talked about one thing," said Emmet. "Time. The Infinite Quality of Time."

"The infinite quality of time?" Daphna repeated, dumbly. "I have no idea what that means."

"I can explain," Emmet offered. But before he began, he started shuffling around the perimeter of the clearing. Daphna used the opportunity to assess the situation. So far so good. She'd found Emmet, and he didn't seem to want to hurt her. Daphna scanned the area, searching for the *Book of Nonsense* or Rash's Ledger, but there was no sign of either.

Then it occurred to her that whatever Emmet was going to say might be worth considering. That is, if he had any idea what he was talking about himself. It was hard to imagine a complicated phrase like, "The infinite quality of time," ever coming out of Emmet's mouth. But then, he probably heard something like it from Rash every day of his life.

"Time is forever," Emmet said, stopping his circuit directly opposite Daphna. "Think about that for a second." He paused and gazed up ruefully at the patches of blue sky visible through the branches over his head. After a moment, he went on.

"There was no beginning to time," he said, "and there won't be an end to it. And that means, even if it's ten trillion years from now, people will be born that look and talk and think exactly the way we have, which means they will be us. It has to happen, eventually. If time is endless, everything has to happen. Everything has to happen over and over and over again. We've had this conversation before, who knows how many times. I only wish it was my turn to kill Rash a long time ago, but I never thought of it. Maybe he could keep some thoughts out of my mind."

Daphna offered no reply to this, amazed now to see Emmet wasn't just parroting words he didn't comprehend. He'd obviously thought about what he was saying. When she'd led him around the other day, he'd just mumbled and stuttered like a moron, like the moron she'd assumed he was. Now she understood that he'd fumbled around her simply because he liked her and must've been nervous.

Daphna tried to refocus on what Emmet was getting at, but it was difficult with all these other thoughts crowding in. She was pretty sure she understood the gist of it, though.

"Emmet, the world isn't infinite," she said, detecting a flaw in his thinking. "It was created at some point—one way or another—and it sure isn't going to be around forever. If we don't blow ourselves up, we're going to cut down all the trees until no one can breathe, or poison all the food and water supplies."

"Of course we will," Emmet agreed, surprising Daphna. "We'll do all those things." He began moving toward her, but stopped suddenly in the center of the Clearing. Did she flinch, or look afraid—or disgusted? She couldn't afford to make him mad right now, not when she needed to get the books from him. Fortunately, Emmet didn't look upset, and he continued on with his lesson.

"Of course we will," he repeated. "I said Time was infinite, not the world. The Earth will be destroyed, in every way you can imagine, but when enough time goes by, other Earths will form, just like the trillions that formed before this one. And when we—you and me and Asterius Rash—when we come around again, things will happen to us with ten billion tiny differences, or just one difference, or they'll happen exactly the same way. One time, Rash will adopt another child from the orphanage and brainwash *him* into feeling like an animal and force *him* to stare at books sixteen hours a day."

"But—"

"And another time, he'll adopt me again, and I won't practice every single Word of Power he makes me put in his Ledger—or I will, but I won't learn the one that makes you not feel pain, and so I'll die the same horrible death he did when the store burns up."

So that's how he survived, Daphna thought. She tried to take in the rest of Emmet's arguments, but wasn't up to it. The nature of his words was confusing enough, but it was just too bizarre to be engaged in philosophical speculation here, in the middle of the woods in Gabriel Park, with an arguably psychotic brute burned badly enough to kill him a dozen times over, one with a crush on her, no less.

And under the surface of this bewilderment her other worries simmered. There was her suddenly nonexistent social life, her ailing father and her insensitivity to her brother, not to mention the small matter of completing the Council's mission of finding and destroying the *Book of Nonsense*. Emmet was going on with his explanations, but Daphna didn't tune back in until his voice took on a much more subdued tone.

"One day," he was saying, his head bowed, his voice dropping low, "one day when we meet again, you won't have to pretend to like me." Emmet shuffled forward until he was standing directly in front of Daphna, who didn't draw away even the slightest bit. Emmet's voice sank to a whisper.

"One day, when you ask me to walk with you," he said, twisting his fingers and trying to look Daphna in the eyes, "we might—maybe we might—hold hands."

The wistful look in Emmet's eyes—they weren't so ruined that Daphna couldn't see it—sapped her of every emotion but one. She felt horribly depressed. A sadness that seemed to have physical weight pushed down like the heel of a hand on her heart. She knew what she was going to do. She was going to play whatever feelings Emmet still had for her against him. What choice did she have? However smart he might actually be, he was dangerous. It didn't really matter that Rash made him that way, did it?

Resolved, Daphna smiled at Emmet. "One day you might meet me right here," she made herself say, giving her hair a flip like Wren always did, though she had no idea if bobbed hair could flip. "And you might give me the Book and the Ledger," she added, "as a sign of the friendship we're going to have next time." Daphna tried to enlarge her dappled eyes the way the woman on the TV talk show had when she looked at the camera.

Emmet returned a forlorn, exhausted smile, but didn't reply at first. As Daphna waited nervously for his response, it occurred to her that his gruesome appearance no longer bothered her, but before she had time to figure out what that meant, Emmet let out a bleat of surprise and then abruptly collapsed like a marionette whose strings had been severed all at once. Daphna dropped to her knees beside him.

"What? What is it, Emmet?" she pleaded.

"Damn," Emmet said. He rolled carefully onto his back.

"What's wrong?" Daphna asked. "Are you okay?"

"Doesn't hurt, but I guess I'm all burnt up inside."

"Do you know any Words to help?"

"Maybe." Emmet screwed up his eyes, thinking, then began intoning a series of odd-sounding Words. They sounded similar to those Daphna heard Rash use under his breath at the ABC.

Strange things immediately started happening in the Clearing. Leaves began to swirl, lifting off the forest floor in a mini-twister. A moment later, they fluttered peacefully back to the ground. While that was happening, bark began to peel off a stand of trees across the way. And something else was going on behind Daphna. She could hear the branches swaying as if in a heavy wind, but she didn't turn to see because Emmet started to rise unsteadily off the ground, the same way the Metro Central's warehouse had. But then he settled down.

"It's no use," he sighed. "I'm too messed up. I think my brain's been cooked."

"Think! Emmet," Daphna encouraged. "Do you know anything else?"

Emmet closed his eyes. His hairless brow furrowed with concentration. Finally, he muttered a Word that sounded like he was spitting out something distasteful. The moment he did, Daphna couldn't breathe. She clutched her throat, and when Emmet saw her, he repeated the Word and then fell silent. Daphna gasped as the air flowed into her again.

"I'm sorry," Emmet whispered. "It's no use—" He looked Daphna firmly in the eyes and said, "I was hoping this life was going to come around. I was sure you were going to make me good. That's why I was looking for you. Can you make me good?"

"I—I—it's okay, Emmet," Daphna said as her eyes welled up. It was impossible to know exactly what she was feeling. Daphna took Emmet's hand. It felt a little bit like the cover of the *Book of Nonsense.*

"You don't have to pretend anymore," Emmet whispered. His voice was soft, almost gentle. "There's no possible way any of my future lives can be worse than this one."

"But I'm not pretending," Daphna pleaded. It came out as a whine. Tears swam before her eyes. She was lying to a dying boy. Or, if she wasn't lying, she wasn't telling the truth, either.

"I believe you," Emmet croaked, his voice cracking now, his eyes beginning to roll in their sockets.

"You can have the books," he said. "I was going to give them to you when I was done with them, anyway. I only learned to use a few Words in Rash's Ledger, but you're smarter.

It's the first Word that chokes people. The last one on the fourth page lets you go wherever you want just by thinking about it. I only got it to work a few times."

"That's what you did at the dump!"

Emmet nodded weakly and waved at something across the way.

"They're over there, under that split log," he said. "I don't think that other book will do anything for you, the one I got back from that old lady. It's all messed up. I took it 'cause Rash was desperate for it. I thought it might have something in it I could use to change my skin back, but it's useless. That's why I went after the Ledger, except I couldn't find anything to help me in there either. I didn't have enough time." Emmet couldn't help but laugh at the irony.

"Thank you, Emmet," Daphna said, softly. "I need to ask you something else," she added. There was no turning back. She was going to work her advantage as far as she could. "Do you know anything about someone called Adem Tarik?"

"Rash talked about him all the time," Emmet said.

"He did? What did he say? Emmet! What

did he say?"

Emmet looked surprised by Daphna's ferocity, but he answered without questioning her.

"Rash was obsessed with finding some kind of magic book that used to belong to Adem Tarik," he explained. "He'd freak out at least once a day and start screaming about how Adem Tarik was a fool for wanting to make Heaven on Earth. Sometimes he'd laugh, but mostly he'd just scream. I kept away from him when he did that. I guess he thought that book over there was it. I don't know."

Daphna's mind spun. This was critical information, but she couldn't think why just then. "Emmet! Emmet! Is there anything else?"

Emmet's eyes had closed again, clearly against his will. But because he wasn't actually suffering, it seemed as though he was just exhausted and unable to keep from falling asleep, like Milton. Daphna knew better though, and after several more urgent pleas, Emmet seemed to revive.

"Sorry," he managed. "Rash told me he stole the book, but he lost it somehow. When we came here, he told me the thirteen year-old he was looking for had something to do with it.

He told me if I found the kid, he'd let me kill someone. But now that I've killed two, I don't feel any better."

"Is that it?" Daphna asked, aware but unable to acknowledge the seething volcano of regret under the surface of Emmet's words.

"Did he say anything else? Emmet!" Daphna cried. "Hold on!" She knew most of this. She knew Rash had come for one of her mother's children to learn the Words of Power for him. She needed more.

"I'm okay," Emmet muttered weakly. His eyes opened to Daphna once again. They seemed to clear out completely for a moment, and he said in a determined voice, "Next time. Next time I'll do better."

Then, without shudder or complaint, he let out a long, slow breath, closed his eyes and went utterly still.

More Monsters

Carefully, Daphna set Emmet's hand down. She said his name, but he didn't reply. She touched his shoulder, but he didn't react. He looked peaceful now, and for that she was glad.

"I'm so sorry," Daphna sighed, and her eyes finally overflowed.

But she got up, angry at her tears. Why had using her new talent, a talent she'd never dared dream of having, make her feel so awful? *You did the right thing*, she told herself, wiping her face. *You had to get the books, and you got them the only way you could.*

Maybe she felt sick because it made her like Wren and Teal, but she'd done a good thing here, an important thing. It wasn't like she was getting some moon-eyed boy to carry her books or deliver ditzy notes to friends. That had to make a difference, didn't it? She wasn't anything like those girls, no matter how much she looked like one of them.

Daphna hardly knew who she was anymore. She paced the perimeter of the Clearing, trying to puzzle things out. The only thing she understood was that she didn't understand anything anymore. But then she had it. Emmet had already told her everything she needed to know.

"Well," Daphna said right out loud—she felt better even before the words passed her lips—"next time, I'll do better, too."

Suddenly, Daphna could focus on the matter at hand. She approached the log Emmet had gestured to and crouched down beside it. Despite its size, it rolled over easily, revealing a cavity below. They were right there, the mutilated *Book of Nonsense* and Rash's Ledger.

Thousands and thousands of years of searching, of fighting, of killing were over. Daphna, daunted by the epic story she'd joined, didn't reach for either book, but rather remained where she was, staring at them, lost in thought about Time. Could time really be infinite? How could it not be?

She'd first learned about the concept of infinity in elementary school, when one character in a cartoon movie asked another to think of the biggest number he could and then told him to add one, and then add one again, and then add one again, on and on.

Well, Daphna thought, *if the world ever ended, there would still be a moment after that, and one after that, even if no one was there to experience it, right*? And as for the first moment of the world—well there still had to be a moment before that, and one before that, forever the other way.

Daphna didn't know what any of it meant. She took a seat, shaking the entangling web of thoughts away, then finally reached out for the precious books. After lifting them out of the hole, she tenderly whisked the dirt off their covers and set them on her lap. She'd looked through the *Book of Nonsense* before, or tried to anyway, when she and her father were taking it to the ABC, thinking it was just a very strange book that might have some value. It had been interesting then, but now it inspired absolute awe. Could a book really belong to God? She didn't know the first thing about the subject, but anything seemed possible at this point.

Carefully, Daphna turned over the nearly shredded cover and looked at a random page. The words were a blur, even more so than they'd been when she'd opened the book with her father and figured she'd gotten carsick. The words were now in rapid flux, and they dizzied her.

Daphna flipped forward, but all the pages looked that way, so she closed it and opened the Ledger instead. Inside its pages were neat lists of fairly legible words. They didn't have explanations, but Daphna didn't find that troubling. They were Words of Power—the closest thing to them, anyway—and they were right there, for her eyes only, thanks to Asterius Rash's centuries of dogged hunting and collecting.

Daphna tried the first Word, the one Emmet had accidentally choked her with, but nothing seemed to happen. She paged through, scanning the lists, trying various Words in a low voice. After a particularly strange one, the Ledger slid to the edge of her hand, paused, then fell to the ground. It didn't work when she tried again, so she closed the book.

Amazed, and not a little terrified, Daphna closed her eyes and sat motionless but for her trembling hands that cradled the books.

Her reverie didn't last long.

Daphna heard voices. People were in the woods nearby. At once, she got to her feet, took one last guilty look at Emmet lying in the center of the clearing, then rushed back toward the park.

Just before emerging from the woods, Daphna veered behind an especially large cedar tree with the two books clutched awkwardly under an arm. A group of fifteen or so boisterous girls were playing Frisbee on the adjacent grassy field. She recognized most of them from school: Ava, Branwen, Jarita, Robin, Yara. They were Pops: the best dressed, the best talkers, the best looking.

Daphna had never claimed to be super close friends with any Pop, but it wasn't like she couldn't go up and talk to each and every one of them. Even if Wren and Teal were liars and users, the rest of them were nice to her, and she didn't do their work for them.

Still, Daphna didn't want to deal with any Pops just yet, so she moved stealthily back into the woods and walked along behind the border of trees. When she felt she was beyond the girls' field of play, Daphna reentered the park, but after no more than two steps, an errant Frisbee hit her smartly in the back of the knee. The books tumbled out of her hands onto the grass.

Daphna was bending down to gather them up when someone called, "Little help!" She cringed at the nasal voice. Wren. And Teal was surely half a step behind because the two were practically joined at the hip.

Their possible presence was the real reason Daphna avoided walking through the game. She wasn't remotely ready for the confrontation. Having no choice, Daphna stood up and turned around when the girls reached her. They looked momentarily stunned in their matching sun visors.

"Daphna!" Wren cried, breaking into a gleaming, perfectly orthodontured grin. She sounded for all the world like she'd just run into her long lost best friend.

"How was camp?" Daphna asked, coldly. She felt like she was a thousand years older than these twits now. How could she ever have admired them?

"Oh, it was awesome," Wren lied, her blue contact lenses shining with wonder at all the fake memories. "Really, you should come next year. It would be so cool to hang with you."

"I thought you weren't getting back until next week."

"Oh, yeah," Teal said. "Um, well—"

"There was a fire!" Wren lied. She barely even paused before coming up with it. "They had to send us home early. That was a bummer, but it was kind of cool in a way. We heard there was one around here, too. We were all just talking about it. Did you see it?"

Daphna seethed thinking of the letters she wrote while waiting for them to send the camp's address. She was suddenly too furious to go on with the charade.

"I know you didn't go to camp," Daphna snarled. "I know you've been using me."

Wren and Teal looked at each other.

"It's nothing personal," Teal said after a long, hideously awkward pause during which Daphna's heart pounded furiously in her chest. Teal looked distressed. "We just—in the summers, we're really too busy—"

"To keep stringing me along," Daphna said. "Yes, I see. Lots of Frisbees to throw. Also to catch. And putting together the Frisbee outfits. I'm sure it's all quite overwhelming."

Wren smirked. She didn't look distressed at all. She looked amused, if slightly surprised.

"We figured you were busy doing next year's

homework, anyway," she said. "I'll drop mine off tomorrow."

"Let's go, Wren," Teal said.

Daphna's face felt like it was ready to catch fire. "I can't believe I ever wanted to be your friend," she fumed. "I can't believe I didn't see how pathetic you two really are."

"*You* calling *us* pathetic?" Wren laughed. "Now that's pathetic!"

"Come on," Teal urged, looking back at the others. "She's not worth it."

"You have no idea what I'm worth, you— you—twit!" Daphna raged.

Now Teal's eyes went narrow.

"You might as well know," she said, her voice a bit shaky, "that every single person over there knows what a sucker you are. We all used to take turns saying something nice to you to make sure you'd keep the answers coming."

"Everyone is going to be so disappointed," Wren put in, pleased her partner was finally joining the fun. "But then again, there's never a shortage of wannabes. By the way, love the outfit you put together."

Daphna looked down and saw that she was covered in clots of that lint-like junk from the dump, and now leaves and twigs were in her hair from the Clearing, too. And despite the fact that her appearance demonstrated just how much distance there was between her concerns and those of these two shallow, spoiled little prima donnas, she was ashamed.

Ashamed of being ashamed, humiliated and incensed, Daphna simply wanted to scream. And she did scream, but what came out was some kind of incomprehensible word. The moment it passed her lips, Wren and Teal doubled over, blue-faced and choking.

Daphna, shocked at first, stared down at them in confusion. When she finally grasped what was happening, she was too flustered to make it stop. Teal's eyes bulged incredibly from their sockets. Wren clutched her chest and tried to scream. They both fell to their knees and looked up at Daphna, terrified.

Daphna gaped down at the strangling girls, less flustered now than simply amazed. Thank goodness they were both thirteen and able to hear the First Tongue. They were literally groveling at her feet. In her wildest revenge fantasy—not that she'd had time to actually imagine one—she'd never have dared hope for such a thing. Wren collapsed and clutched at Daphna's shoe.

Enough was enough, though. It took several tries, but Daphna managed to pronounce the Word again. Immediately, the girls rolled onto their sides, sucking in air. The moment they could, they got back to their feet and, massaging their throats, staggered away without their Frisbee.

Daphna watched the girls rejoin the other Pops before tucking the books back under her arm and heading off. Did any of that just happen? Shouldn't she be feeling a whole lot worse if it did?

Next time, Daphna told herself, *next time I'll handle things better*. But she had to say this repeatedly in her head as she walked. It was the only way to drown out the other little voice in there, the one telling her that if she lived forty billion lives, she'd never want to handle it any other way.

mixed (up) messages

Second thoughts gnawed at Dexter as he sprinted away from the park. It was he, not his sister, who should've gone into the woods. Yes, Daphna had logic on her side, but he was a boy. She was a girl. But that was stupid, wasn't it? Dex didn't know. He did know he'd get nothing out of Emmet if he went in, except possibly two oversized hands around his throat that wouldn't let go until he was dead. He wasn't going to confuse his newfound ability to take a punch with committing—

The blaring of a furious horn made Dex suddenly stop. Only when the car passed did he realize he'd charged blindly across a street—and how close he'd come to getting hit. Dex leapt onto the opposite sidewalk and stood there hunched over with his hands on his knees, trying to steady his fraying nerves.

I should go back, Dex thought when he recovered, but then he looked up to find he was standing right outside the R & R. There was only one thing to do, it having actually been too late to change the plan for nearly ten minutes. He sped in through the Home's automatic doors, hurried across the lobby and burst into his father's room.

"What's going on?" Latty yelped. She was sitting in a chair pulled up next to Milton's bed. He was sitting up with his laptop computer on the food tray, looking surprisingly refreshed and alert.

At first, Dex thought Milton must've told Latty the story he and Daphna told him, and she was furious they'd gone against her wishes. But his father didn't look concerned at all.

Then Dex realized how his entrance must have looked. He still had some of that fluffy junk from the dump stuck to his clothes, and he was sweating profusely.

"Nothing's going on," he said, "just thought you might be wondering where we were."

When Latty looked confused, he added, "There was an—accident at the dump, but we were nowhere near it. There was all this stuff there—couches with their insides all pulled out—we were messing with it."

"An accident?" Latty cried through the

hand that shot to her mouth. Then, inexplicably, her face purpled, and she began to cry.

Dex had no idea what to say. Latty was clearly going to pieces. He glanced at his father, who returned a knowing look. Dex had no idea what it meant.

"Ah, hey, Dad," he offered. "How's it going?"

"Hi, Dex," Milton said. He sounded quite cheerful, though his voice was hoarse.

Latty stood up. "If you're here to keep your father company," she sniffled, pulling herself back together, "I may just run home to get the house organized and start working on dinner. The kids will bring you something later tonight, Milton. That lunch they wheeled in here was criminal. Is Daphna home?"

"She's coming here in a bit," Dex said.

"I hope she hurries," said Latty, voicing his thoughts precisely. "I feel much better when you two are here with your father, safe and sound." Then she added, with an only half-joking wink, "You two can protect him from that Evelyn woman."

Milton rolled his eyes good-naturedly.

After extracting a few tissues from her purse, Latty hurried out, though not before passing Dexter to brush and straighten his shirt. When she had him by the collar, she leaned over and whispered, "Don't forget what you promised." Then she straightened up and hurried out the door.

Dex looked at his father, unsure what to say next. "What's wrong with her?" he managed.

"Oh, you know Latona," Milton said with a tolerant shrug. "If you think she worries over you guys too much, you don't know the half of it. Trust me."

"But why does she have to worry so much? It doesn't seem healthy."

"You two are her life," Milton said, "and you're all she has of your mother. In fact, it was Latty who talked her into trying to have kids in the first place. Your mom thought she was too old. And of course Latona has no family of her own—"

Dex had never considered Latty's personal life. He'd assumed she had some kind of family, somewhere, though she clearly didn't ever see them now that he thought about it. Of course, neither he nor Daphna had extended family, either. Maybe Latty was trying to make up for all that.

"What's she got against the lady who runs this place, anyway?" Dex asked.

Milton chuckled. "Just like they say," he said, "the more things change, the more they stay the same."

"What do you mean?"

"Oh, well, do you remember how I met Evelyn? I guess how we all met her, really. You and Daphna were with me after all. We all sat together on the same flight from New York to Portland. We'd connected from Jerusalem, and she was moving from New York City.

"Anyway, I guess she took a liking to me, and to you two, as well. Latty could see this when we all walked off the plane together, or at least when she saw Evelyn give me her phone number. The truth was I found her a bit aggressive for my tastes. Anyway, Latty took an immediate dislike to her."

Dex struggled to keep a straight face. A woman hitting on his father? The very idea was laughable. The story was over, but he didn't know how to keep the conversation going. It seemed his father didn't either.

After an awkward silence, Milton said, "Oh! How could I have forgotten? Latty tells me you and your sister are collaborating on a project about city waste."

"Ahh—"

"It just so happens I know someone who used to have an interesting history of garbage if you're interested—my old friend and colleague Berny Quartich. The odder the topic, the more likely he is to have it! Since I woke up I've been feeling fantastic, other than the sore throat and strange dreams, anyway. So when Latty told me what you were up to, I e-mailed him. He already wrote back and said he still has it. Here, have a look."

Panic rose in Dex like a geyser. He was nowhere near ready to tell his father about his reading problem. He wasn't so sure about this syndrome thing. Daphna probably didn't remember it right.

"Ah—sure," Dex stalled, "but you said you're having strange dreams?"

"Yes," said Milton. "One, actually."

"What is it?"

"I keep dreaming that I'm walking down a stone street in Malatya—"

"That town in Turkey you went to!"

"I've been there before," Milton said, "but

not for some time. I'll be going this summer, actually, so I guess it's on my mind."

"Okay," said Dex, deflated to see there'd been no change in his father's memory. "So what happens?" he asked.

"Well, I do know the town, but not this street because it's not in the main area of commercial activity. It's lined with quiet little shops."

"Do you go in one?"

"Yes, a coffee house, the kind where they read your fortune in the grounds of your cup. Fikret Cihan's Coffee House. I just remembered that."

"Weird," Dex said. "You don't even drink coffee." He was beginning to suspect that this was a memory, not a dream. "Do you get your fortune read?"

"No," Milton said. "I ask the proprietor, Fikret Cihan, about an author I'm curious about. He tells me he hasn't heard of him, but then suddenly someone I hadn't seen in the back of the shop, an ancient looking old fellow sitting under a lamp copying text from a book, lets loose an awful, soul-piercing cry. He falls out of his seat with the book he was copying and literally begins crawling toward me with it. There is all kinds of confusion in Turkish, but eventually this Fikret brings me the old man's book and positively begs me to take it away that instant. It's in absolutely awful shape."

"*Then what?*"

"Well," Milton said, looking slightly taken aback by Dexter's fervor, "I take it, give him my card, and walk back outside. And that's the end of the dream."

Dex, certain now that this was how his father found the *Book of Nonsense*, decided to take a risk. "This author, Dad, that you were asking about—"

"I don't think it's an important detail, Dexter. I can't actually remem—"

"Any chance it was Adem Tarik?"

Dex held his breath.

"That name," Milton said, "it does sound familiar. Where did you hear it?"

"Um," Dex said, "you said it when you were sleeping."

"Perhaps that was it then. But enough of this nonsense," said Milton. "It's you I want to talk about. I'm ashamed to say there's so much about you I don't know. I really would like to help with your project. Shall we respond to this e-mail?"

"Actually, Dad," Dex said, "we've decided to change our topic."

"Oh, to what?"

"We're not sure," Dexter replied, but he'd seized on an idea. "Maybe you can help. We're supposed to interview someone in an unusual line of work, and I was thinking—"

"You—you don't mean you want to interview me, do you?" Milton asked, misunderstanding. His eyebrows had piled together and his lips were parted in surprise. "Don't tell me after all this time, you've finally come around—"

"Bookscouting is pretty cool," Dex said, feeling a sharp stab about how pleased his father looked, about how easy it would've been to show just a little interest all these years. "We'd like to interview you," he lied, struggling to keep the conversation turning to his purpose, "but you gave me another idea. I'm thinking it can't get any more unusual than reading fortunes in a Turkish Coffee House. How 'bout we check to see if there really is a Fikret Cihan's Coffee House in Turkey?"

"Well," Milton said, "why not? Let's see

what we can do." He clicked around on his computer and opened up a search engine. After a moment he said, "Well, I'll be. There is. In Malatya, Turkey! And with a website in both English and Turkish, no less. But I really don't recall ever—I'll have to check with Latty. She plans all my itineraries down to the last detail, even restaurants. She'd know—"

"You sure you want to freak her out with all this?" Dex asked, alarmed.

"Upon reflection," Milton replied, smiling but serious, "not on your life."

"Does the website have a phone number?" Dex asked, allowing a tiny sigh.

"He's got an e-mail address. Here, I'll open an e-mail to him. There. We can send a note. Why don't you come around and—"

Again, the panic.

"*Hellooo* in there!"

A lanky woman stepped into the room, rescuing Dex. She was so tall, thin and full of awkward angles, that all Dex could think of when he saw her were those hanging projects kids make in elementary school out of linked-up coat hangers. She was blushing as she pushed her tiny glasses up her nose. It was Evelyn

Idun, Director of the Home.

After she'd arranged Milton's transfer from the hospital, she'd made sure he got a room near her desk in the lobby so she wouldn't have to go far to check on him. When Dex had pushed his father's wheelchair into the building that morning, she'd made a big fuss and promised the twins she'd have him back on his feet in no time.

"Hello there, Evelyn," Milton said, offering a genuine but hesitant smile.

"You look fantastic!" Evelyn declared, marching right to Milton's bedside. "The color has come back to your face." She put the back of her long-fingered hand on his forehead. Milton blinked, looking slightly overwhelmed.

"Amazing!" Evelyn said. "Though I don't like the sound of that voice. Let's do some walking, shall we? You can do it. Two minutes, I promise."

Milton looked unsure.

"Go ahead, Dad," Dex urged. "Maybe I'll e-mail the guy while you're out."

"Very well, then," said Milton, as if he had a choice. Evelyn was already hauling him out of bed and getting him situated behind his rolling walker. As they inched to the door, she complained that he never returned her calls. Milton said something about the messages probably getting lost on Latty's desk, but then they were gone.

The screen saver came up on the laptop, attracting Dex's attention. After a big sigh, he sat on the bed and touched a key, bringing up the e-mail form his father had opened. It was perfect the way things were working out. Perfect, except for the fact that Dex couldn't type.

As part of his lifelong campaign to camouflage his reading problem, he'd kept away from computers. When he had no choice, he'd sit and click away, pretending to know what he was doing, then stop and quit if anyone came to see what he was up to. Teachers assumed he was messing around with the computer's hard drive or visiting forbidden sites on the web, and that was fine by him because it often got him kicked off.

But Dex wasn't going to lose this opportunity. He was going to figure out what this "dream" meant. If it were true, it was hard to believe. How in the world could his father wander into a random coffee house in Turkey and have some old geezer force a book on him that people had been chasing for millennia, only to wind up bringing it to another old geezer in Portland, Oregon, who wanted it to enslave the world? The coincidence was too much. He'd have to be some kind of—puppet.

Of course! Dex thought, jolted. He was a puppet. He wasn't controlling his thoughts and actions! Someone else was—and there was no doubt in Dexter's mind that this someone was Adem Tarik. Part of his dad knew it, Dex realized, and that's why he'd been saying he wasn't a bad man!

Dex concentrated for a moment on the screen, but almost instantly, the usual, crippling stress arose. It brought an acrid taste to his tongue and made him start to sweat. He glanced down at the keyboard, but the letters seemed to sway and blend, and now the screen shimmied in his vision.

Dex looked away, defeated that quickly. Furious, though not surprised, he pounded out some random letters and watched the meaningless symbols squirm across the screen. He could make out the large icon with an envelope halfway into a mailbox. *Screw it*, Dex fumed. He clicked it, sending off his jumbled letter.

"Dex!" someone called. It was Daphna, slipping into the room wearing a backpack and a strange, flushed look on her face.

Dexter jumped off the bed. His sister had obviously gone home to shower and change, which irritated him, but even so, he'd never been so happy to see her in his life.

"What happened?" he asked. "Did you find him? Did you get the books?"

"Coming through!" Evelyn appeared in the door at that moment, just ahead of Milton. "Daphna, darling!" she cried. Dex knew Evelyn thought Daphna was the world's greatest kid for reading to the old folks.

"Hi, Evelyn," Daphna said.

Evelyn grinned, but then turned back to her charge.

"Let's get you back into bed," she said, walking Milton slowly across the room. Halfway there, she looked at the twins and said, "Your father's doing super! Far better than I expected at this point."

Dex and Daphna smiled at this news.

"I'd love to stay and chat," Evelyn told them

when Milton was comfortable again, "but I've got to go deal with the police. I still can't believe what happened! You two must be devastated. I know I said it before but, Daphna, your entire group murdered in cold blood!" Daphna nodded and looked away. She was devastated, even if she didn't have two seconds to notice it.

"Anyway," Evelyn continued, "I shudder to think what kind of mess the police made of the Records Room. This is all too bizarre and awful if you ask me. That Mrs. Scharlach! She seemed like such a nice old lady!" Evelyn offered a sympathetic smile and then left the room shaking her head.

The moment she'd gone, Dexter bugged his eyes at Daphna to let her know he wanted the news. She bugged her eyes back as she took the pack off her shoulder.

"Dad," Daphna said, "remember that book we were telling you about, the really messed up one that makes no sense? The one you gave away and were trying to get back? Well, I just happened to find it. Here it is." Daphna pulled the mangled, decrepit *Book of Nonsense* out and handed it over to her father. Dex looked on, amazed by his sister's ability to get things done.

Blinking, Milton took the book and examined it carefully.

"You know what?" he said. "This looks like a book I picked up for your birthday, kids. Did you find it in the house?"

"Um, yeah, Dad. It was under your bed. I was vacuuming. I'm sorry if I ruined the surprise. Why did you get us such a crazy book?"

"No reason," said Milton, though he looked rather unconvinced. "Just a curiosity. I seem to have ruined books on my mind—"

"Thanks, Dad," Daphna sighed, taking the book back and trying not to sound disgusted. But it didn't matter. Milton had drifted off to sleep.

Dex waited a moment, then turned to Daphna and asked, "Did you get the Ledger, too?"

Daphna didn't respond at first. She seemed interested in something on the floor. Then she looked up, though not at Dex, and said, "No, Emmet told me he destroyed it. He died."

"He died? That's incredible!" Dex cried. "I don't know how you do it!" He shared what he'd learned: his father's "dream" and his theory that Adem Tarik was somehow still involved in all this, somehow controlling Milton.

Daphna, whose face had uncharacteristically dimmed in the face of her brother's praise, lit up again with all this new information.

"Dex," she said, "Emmet told me that Rash ranted about Adem Tarik every day, about what a loser he was for wanting to create Heaven on Earth. Do you see?"

"He was the Teacher!" Dex cried. "He recruited the thirty-six kids to learn the First Tongue! But—but, why would he call Mom and send her into those caves? It was his book. Why wouldn't he get it himself if he knew where it was?"

"I don't know," Daphna replied. "Maybe it was too risky. But don't you see, that does explain why Mom would have gone on such a dangerous trip after she'd quit the search! Even if she'd already sold the store!"

"Yes," Dexter agreed. "She would've thought the search might end once and for all. Did Emmet tell you anything else about Adem Tarik?"

"No, nothing," Daphna admitted. "We've got nothing to go on."

"Not completely nothing," Dex said. He'd forgotten to mention that Milton had found a website for the coffee shop he'd dreamed about.

"I sent that Fikret guy an e-mail," Dex said after explaining. "But it made no sense. I was mad and just pounded on the keys. You could write, though, and ask him about Dad's visit."

"That's great," Daphna said, brightening up further. "I'll do that later tonight."

Milton stirred in his bed just then. "I—not a bad man," he said. "Adem Tarik—I—I—"

The twins waited him out, and when he seemed done, Dex said, "Okay, but there's something we'd better do ASAP."

"What's that?"

"We need to destroy that book. Finish the job for the Council once and for all."

Daphna hesitated. "Are you sure, Dex?" she asked, surprising him. "I've been thinking it over. I know people misused the First Tongue when they knew it, but does that mean people would misuse it again? Aren't we much more civilized now? Think of the power, Dex. Think of all the problems that could be solved. Think of the justice that could be served. If I learned it, I could teach it to you."

Dex was impressed by Daphna's enthusiasm, but any second thoughts she might have stirred just got wiped out. He'd been feeling a lot less angry at her since he spilled the beans about not being able to read, but the thought of her, already Miss Overachiever of the Universe, teaching him like a toddler—well, that just wasn't going to happen, not in this lifetime. Dex was sure he'd never be able to learn it, anyway.

"No," he insisted, "don't you think the Council considered that? If they didn't want it around when they were the only ones who knew it, it must be bad news. People aren't meant to have that kind of power. Look what Picker was doing with it! I think we should burn it."

"I don't know," Daphna replied. A pained look crossed her face. "I don't think I could do it."

The thought of burning a book, rare or not, magical or mystical or otherwise, didn't phase Dex. But he knew Daphna could barely stomach seeing a dog-eared page in a worn-out paperback she didn't even like.

"Daphna," he persisted, "Mrs. Tapi was trying to burn the book when Emmet got her, remember? That's what the Council wanted. For crying out loud, you're standing there holding a book that supposedly belonged to God. Do you think you're meant to drag it around like some overdue library book?"

"You're right," Daphna conceded. "You're right." Then she looked down at the book in her hands.

"By the way," she said, "the pages are all changing. They're blurry. At least they were. Maybe they stopped, or maybe Dad's just too whacked out to know the difference. I almost puked looking at them."

"So?"

"So, I was wondering if this is what it looks like to you when you read regular books." Daphna held the book out for Dex, who took it with mild curiosity. He opened to the middle somewhere and looked down at a page. Immediately, his eyes dilated into two spotted green moons. He snapped the book shut.

Daphna was genuinely hoping to get some insight into what Dex had to deal with, but he was staring down at the book's tattered cover, his mind suddenly somewhere else.

"Am I right?" she asked. "Are they moving again?"

"Yeah," Dex muttered, not lifting his eyes from the book.

Daphna looked at her brother. His cheeks,

crimson when she'd come in, had gone a deeper red, and he looked almost clammy. "Are you okay?" she asked.

"That's—that's exactly it," Dex explained, massaging his forehead now. After a moment, he looked up, though there was no focus to his vision. "Only—it's a lot worse," he added. "I feel kinda sick now."

"Sorry," said Daphna, taking the book back, "it did the same thing to me. So, when do you want to do it?"

"What?"

"Burn it. If we do it here, we'll probably set off the alarm and Evelyn will have pandemonium on her hands again."

"Speaking of Evelyn," Dex said, regaining his focus, "I just got an idea. She said something about a Records Room, right? Maybe we can get in there and read up on all those old people in your group. They were all taught by Adem Tarik, right? Maybe we can find some clues."

"Great idea!" Daphna said.

Dex had to force himself not to look pleased.

"But," Daphna said, "let's go and do our own things for a while."

Dex looked skeptical, so she explained.

"Look, first of all I'm starving. And, anyway, if we suddenly seem like we're best friends, Latty's eventually going to think something is up. I know, we'll tell Latty we want to stay overnight with Dad. They have cots here. On the way over, we'll burn the book. Then, when everyone's asleep, we'll break into the Records Room. All the night nurses are on the second floor."

"Okay," Dex agreed, but then, with a trace of challenge in his voice, he said, "How 'bout I hold on to the book until then—so you won't get too attached."

Daphna's reply came after only a moment's hesitation. "I suppose that's reasonable," she said and then handed the book over.

Dex received it with no small measure of surprise. He felt guilty for the surge of suspicion he'd felt, but forgot about it in a sudden rush to get going. He considered the incredible, fragile old book for a few seconds, then turned and left the room, too swept up in his own swirling imagination even to think of saying good-bye.

Daphna, distracted by her own considerations, thought nothing of her brother's hasty departure. In fact, she was pleased to have a chance to make sure the Ledger was still secure in her bag. She felt sorry for lying. She hadn't planned to do it, just like she hadn't planned to flirt with Emmet or use that Word to choke Wren and Teal. It all just happened. Things were just happening, and the best she could do was react.

The point is, Daphna told herself as she re-zipped her bag, *there's no use worrying about it*. In fact, she realized, if Emmet was right, there was no use worrying about anything. If events repeated themselves ten trillion times, she was just doing whatever she happened to be doing this time around. It seemed like the only rational thing to do was just to go with the flow.

Besides, if she told Dex the truth now, he'd stop trusting her altogether. There'd be a screaming match, for sure. And what was the point of asking for trouble before it was due?

burning desires

Everything went according to plan. Latty, who'd seen the news about a "bizarre incident" at the dump, was reluctant to let the kids leave after dinner. But she was touched that they wanted to stay by Milton's side.

After what appeared to be a rather tormented internal debate, she sent them off with a container of Min-hun-t'ang soup and several pleas to do anything and everything they could to make sure their father didn't think about what happened in those caves.

"And don't worry," Daphna teased, putting her backpack over a shoulder at the door, "we'll protect him from that woman!"

Latty smiled, accepting the gibe, and waved her off.

Daphna turned to leave and saw that Dex was already hurrying down the road. He also had his backpack over a shoulder and was carrying a large tin can. She rushed after him as best she could carrying the soup.

"Slow down, Dex!" Daphna hollered as her brother turned into an alley up ahead. When she rounded the corner, she saw him at the far end, stooping over the can, which he'd set on the ground.

"I said wait up, Dexter!" Daphna protested, reaching him at last. Dex lit a match and dropped it into the can. Instantly, multi-colored flames leapt up. Daphna jumped back. "What's going on? Why's it burning like that?"

"Lighter fluid," Dex answered. "I'm sorry I didn't wait Daphna, but I had this huge feeling you were going to try to talk me out of it."

Daphna looked cross, so Dexter added, "You're good at that. I didn't want to give you the chance," which took the teeth out of her glare. Brother and sister watched the flames transform the book into a pile of layered black tissue. It didn't take long.

"So it's done," said Daphna when the last glowing red sliver faded to gray.

"Finally," Dex sighed. There was a dumpster in the alley, so when the can cooled enough, Dex tossed the whole thing in.

"It sort of feels anticlimactic, though, doesn't it?" Daphna said when it thunked inside.

"What do you mean?"

"I mean it all seems too easy. We got the book and burned it. After all the Council went through—and for so long. It feels weird."

"We went through a lot, too, Daphna. I don't how you can say it was easy. We were almost killed, like two hundred times."

"I know. Believe me, I know. I just meant it seemed too easy to destroy. I mean, doesn't it blow you away to think that book might really have belonged to God?"

"Yeah. I guess," said Dex.

"You guess?"

Dex ignored his sister's tone. He'd never thought seriously about the idea of God. The few times he'd tried, it felt not unlike looking at the pages of a book—dizzying and pointless. Anyway, this was hardly the moment to start contemplating the subject again.

"So, what have you been doing all day?" he asked.

Daphna considered pressing her point. It seemed important that Dex understand the incredible significance of what they'd just done. But then she thought, *Why?* He either appreciated it or he didn't.

Again, trying to avoid thinking the worst about her brother, it occurred to Daphna that though he'd been totally absorbed in the search for answers about the various mysteries surrounding the book, he hadn't expressed much fascination with the book itself. And why would he if he couldn't read it? A book that belonged to God would be nothing but the ultimate cruel joke to him.

"I just kind of hung out in my room," Daphna said, attempting to sound warmer. "I really needed some time to think about everything that's happened. I wanted to think about the Dwarves. It's all been too much. We've seen people die, Dexter. The whole world seems like it flipped upside down since we turned thirteen. What did you do?"

"Oh, I just hung out in my room, too, with an ice pack. My face is still killing me. Of course," Dex added, "yours is killing me worse."

"Ha ha. Never heard that one before."

"Let's go," Dex said with a renewed sense of urgency. "We've got to figure out a way to break into that room."

Daphna smiled, wryly. "Oh, that," she said. "I'm not worried about that at all."

"Why not?"

Daphna smiled again. "Trust me," she said, then walked swiftly out of the alley. This time Dex had to hurry to catch up to her.

"Daphna!" Someone had dashed out of a restaurant as the twins hurried by. "Daphna!" she called again. The twins stopped and turned. Daphna saw who it was and couldn't speak.

"Hey, Wren," said Dex.

"Ah, hi," Wren replied, giving him a dismissive once-over. Dex knew she hadn't the slightest idea who he was.

"Anyway," she said, turning away from him, "Daphna, I'm glad I ran into you. How are you?"

"Um, I'm—I'm good. Thanks," Daphna stuttered. "We're kind of in a hurry, though."

"That's cool," Wren said. "I just wanted to let you know I'm having a party next Sunday night. A week from today. Just for fun you know, the last hurrah and all that before school starts. Just us girls. I'd love you to come. Around seven?"

Since he was basically invisible to her, Dex watched Wren closely as she spoke. Something was clearly not right. Aside from the obvious, that his sister was being invited to a Pop party, there was something about the indifferent tone Wren was affecting. It was covering something up. Something—he didn't know the word— predatory? It was there in her cool expression as well. But that's how Pops always seemed. He'd just never gotten this close to one before.

Daphna didn't seem able to hold up her end of the conversation. She was probably speechless now that her fondest dream was actually coming true.

"She'd love to," he said for her, but not without bitterness. Why did everyone have to keep mentioning that school was starting up again?

"Great!" Wren chirped, though she gave Dex a look that made him feel like he was a repellent species with which she was only passingly familiar. "By the way, cute bag!" she added, then disappeared back into the restaurant.

The twins looked through the front window and saw Teal at a table with some other Pops. She smiled and waved, though her smile looked oddly anxious to Dex.

Daphna hurried down the road, so Dex had to catch up again.

"What was that all about?" he asked, coming alongside. "Did I just see what I think I saw? Did she really just invite you to a party? I thought you had to be a Pop to go to a Pop party."

Daphna shrugged, looking both pleased and somehow guilty, like she'd just been caught cheating or something.

"You heard her," she said.

"But you're not a Pop." Dex scrutinized his sister. She certainly didn't look like her dreams had just come true. On the other hand, she had a bit of a smirk she was trying to hide.

"I don't get it," Dex said.

Daphna turned a sharp eye on her brother, but then collected herself. "I ran into her," she said, coolly. "Turns out they did lie about going to camp, but they apologized. So we're cool. Now let's get a move on or we'll—Oh, gosh—"

They'd reached the burned out hulk of the ABC. The twins stopped and stood there gaping at the collapsed front room. A line of yellow tape strung around rubber poles cordoned off what used to be the entrance. The place looked desolate.

"Wow," said Dex, "creepy."

"Hey! It's them!" someone shouted. The

twins tensed. Six boys stepped out from behind the far side of the building.

"Run, Daphna!" Dex yelled, dropping his bag.

Daphna was too stunned to react. Dex grabbed her by the arm, causing her to drop both her bag and the soup, and tried to pull her away. But because they both reached back for their bags, the twins wound up in a tangled clutch, and then it was too late. The boys dragged them toward the steps leading down behind the warehouse.

Rough hands pushed and pulled them down the stairs and then shoved them up against the blackened rear wall of the building. Dirty fingers jammed over their mouths.

"Well, well, well, well, well," sneered a gangling boy with ferocious red hair. He looked back over his shoulder twice as he spoke, though no one was there.

Dexter recognized this hooligan. He'd been there in the park with his gang when Emmet made Dex piss himself. Emmet had shouted at him to keep away. Dex was scared, there was no doubt about it, but something deep inside whispered that this might just be a chance to redeem himself.

Daphna was terrified, plain and simple.

She had no idea who these boys were. Some of them looked like the kids at school who were always getting suspended, but she never went anywhere near any of them.

"You got a strange name," the redhead said to the twins. "Wax. What's up with that? Are you made of wax or something? If you caught on fire, would you melt?"

Dex and Daphna tried to look at each other to gauge the seriousness of this threat. For their efforts, they got their skulls slammed into the wall. The redhead took a lighter out of his jeans pocket and flicked it. A tall blue flame jutted out like a blade.

"Go, Antin! Go, Antin!" sang the boy with his disgusting hand on Daphna's mouth.

"Shut up," Antin barked. Then he said, "We've become very interested in fire lately."

He stepped forward and waved the flame in Dex's face, revealing his herky-jerky black pupils. "Do you have any idea why we might be so interested in fire lately?"

Dex and Daphna managed to shake their heads.

"Tell 'em," the same other boy urged.

"Shut up. I'll tell you why," Antin said, stepping toward Daphna now with the flame. She recoiled from the bloodthirsty look in his eyes.

"For one thing," he said, "this old place just went up. Very interesting, fires. They can really mess you up. You ever see how much a fire can mess a person up?"

Daphna had no idea how to respond to this. She was too frightened even to speculate about what was going on.

Antin didn't seem interested in her answer, anyway. He snapped the lighter shut and crammed it back into his pocket.

"Funny you should ask," he said, looking over his shoulder. "Here, I'll show you."

At his command, a boy with tattoos on his hands pulled aside a large piece of plywood resting against the wall, exposing a hole. Other boys pushed the twins through, then covered the hole behind them blotting out the light like the door to a dungeon.

It wasn't completely dark inside. They were in some sort of basement or lower storage area. Portions of the warehouse's floor above had collapsed, so the ground was strewn with debris that seemed to include charred books. A series of dim, flickering flashlights were set up in a half circle in the center of the space, projecting weak beams at something large and lumpy under a sheet. Little else was visible, making the object appear to float in an empty black sea.

"Over here," Antin ordered. He'd moved up ahead and was squatting down at one end of the thing. Then, for some reason, he suddenly swung his light toward the back of the storage area. He moved it around a moment, but quickly turned his attention back to whatever was on the floor.

When Dex and Daphna were pushed forward, he snatched the sheet away like a magician. There were no flowers or birds or bunny rabbits in this trick. It was Emmet. Daphna looked down sadly at the body. The smell before was awful; now it was atrocious.

Dex was prepared for neither the sight nor the smell, and the shock, combined with the rank vapor he'd sucked into his throat, caused him to start heaving. The boys holding him leapt away, letting him fall to a knee and vomit on the floor. Everyone laughed.

So this was his redemption.

"We found him," Antin said, hauling Dex to his feet.

"So?" said Daphna. Seeing Emmet had somehow calmed her, and she'd been able to gather her thoughts a bit. She was desperate to get her bag before she lost the Ledger, but she didn't want to use her Word unless she absolutely had to.

"Sooo," Antin said, turning to Daphna with mock patience, "we want the scoop." He shone the flashlight at the body again. "What do you two know about good ol' Emmet here getting toasted?"

"Nothing," Dex insisted. "We don't know anything about it."

"Don't be stupid, even if you are the stupid one," Antin spat, looking back and aiming his light in Dexter's face. "We found him in your little hideout." Dex must have looked dismayed, because Antin laughed.

"The other day," he explained, "after you and him put on that little show in the park, we saw him follow you into the woods. So I did a little following myself. He watched you crying like a sissy for a long time before he took off." Antin turned to Daphna then and said, "We found Mr. Well Done here right before he croaked."

Now it was Daphna's turn to look dismayed.

She must have been wrong about Emmet being dead! She'd walked away from him, and he wasn't dead. These boys, these sick boys, must have been the people she heard in the woods.

"And guess what his dying word was," Antin said, giving a wildly exaggerated sniffle.

"I—I don't know," Daphna whispered.

"Nope," Antin quipped. Then he choked up with phony emotion and said, "His last word was—it was—'Daphna.' Isn't that touching? Anyone have a snot rag? I may weep." Approving snickers met this remark. Daphna dropped her head and fell silent.

"So what's the story?" Antin asked, switching to another voice, this one gossipy. "You and Emmet have a little thing going, or what?"

"No!" Daphna cried, disgusted by the mere suggestion. But Antin had given her an idea. It worked once, so— "I only got to know Emmet so I could ask him to help me meet you," Daphna said shyly. She was still using the poor boy. "I'm always too scared when I see you around."

"Why's that?" Antin asked, suddenly interested.

"'Cause—'cause—" Daphna sputtered. Her

insides felt like they were rebelling. She didn't think she could go through with it without throwing up like Dexter had. No more words would come out.

"Well?" Antin said, the edge creeping back into his voice. Now the light was directly in her face.

Next time, Daphna told herself. It was now her motto. "I just think you're kind of cute is all," she said.

burning desires (part ii)

"Daphna!" Dex yelled in disbelief, but two boys grabbed him and twisted his arm behind his back so far he couldn't speak.

"Fellas, fellas!" Antin said, turning round. "Did you hear that? Daphna here's got the hots for me!" He turned back to Daphna and said, "You're one of those good girls who go for bad boys, is that it?" All the boys in the room laughed, malevolent cackles in the dimly blinking dark.

"Why don't we go outside and talk about it," Daphna asked. She couldn't tell if she had the upper hand. It didn't feel like it had with Emmet. Not at all.

"Sure," Antin said. "Noooo problem." But he didn't move.

Daphna was rapidly losing her nerve. "Can we go now?" she asked.

Antin chuckled. "Sorry, Babe, business

before pleasure. That's what I call my girlfriends—'Babe'—hope you don't mind. So, how
'bout you just tell me what old Emmet here was
looking for."

"I told you," Daphna replied, "we have no
idea."

"That's right," Antin said, "you did say
that." He took a few steps toward Daphna, and
the next thing she knew a vicious slap snapped
her head to the side and sent her sprawling.
She never saw it coming. The boys holding Dex
clenched him even harder, but he didn't try to
move. He could see his sister's silhouette crumpled on the ground, but he could not react to it.
He couldn't feel anything because his mind was
spinning away.

"Oh, I guess I shoulda told you," Antin said,
helping Daphna, stunned and disoriented, to
her feet. "That's what I do when my girlfriends
lie to me."

Antin walked over to Dex and put his arm
around his shoulder like they were old-time
buddies. "Chicks," he said. "Can't do anything
with them, right? 'Specially the good-lookin'
ones. So, what's the story, man?"

"We don't know any story," Dex whined

when someone took a hand off his mouth. His arms were going to break if they didn't let up.

"I'll tell you a story then," Antin said. "When that freakshow showed up and started scaring kids off the streets around here, he was messing with our territory. We went to take care of him, but he told us he and the old man were up to something major. He said he'd cut us in on it if we backed off in the neighborhood for a while."

When neither Dex nor Daphna responded to this, Antin continued. "Soooo," he said, "when we found him all extra crispy-like in the woods, we tried to beat the story out of him for a while. But the big idiot wouldn't spill the beans no matter what we did—too stupid to feel pain, I guess."

The twins remained silent.

"Soooo," Antin went on, "old Antiny here had to do some figuring on his own, and this is how he figured it: Emmet here's burnt up, right? Good. And this place burned, right? Good connection, right? Solid. And that freak wrings your neck. You with me? And he croaks out your name before going kaput. Any of this making sense? Oh, wait, your old man sells books, right? Found that out, too. And that old books can be worth a lot of money. You following me? Been all kinds of vultures around here sneaking off with burnt books. How this crap could be worth anything is beyond me. Lookit—" Antin bent down and picked up a book and opened it. It was too dark to see what it looked like, but it seemed heavy.

"Just names," he said. "Like a gazillion names on every single page. Most of the books down here are just as stupid." He tossed it away. "Anyway," he said. "So what's the deal?"

"We told you—" Dex tried, but it was a feeble protest.

"Save it," Antin snapped. "We want to know what Emmet and the old dude were after. I knew you'd come snooping around here soon enough. So, unless one of you tells me exactly what I want to know, right now, we are gonna start melting some wax around—"

"How dare you!" Daphna suddenly screamed. Her cheek was still smarting, but her head was clear. She hadn't heard anything past the news that the gang had beaten Emmet. She leapt at Antin, already punching and kicking. She wanted to tear his hair. She wanted to scrape his eyes out for what he'd done to that poor, lonely, dying boy.

Though she'd never physically attacked anyone before, all of the anger and frustration she'd been feeling about so many things burst out in a singular desire to hurt. Daphna wailed her arms and legs indiscriminately, trying to claw at the arms and hands struggling to get hold of her. Enough was enough, she was going to choke every last evil boy there with her Word—but now hands were on her mouth. She couldn't speak. She could barely breathe.

Antin started laughing again when Daphna was finally subdued. "I guess we know who wears the pants in the family," he sneered. "And speaking of pants, did your brother tell you what happened when old Emmet here—"

"He's gone!" someone shouted.

The boys who'd remained with Dex wheeled around to see where he was, but just then there was a violent whacking sound. Someone on the fringes of the group let out a whelp of pain and collapsed.

Moments later, there was a second smack, then another cry as a second boy fell. Bedlam ensued as everyone scrambled in a riot to get out. The blinking flashlights were kicked around in the mad rush and sent spinning in all directions like crazy, feeble searchlights. It was impossible to see where anything was. Cries followed one upon another as more boys crumpled in pain.

Daphna heard the repeated smacking and the heavy thumps of bodies hitting the floor around her, but she couldn't see what was making them fall. The lights were here, then there, whirling around. She caught a glimpse of one boy stagger as if he'd been hit in the back, but for the life of her couldn't see what hit him. Terrified, she crouched on the floor.

"Daphna!" It was Dexter. He was somewhere nearby, but she couldn't see him.

"What's going on, Dex? I'm scared," she whispered.

"Come on," Dex urged.

Daphna couldn't see where to go, but suddenly the board blocking the hole in the wall was pushed aside. She ran for it, getting only a brief glance back inside at the strewn bodies clutching heads, guts and legs. Once out into the light, Daphna found her brother holding a broken piece of rafter. He tossed it aside, grabbed her by the arm and pulled her back up to the street. It was getting dark.

"My bag!" Daphna cried leaping to scoop it up. Dex grabbed his own, and the pair sprinted away. They ran full out until they reached the R & R but pulled up before going inside.

"How—when—I didn't know you could—what happened in there?" Daphna panted.

Dex, shaking and wheezing, said, "It was dark—they let go when you—I surprised them—"

Daphna, also shaking uncontrollably, waited for more of an explanation, but none came. It was as if Dex thought it was no big deal to beat up half a dozen juvenile delinquents. Before she could ask anything further, he stepped around her and hurried into the lobby, so she followed, impressed with her brother like never before.

(not) breaking
and entering

After composing themselves as best they could, Dex and Daphna stepped into their father's room. They found him working on his computer in bed. Daphna, trembling still as her adrenaline ebbed, noticed immediately he was typing much faster than usual.

"Isn't it amazing?" Milton whispered when she pointed it out. He apparently didn't want to strain his voice, which sounded like sandpaper now, but he flexed his fingers above the keyboard. "My arthritis isn't bothering me at all," he said. "It's been years since my hands felt so good. And my hip! It hurts so much less than—are you two okay? You're both pale. And Daphna, now *your* face is bruised. Did something happen? The two of you look like you've been through a war."

"Oh," said Dex, thinking his father had no idea how right he was. "We—raced," he lied, dropping his bag on the floor. "Daphna wiped out."

It was difficult to speak in a normal voice with his heart still throbbing. Dexter was on a high like he'd never experienced before. He could barely contain the urge to prance about and scream and pump his fists in the air. He'd just routed an entire gang. He, Dexter Wax, had just routed an entire gang. With every swing of that board he was taking out more than just those psychos. He was taking out the cruel kids in elementary school who challenged him to spell three letter words on the playground; he was taking out the domineering Pops in middle school who walked all over everyone; he was taking out every adult who'd ever lectured him about his lackadaisical attitude toward life and learning. This wasn't exactly the way he'd been hoping to start asserting himself, but it sure felt good.

Dex felt like some kind of superhero, and now maybe he'd have the confidence to find a way to feel like this all the time. He did wonder if maybe he'd used more force than was strictly necessary, but it wasn't like he hadn't been driven to it. He'd figure it out later, when he had some time to think.

"I tripped on a curb," Daphna explained. She put a hand to her cheek, feeling the pain now that her father had pointed out the bruise. Then she suddenly realized they'd lost the soup.

"Ah, I'm really sorry, Dad," she said, "but I kind of dropped the dinner Latty made for you, when I fell. It was your favorite again."

Milton offered a dismissive wave. "Don't worry about it," he said. "Evelyn brought me a great meal. She ordered out. Are you sure you're okay?"

"Sure, Dad," Daphna said. "Are you getting sick?"

"Evelyn thinks I'm getting laryngitis of all things. When it rains it pours, eh?"

"She likes you, huh?" Daphna asked, walking over to one of the two cots Evelyn had brought in. She stashed her bag underneath one and then sat on her hands to make them stop shaking.

Milton blushed a bit, which was not something the twins had ever seen before.

"Evelyn has never been anything but kind to me," he whispered, "though I'm afraid I've been too wrapped up in my business to appreciate it. Anyway," he said, changing the subject, "I'm really looking forward to this new trip to the Middle East. I've got a feeling I'm going to find something of great importance this time. But don't you guys worry, I'll be back before your birthday. I wouldn't miss this one for the world."

Dex and Daphna flashed each other a vexed glance but agreed to let this go. He'd said the very same thing before he left on the trip nearly two months ago.

"Oh, Dex," Milton added, "speaking of the Middle East, I got a very strange e-mail from that Turkish Coffee House owner you must have contacted, Fikret Cihan."

Daphna looked at Dex, perplexed.

"You did?" Dex said.

"Yes, and he seemed extremely upset. What in the world did you write?"

"Nothing—I—What did it say?"

"He said your message—or my message, since it came from my account—was an intolerable insult. He said his grandfather is dead, but that it's all already on the way, though he didn't say what 'it' was. He said if

I don't explain immediately, he'll come here personally to take it all back. Do you have any idea what he's talking about?"

"I have no idea," Dex replied.

"Did you ask him to send something?"

"Um, yeah," said Dex. It was easy enough coming up with a reasonable explanation for that. "I asked him to send me answers to the questions I was supposed to ask, for our assignment, I mean—and also, if he had any authentic items we could use for the presentation. Maybe he sent a bunch of stuff?"

"But he sounded so angry."

"Maybe my typing was bad or he took something I wrote the wrong way. Maybe his English isn't all that great."

"Well," said Milton, "I suppose anything is possible. Maybe I'll send him a quick note, just for clarification."

"I'll do it, Dad. Don't worry about it. It's probably my fault."

"All right," Milton said. "I am a bit tired." He apologized for being so tired all the time.

"That's okay, Dad," Daphna told him. "We're pretty tired, too." Milton seemed relieved to hear this, so the twins took turns in the bathroom getting into their pajamas, then turned off the light and climbed into their cots.

For a few minutes, they laid in the dark wondering how they'd know when their father fell asleep. But that turned out to be no problem at all because within five minutes, he was muttering, "Not a bad man—not—I—Adem Tarik—Adem Tarik."

The twins sat up when he stopped.

"When do you want to do it?" Dex whispered.

"We've got to wait until everyone's asleep," Daphna whispered back. "I'm gonna stay up reading. It's been like, forever. I'll wake you up." Then, with no further comment, Daphna curled into her sleeping bag and switched a flashlight on inside.

Dex glanced at Milton, then slid deep into his bag and switched his own light on.

"Dex!" It was Daphna, whisper-shouting his name. Dex flipped his flashlight off and sat up out of his bag in a haze.

"It's one a.m.," Daphna said, noting how tired her brother looked. His hair was shooting out in even crazier directions than usual. She was tired, too, of course, and was afraid to see what her hair looked like. "What were you do-ing in there? Sleeping with your light on?"

"Yeah," Dex said, blinking away the daze. "You look like crap."

"Thank you so much. Let's go, already."

The twins sneaked out of the room and padded cautiously into the lobby. Some of the overhead lights were dimly lit, so it wasn't too difficult to see. Dex walked directly to the door behind Evelyn's desk, clearly labeled, 'Records Room' and tried the knob.

"Locked," he said, twisting it round. "Check the desk for keys."

Daphna, already standing next to the desk, tried the drawers, all of which were unlocked. She looked up, shaking her head.

Dex scanned the lobby for ideas. He looked up, remembering how he'd gotten into the ABC, and sure enough, another idea came to him. He walked over to Daphna and point-ed up at the ceiling, which was made of square panels resting on thin metal strips.

"Those lift right up," Dexter whispered, "same as in school. I might be able to crawl into a vent that leads in there."

Daphna thought this was a terrible idea.

Dexter was going to get himself killed pulling a stunt like that. On second thought, it gave her a perfect opportunity.

"Well," she whispered, "go grab a flashlight. It's probably pitch black up there."

"Right."

When Dex was gone, Daphna immediately focused all her attention on the Records Room door. Then she closed her eyes and thought about being behind it as intensely as she could. Slowly and clearly, she spoke the Word Emmet told her about, the one he'd used to get to the dump—the one, incredibly, that took her from her bedroom to her closet that afternoon. Twice.

Daphna felt nothing, but she opened her eyes and smiled. She was surrounded by tall gray filing cabinets in a dark and cramped little room. It worked again! It was incredible. She'd felt absolutely nothing, yet, there she was. There wasn't time to dwell on it.

Daphna hurried to the door, opened it, and stepped back into the lobby. Dex was just coming back in with his flashlight.

"What? It was—How—?"

"Shhh. It was unlocked."

"But—I tried it!"

"Shhh! It sticks a bit. Come on already."

Dex looked at Daphna a moment and recalled how certain she'd been they'd get in. He tried to picture how well he'd worked the knob. The truth was, he was too groggy to remember. Maybe it was sticky. Dex slipped into the office behind his sister, slapping himself lightly on the cheeks.

Fortunately, the door had no window, so the twins were able to turn on the light and move around freely. The narrow little room was lined with cabinets, labeled alphabetically. Daphna dove right into the W's.

A familiar grunt of self-loathing burst out of Dex before he could stifle it. It was obvious he was going to be of no use, so he sat on the floor. He wished bashing things with heavy objects was necessary again.

Daphna looked up and saw the disgruntled look on her brother's face. She hurried her search through the drawer she'd opened and pulled a file free.

"Dad's," she said, holding it up, but Dex only shrugged. Daphna flipped through the sheets inside, but at the same time asked, "Do you have any idea what that guy, Cifan—whoever Cifan—would've sent Dad?"

"Fikret Cihan," Dex said. "And I have no idea."

"That's really weird. And you say you only typed a bunch of gibberish in the e-mail?"

"Yeah. Maybe he could tell I was pissed, or maybe I typed out, 'Your grandfather's a nut,' in Turkish or something."

"Why would his grandfather have the *Book of Nonsense* anyway?" Daphna asked. "And why would he force it on Dad like that, just because he came in and asked about Adem Tarik?"

"Well," said Dex, "Adem Tarik must have given the book to him, and maybe he figured Dad was there to get it back for him."

"Yeah, that makes sense," Daphna said. She put Milton's file back, disappointed that it had failed to explain pretty much anything.

"Nothing interesting?" Dex asked.

"It's all just medical forms from the hospital," she explained, pulling the drawer out as far as it would go.

"Hey," she said, "there's a huge book in the back here with some kind of straps on it. She reached for it, but noticed a second file with her father's name on it. It was the last one. "Look at this—" she said, lifting its contents out. "It's for Dad."

"A present?" Dex asked. Daphna was showing him a thin rectangular gift of some kind.

"It feels like a book," Daphna said, "but it's almost totally flat. Oh, that's weird—"

"What?"

"There's a tiny card attached that says, 'For my soul mate.' It's from Evelyn."

"Probably some book she thinks Dad wants," Dex said. "She was hitting on him when they met, on the plane ride we all took moving here. That's why Latty doesn't like her."

"Someone hitting on Dad," Daphna laughed. "That's about the biggest joke I've ever heard. And to still like him thirteen years later—that's kind of pathetic, actually."

"Yeah, it's like she's obsessed or some—Wait a minute!" Dex cried. "What if she's some kind of stalker? It's kind of a coincidence that she happened to be on that flight from New York with us, isn't it? Maybe she's been following Dad!"

"What? Shh! I don't know, Dex. If you think about it, it's a coincidence that you meet anyone."

"But what if she really lived in Israel, and knew him there, and was in love with him, but he didn't know her—and then he married Mom. What if she was really jealous?"

"So she sent Mom away to get killed, and then followed Dad to Portland? Is that what you're saying?"

"Well, isn't that the kind of thing insanely jealous people do? I'll bet you Latty suspects as much, and that's why she's hated her all these years!"

"But," Daphna replied, "are you saying Evelyn Idun is Adem Tarik?"

"Maybe!"

"Dex, keep your voice down!" Daphna was skeptical. "Okay," she said, "let's say she's Adem Tarik, forgetting for a second that Ruby called their teacher a 'he.' I do remember that."

"So what! She also said the Council was called The Nine! She was a liar!"

"True," Daphna conceded. "So let's say she wants to get Mom killed. Why? Let's say she's jealous and in love with Dad for some crazy reason. So she lures Mom into the caves and gets her killed. But Dad was there, too. He could easily have been killed as well. He almost was."

"Us! That's why!" Dex said. "Maybe Mom and Dad were both supposed to be killed in the caves! Maybe she was going to try to adopt us or something!"

"Okay," Daphna pressed, "but how does that fit with being obsessed with Dad or calling him her soul mate all these years later? Wouldn't she have tried to kill him again in the last thirteen years?"

"Dad wasn't supposed to go to the caves," Dex declared, adjusting his theory. "She probably figured he'd stay home with us when Mom went for the book! She doesn't want to kill Dad, Daphna. She wants to marry him!"

Daphna had no reply to this. She had to think about it.

"We should at least try to find out if Evelyn ever lived in Israel," Dex urged. "We should go search her stuff."

"Dex, not everything is a crazy conspiracy, you know."

"Let's open that gift!"

Daphna hesitated, doubting they'd be able to re-wrap it if it was nothing important.

"Not yet," she decided. "Let's slow down, Dex. I have to admit your theory isn't totally insane, but it's only a theory, and it's only our first theory. It doesn't even begin to explain how she could have been the Council kids' original teacher. Let's do what we came in here to do. If we don't learn anything else, we'll tear apart everything Evelyn owns."

"Fine, whatever," Dex snapped. Daphna couldn't stand not being the one who figured everything out. The euphoria he'd felt after leaving the ABC had begun slipping away when he'd come into the Records Room. Now it was gone completely.

Daphna, disturbed by the totally unnecessary harshness in Dex's voice, put the gift back into its file and put the file away. Then she moved to another drawer while he glowered at the floor. It was strange. As long as Daphna could remember, Dex had been falling in and out of his sulky moods, but so much had happened in just the last few days that it seemed part of another time, another life even.

"Here's Mrs. Tapi's file," she said, pulling out another folder, hoping to move things along. "She's got a phony birth certificate here. I'll bet most of this stuff is phony. It must've been hard for them, having to reinvent themselves every generation. It says she was a librarian." Daphna knew she was talking to herself, but it helped her ignore the stifling atmosphere Dex was creating in the already stuffy little room.

"Here's something called an 'Intake Interview Report' from the Home's psychologist," she said. "The rest home residents must have to do that." Daphna began reading it to herself as Dex watched with little enthusiasm.

"Not very interesting," she concluded. "Though it's kind of sad. It says when she was younger she lost a newborn baby and still seemed upset about it."

"Nothing about Adem Tarik, though?" Dex asked. "Like an address?"

"I wish," Daphna said, pleased Dex was at least paying attention.

"Here's Mr. Bergelmir' file." Daphna read through and put it back.

"Nothing," was her conclusion again. "Just more fake background info. He was a bookbinder. Nothing interesting in the Intake Interview. Let me get Mr. Dwyfan." Daphna skimmed through the file, then put it back.

"Nada," she moaned. "He was a publisher."

"That makes sense."

"What?" Daphna asked, pulling out another file.

"They were all in jobs related to books."

"Right, of course—Hey, this is strange—"

"What?"

"I've got Mrs. Kunyan. In her interview she said the most difficult ordeal of her life was giving birth to a stillborn baby."

"What's strange about that?"

Daphna, her interest piqued, pulled out a thick file with Mrs. Deucalion's name on it and read through papers for a while. Despite himself, Dexter grew increasingly curious as she read. Finally, Daphna looked up at him and held out a blue sheet of paper. "Her medical report," she said. "Guess what."

Dex had no idea what she was talking about. "What?"

"Under 'Health Notes,' it says she suffered some internal damage due to a complicated miscarriage."

"And?"

"Don't you see, Dex? All three of the women on the Council lost babies."

"What does that mean?"

"I don't know," said Daphna, "but Mom

was on the Council, and we didn't die."

"Wait a minute!" Dex cried, jumping to his feet. Maybe he had been too hasty condemning Evelyn.

"Shh! What?"

"I just remembered something Mrs. Tapi said in the park before Emmet got her!" Dex tried to keep his voice down, but it was difficult. "She said that when Mom told the Council she was quitting the search, they weren't surprised. She said—I remember her exact words—she said they weren't surprised because 'several of us did the same over the years, though our own tragedies brought each of us back.'"

"That's right!" Daphna cried. "They all left the search to have babies, even though they were all so old. But they all lost them—the tragedies— so they all went back. What does it mean? Why were they all trying to have babies?"

"I don't know," Dex said. "Didn't Mom say she just wanted a normal life in her note?"

"The note!" Daphna fumbled it out of her pocket once again. It was starting to tear.

family matters

My Dearest Children,

I am writing to you now, just minutes before I leave on a most unexpected journey.

For so very long I have been searching for a book. This search has consumed my time in this world and denied me what I truly seek, what we all seek: to live, to love. May you never know loneliness like I have known. May you be surrounded by those who love you all the days of your lives. How blessed you are to have each other!

I broke my word, Children, and renounced the search. I found Love. Uttering those two small, simple words, "I do," set me free. And now I have you and my joy knows no bounds.

Only now it seems that the book may be within reach. I am going to find out. I expect the best, but something I cannot put my finger on worries me, and so I must write you this note. There is a man, Asterius Rash, who will go to any length to find this dangerous book, including murdering children. Should you ever cross his path, run! Under no circumstances should you have anything to do with this vile man.

It is my profound wish that you never read this note, for if you do, it will be because I am gone. I love you so much. I must admit I did not think it possible that you two could ever be. Two little miracles! Latona did me the greatest favor in my long life when she encouraged me to try for you. I need you both to

"*STOP READING!*" Dex ordered in a barely stifled scream.

"What?" Daphna cried. "We've got to be quiet! You scared me to death! *What?*"

"Daphna," Dex said, coolly, "what if it wasn't actually the women's idea to have kids. Or, what if someone took advantage of the fact they all wanted to and talked them into trying, someone who wanted them to have children for some reason. You just read the answer, Daphna. 'Latona did me the greatest favor in my long life when she encouraged me to try for you.' Dad told me the same thing earlier today!"

"Oh, my God, Dex," Daphna gasped. "Latty! Oh, my God, Dex. Oh, my God!"

"She took that supposed phone call," Dex realized. "There was no call! And she's the only one who had a story to tell about what happened in the caves. I think she's Adem Tarik! She probably just faked those cuts and bruises! And—and—"

"It makes perfect sense!" Daphna shouted, unable to keep her own voice down. "At some point she works her way into one of the female Councilor's lives. She sets them up with some man, then talks her into having a child, but the baby dies, so she moves on to the next one, and the next one, until she gets to Mom. Mom's kids are born okay, but just to make sure, she waits a few months—"

"That's why Dad went into a coffee shop when he doesn't even drink coffee!" Dex said. "Latty plans his itineraries!" Dex slapped himself in the forehead. There it was, the explanation that kept eluding him, keeping a germ of doubt about his father festering. It all made sense now.

"Latty killed Mom, Dexter!" Daphna cried. "She probably tried to kill Dad, too! Oh, my God!"

"No," Dex said, "not Dad. We'd've been sent away to some foster home or something. She needed him alive so she could move into our house. She probably knocked him over the head and pushed Mom over the edge before the collapse ever happened! Or, for all we know, she used the First Tongue to cause that collapse, or give Dad amnesia about it. Dad gets better and she keeps him running all over the world on wild goose chases so he'll never meet a new wife who might not want her around—"

"Which explains why she hates Evelyn!"

Daphna said. "And then she stays at home and barely ever lets us out of her sight!" Daphna was reeling. "And that's why she's so freaked out about him remembering what happened in the caves! Dex, what are we going to do? I feel sick. I think I'm going to throw up."

"We've got to think this through, Daphna," Dex insisted, feeling a lot calmer than he would've expected. "We've got to figure out what she wants with us."

Daphna, nearly hyperventilating now, tried to get a grip on herself. "She's been waiting for us to turn thirteen, like everyone else!"

"That's got to be true," Dex agreed. "But what for? If she sent Dad to Turkey for the *Book of Nonsense*, why didn't she get it from him right away when he got home?"

Daphna understood. "Dad got in early! Latty was shopping, and I made him take me to the ABC the second he got out of his cab. He never even went in the house! Rash got the book from him right away. Remember how she freaked out when Dad mentioned Rash's name? She said it was just an awful name. She must've realized her plans had gotten screwed up!"

"Okay, but she didn't seem to want Dad to

get it back."

"That's true," Daphna agreed. "In fact, I think she was avoiding Rash. I didn't really think about it at the time, but she didn't go into the ABC with Dad when they got there with that Latin book. With Dad halfway crazed, she said she was going to the toy store to buy us gifts!"

"She couldn't go in," Dex said, amazed at the obviousness. "She couldn't risk Rash recognizing her."

"What does she want? If she is Adem Tarik, what was all that about making Heaven on Earth?"

"Nice way of going about it," Dex spat, "murdering people. She probably gave that book to Rash way back when and told him to start the War of Words. Hey! Maybe she wanted the book to get back to Rash so he could try again!"

Exhausted by all this speculation, the twins just breathed, letting the information sink in. They'd known Latty their whole lives! She was the closest thing to a mother they had.

After a while, Daphna said, "What should we do, Dex? How are we going to find out what she wants from us? I, for one, don't want to wait around for her to—whatever."

"Me neither," Dex agreed. "We've got to flush her out."

"Hey," Daphna said, swelling with anger. "Let's scare her. Let's let her know she's been found out and see what she does."

"How?"

"I don't know. Maybe we could write her a note or something."

"Tonight?"

"I could do it."

"It's like, two in the morning or something, Daphna." Dex could see his sister was serious, and after letting her deal with Emmet, he felt he had no choice but to offer to go himself. It wouldn't be too difficult.

It was plain to Daphna that Dexter hated her idea, again, and that this time he was going to insist on doing it himself. "I'll take care of it," she said, not giving him time. She slipped past her brother and out of the room while he was still getting to his feet.

By the time Dex hurried into the lobby after his sister, she was gone. He looked around, confused. How could she have gotten out so quickly?

Dex paced to the entrance to see if she was

just outside. It was too dark to see, but he did notice a little gray box on the wall next to the doors. It was a security panel with a blinking red light. The door was armed. Daphna must've headed for another exit. Dex chose the closest hall, his father's, and hustled down it, looking for another way out. The place was difficult to navigate because halls crisscrossed one another. He hadn't ever spent much time on the first floor, not that it would've made much difference. Daphna could've gone any which way.

Eventually, Dex found another door, but it was armed, too, as was the third and fourth he happened upon. By that time, he was too frustrated to care where Daphna was. He didn't even know where he was. There were mounted signs of course, but they did him no good.

Dex raged up and down random halls, growing more and more aggravated until by sheer luck he found himself back in the lobby. After closing up the Records Room, he stalked back to his father's room, fed up again with just about everything.

departures and arrivals

Dex sat on his cot and sulked. But after what seemed like no more than fifteen minutes, Daphna walked in. He'd wandered the halls for a while, but long enough for her to run home, sneak into the house, leave a note and run back? She didn't even look winded. *Not stinking likely*, Dex thought, but maybe she couldn't get out of the building. "Did you already—?"

"Shhh!" Daphna warned. "I went through the service doors downstairs—I sprinted! It's scary out there—I was afraid of running into those animals again." Noting her brother's disbelieving air, Daphna flushed with displeasure and said, "Do you want to know what happened or what?"

Dex did, so he pushed aside his rekindled distrust for the moment.

"Well," Daphna whispered, "on my way over, I started thinking maybe the direct approach wasn't the best plan. I mean, what do we think Latty'd do if we just came out and accused her of killing Mom? She'd deny it, obviously."

"So what did you write?"

"Well, first I wrote she shouldn't be alarmed that the note was delivered in the middle of the night. I said one of the nurses was getting off shift and lives right near us and didn't mind dropping it off."

"Okay, so what did it say?"

"I said we wanted to warn her about Dad before she came today."

"Warn her? About what?"

"Well, I said Dad's been talking more in his sleep and that he mumbled something like Mom didn't really slip off that ledge in the cave, that she was pushed. I wrote he sat up and yelled that she was murdered and then started saying he thinks he might know who Adem Tarik is. See, this way, she'll think she hasn't quite been found out yet, but she'll definitely think she's going to be. I figure she'll have to do something right away, and we'll be watching. If we're wrong, she'll just blow it off as more kooky mumbling.

"So anyway, I put it on the mat, and made a lot of noise like by accident, then hid. When I saw the front light come on, I ran back. It all took, like, five minutes. She must've been up."

"Not bad," Dex said, but with little enthusiasm. It was a clever idea. He'd never have thought of all that. Still, Daphna was up to something, and it was starting to get under his skin.

"Not bad?"

Dex could see Daphna was fishing for a compliment, but she wasn't going to get one. "I guess we'll just have to wait and see what it does to her," was the best he could offer.

"I guess so!" Daphna snapped. Dexter was acting like he couldn't care less that the person they'd spent the most time with in their lives murdered their mother.

Maybe he's in shock about it, she thought. It was shocking news after all. Perhaps she'd overlooked that possibility because what she felt wasn't shock, at least not anymore. She'd been lied to by the one person in her life she'd continually confided in, even if it had been a while since she and Latty had really talked. Not only had her supposed friends at school turned out to be frauds, her supposed best friend at home had, too.

What Daphna felt now was pure fury. If

Latty really was Adem Tarik—if she really did kill their mother—she needed to pay. Dex could react however he wanted, Daphna decided, but if she had to lie, cheat or steal, she was going to do whatever she had to do to get revenge. And if that wasn't the noblest way to react to these developments, well, she'd learn to take betrayal better next time around.

The words of Ruby Scharlach came back to Daphna just then. She'd told Dex that sometimes even those closest to you cannot be trusted. The irony of her remark was a bitter pill to swallow. Irate on several levels, Daphna climbed into her sleeping bag without offering her brother a goodnight.

Dex, having no intention of saying goodnight either, did the same. Both twins burrowed churlishly into their bags, so neither noticed the other's flashlight come on, nor did either comment when, ten minutes later, their father started mumbling in what was now a Rash-like raspy voice, "Adem Tarik, Adem Tarik—I—am—I—not a bad man."

"Kids! Kids! Up and at 'em! Kids!"
Dex and Daphna both jerked to woozy

attention and flipped their lights off. Neither had slept a wink.

"Rise and shine! Hello?" It was Milton, sounding like he was gargling steel wool.

Dex freed his head from his bag and blinked groggily at his wide-eyed father, sitting up in bed. A moment later, Daphna's head emerged. She had dark circles under her eyes.

"What gives?" Milton asked, noting the twins' equally bleary looks. "Are those cots that bad? I wanted to let you sleep, but it's already eleven, and I'm wondering where Latty is. She should've been here an hour ago, and there's no answer at home. I'm hoping one of you wouldn't mind running over to see what's what. I almost feel good enough to do it myself, but Evelyn would have my head if she knew I was even thinking about—"

Both Dex and Daphna were on their feet. "We'll both go," they said.

Daphna rushed into the bathroom before Milton could get another word out. He looked quizzically at Dex.

"I think she just really wants her own shower," Dex offered by way of explanation. "I just want some more sleep. The cot was a little lumpy." Dex noticed a tray of bagels and apples had appeared in the room. He grabbed one of each.

"I'm sorry about that, Dex. I could talk to Evelyn. But to tell you the truth, I don't think I'll be in here much longer."

"That's okay," Dex said. Daphna rushed back out just then, so he hurried into the bathroom behind her.

"Sorry to bolt out of here, Dad," Daphna said, grabbing her own bagel and apple.

"That's fine. I'm going to be doing some heavy duty walking today."

Dex reappeared, so the twins put on their backpacks, said good-bye to their father and hurried straight outside. They walked home eating ravenously, anxious to learn what Latty's absence meant.

The moment their house came into view, it was obvious something was amiss. Every light was on, and the front door was standing open. The car was also gone, which meant Latty was, too.

The twins dashed inside ready for—they didn't know what they were ready for. What they found was about the only thing they hadn't expected: that is, nothing. Nothing seemed wrong. Dex and Daphna looked around the living room and then walked into the kitchen. They came back out, shrugging. Both had a sense they were missing something.

"Something's weird," Daphna concluded. "I just can't figure out what."

"Yeah," Dex concurred. "It's different in here." The twins remained standing where they were, looking at everything as if for the first time.

"What is it?" whispered Daphna, turning about, scanning the bookshelves and coffee table and couch.

Dex was doing the same. He turned himself in a full circle before his eyes settled on the mantle above the fireplace.

"Look," he said, pointing to the blank space on the wall above it.

"Mom's picture!" Daphna hurried over and put her hand on the wall. She had no idea what it meant that it was gone. It was strange not to have noticed right away.

Dex turned to look at the collection of small, framed photos on the shelves and coffee table. They weren't there.

Daphna, certain what she'd find, rushed to the built-in cabinet below the shelves and threw open the doors. "All our photo albums!" she cried. "They're gone!"

Dex hurried into Milton's room and immediately called out, "They're all gone in here, too—even the giant one of Mom over his bed!"

Daphna noted the same in the kitchen and in the office. Then, at the same moment, both of them ran to Latty's room.

It was deserted.

There was a stripped mattress, an empty closet and barren dressers. It was as if it were an unused spare room. The twins, stunned by the sight, backed into the living room and sat down on the couch. Whatever they thought the letter might make Latty do, this wasn't it.

"It's like our past just got stolen," Daphna muttered, staring dumbly at the front door, still ajar.

"Why'd she take the pictures?" Dex asked. He was so tired, it came out as a whine. "Why'd she have to do that? Those pictures of Mom were all we had of her." Dex hadn't allowed himself time to think much about Latty's treachery. He hadn't entirely decided to believe it. But now—

"She's evil," Daphna snarled, feeling prickles on the back of her neck. "She wanted to hurt us on her way out. We were right, Dex. We've been living with Adem Tarik for thirteen years! We've been living with the person who killed our mother our entire lives. She took Mom's body once, and now she's taken her memory!"

These last words exploded out of Daphna. The guilt she'd already felt for being ashamed of her mother's old-looking face in those pictures hit her like a wrecking ball. Now they were gone. But Daphna was too crushed to rage for long. She suddenly felt empty and frail, and she wished she'd slept at least a little bit last night.

"What are we going to do, now, Dex?" she asked, whining herself. "I didn't think this far ahead. We've got to find her. We've got to find her and make her pay."

Dexter got up and paced around the living room. He'd never seen such a savage look on his sister's face before. He was angry, too, but she looked downright murderous. He did suppose Daphna was a lot closer to Latty than he was, though it didn't seem like it recently.

He had no idea what they could do now. What were they going to tell their father? Could they stall his coming home? Could they make a new effort to get him to remember everything so he'd understand, once and for all? Did they really want to make him remember seeing his wife get murdered?

"Hey, what's this?" Dex asked. He'd just crossed to the door and was about to close it when a long delivery truck pulled into their driveway. Daphna got up and hurried over.

The truck stopped alongside the house, and a muscular deliveryman hopped out with a clipboard in his hand. He approached the twins, who'd come out on the porch, and asked if a Milton Wax lived there. A pin on his work shirt said 'Ireneo Funes.'

"Ah, yeah," said Dex. "But he's in the hospital."

Ireneo looked disappointed. "Either of you eighteen?" The twins shook their heads, but he looked like he knew they weren't anyway. "Anyone home who is?"

"No, but we can sign," Daphna offered. "We're responsible."

"No can do. Could lose my job." Ireneo tore a card from a pad and handed it to Daphna. "Have your father give us a call to arrange another time for delivery."

"Really, we're very respons—" Daphna insisted, but Ireneo was already heading back to his truck.

"Do something, Dexter!" Daphna whispered. There was no possible way she was going to flirt with a grown man, but she was too worn out to think of anything else. "It's gotta be from that guy in Turkey! The stuff he said was on the way!"

Dexter hurried after Ireneo, who'd climbed back into his seat. Daphna heard him say something, then he came running by her and back into the house.

"I'll be one second!" he shouted.

Daphna was pleasantly surprised at her brother's lack of hesitation and extremely curious to know what he was doing. She walked casually over to the far side of the truck to see if Ireneo might say anything to her, but she found him sitting in his seat, staring through the windshield with a dull, slightly misty look in his eyes. She cleared her throat, but he didn't respond. He had that expression some kids get in school when they're so bored they have no idea where they are anymore.

"Ah, sir?" Daphna tried, growing concerned. She was about to lean in to get a closer look at Ireneo's eyes, but Dex called out from the house that he was coming. When he appeared at the driver's side door, Ireneo turned and blinked at him.

"I was hoping you could make an exception?" Dex said, holding out a bulging envelope.

"Huh? I've got to get go—"

"An exception," Dex repeated, putting the envelope into Ireneo's puzzled hands. "I'm sure they let you make exceptions sometimes. You know, about the age requirement."

Ireneo opened the envelope, but immediately squeezed it shut again. Daphna had seen enough to understand, a fat flash of green. Suddenly, Ireneo was climbing back out of the truck.

"You're right," he said, shoving the envelope into a long pocket on the side of his pants. He strode around behind the truck and the twins followed after. "They do make exceptions for minors, like, for times when the only adult is ill. You can go ahead and sign your father's name." Ireneo handed his clipboard to Dex, then began unlatching the cargo door.

"No problem," said Dex, scribbling away with relish. "We really appreciate—" Dex stopped short when the door rolled up. Both twins stared, transfixed, into the truck. Inside were boxes, hundreds and hundreds of boxes, all the size of milk crates, all with their father's name and address on them.

"Is this all for us?" Daphna asked.

Ireneo nodded. He began pulling boxes out and setting them on the driveway.

"Can we see what's in them?" Dex asked. Nodding again, Ireneo pulled a box cutter out of his back pocket and sliced open a box he'd set down. Then he went back to unloading.

The twins leapt to the box and pried up the flaps like it was the birthday gift they hadn't received. Inside were thick bundles of low-quality paper tied up with string. Dex fell back as if he'd discovered his present was a wasp's nest. Daphna, on the other hand, was thoroughly intrigued. She pulled a bundle out, untied it, and fingered through some pages. Her eyes grew wider. After a while, she put the bundle back in and pulled out another, then two more.

"Are all the boxes full of the same thing?" she asked, turning to Ireneo. He shrugged and tossed her the cutter.

"What are they?" Dex asked.

"Hold on," Daphna replied, cutting open two other boxes. They were both filled with the same bundles. She pulled a few out and flipped through them, then put them back. "There must be thousands of these in that many boxes," she said, slightly awed.

"Yeah, but what are they, Daphna?"

"Sir," Daphna asked, "is this all from Turkey?"

Ireneo took the clipboard back from Dex, checked it over and said, "Yeah, from Fikret Cihan."

Daphna was enjoying keeping him in suspense, Dex could tell, and he decided to let her know what he thought about it. He turned to Ireneo and asked if he'd mind giving him a moment to talk with his sister in private. Ireneo had no problem with this. He stepped back around front and climbed inside the truck.

"Dex, how much money did you give him?"

"I don't know. I just grabbed a couple handfuls."

"But why was he just sitting there, all spaced out when you went inside?"

Dex sighed. "I have no idea," he said.

"It was weird," Daphna insisted.

"Are you going to tell me what these stupid papers are or not?"

"Just lists of random words," Daphna said. "Bizarre ones. They're copies of the *Book of Nonsense*, Dexter. The old guy who gave Dad the Book—that's what he was doing when Dad came into that shop!"

"He was copying it in case the First Tongue reappeared, and he had to keep copying because, for all he knew, it might appear only one Word of Power at a time."

Dex looked into the truck and said with wonder, "He must have been doing it for his entire life. I bet he had no idea what he was doing it for."

"But he sure knew *who* he was doing it for!" Daphna cried, "Adem Tarik!, who was busy trying to get Council members to have babies!"

"Dex," said Daphna. "Latty sent Dad to get the *Book of Nonsense*, but also to get all these papers. Maybe that explains why she didn't care about the actual book when Dad brought it back! She had to know everyone would come and start killing each other over it. It was a lure! What she really wanted were the copies!" Daphna's temper flared up wildly again. "I mean, there was no way the First Tongue was just going to happen to be in the original book just because we turned thirteen!"

Dex shrugged, as if not entirely convinced. Then he seemed to think of something. "But, that's strange," he said.

"What's strange?"

"Well, the only reason anyone would want the *Book of Nonsense*, or those copies, would be to learn the First Tongue, right? And that's strange because Adem Tarik should already know it, right? She wasn't part of the Council. She didn't make herself forget it like they did. She taught the kids the language in the first place. If she wanted the book back, she could've writen her own copy of it, right?"

"Yeah," Daphna agreed, "but I guess not. I don't know what that means, and I'm way too tired to figure it out."

"Yeah, me—No, wait a minute. Remember

what Ruby told us about how the kids had to learn the Words of Power?"

"No, Dex," Daphna sighed. "I really don't."

"She said they had to puzzle out the Words themselves."

"She can't do it!" Daphna cried. "Maybe her plan all along was to have the kids learn the language so they could teach it to her! Maybe she was blind, like Rash! Maybe that's what she wants with us!"

"That would make sense," Dex replied, "except for one small thing."

"What's that?"

"Latty isn't blind."

"Oh, right," Daphna said. "I told you I was too tired. I give up, Dex. I can't deal any more."

"Me neither. And anyway, whatever the truth is, we better get busy."

"What do you mean?"

"By the looks of it, we're gonna be spending the next ten hours burning paper."

tired ideas

Dex had to bring out another envelope, but it wasn't too thick, and it helped Ireneo forget the deadlines that started worrying him again. It took nearly ninety minutes, but he and the twins managed to haul all the boxes into the living room. They were stacked everywhere. Awkward piles overwhelmed the couch, the chairs, the shelves, the coffee table and the floor. The tallest stacks reached as high as the twins' shoulders.

When Ireneo finally left, Daphna called Milton. She told him Latty wasn't feeling well and that she and Dex were staying home with her. He said that was fine because he was going to see a bunch of doctors all day anyway. Evelyn wanted them to confirm that he was recovering as fast as she thought he was. He said he might even try to talk them into sending him home in the morning if it went well.

As good as this news was, it made the twins frantic. They very briefly considered letting their father see all the bundles, thinking the incredible number of them alone might make their story more believable. But that was a long shot, and they quickly agreed it was more important to destroy any remaining source of Words of Power.

Though thoroughly exhausted, neither thought they could afford to rest at all. So, as soon as their minds were made up, the pair cleared a path through the boxes to the fireplace. Dex used one of the bundles from an opened box to get a fire started, and Daphna, sitting on the hearth, began feeding them in a few at a time once the flames took hold.

It was slow going, incinerating that much paper. The fireplace was only so large, and putting too many bundles in at once choked the flames. Also, scoops of ash had to be hauled out when it heaped up too high.

For a while, Dex tore out pages from the bundles for Daphna to throw in one at a time. They burned better, but it soon became obvious it would take days to do it all that way. The twins had no choice but to feed in the full bundles and wait. Feed and wait and scoop. Feed and wait and scoop. Both were too tired to talk. After a while, the repetition and the quiet and the steady heat from the fire finally got to Daphna. Leaning against the side of the fireplace, she nodded off.

"Daphna!" said Dex, poking her in the leg with a bundle.

Daphna jolted awake and suddenly asked, "Did you tell that delivery guy what you were doing when you went into the house?" She'd been thinking about it as she fell asleep, about the way Ireneo said he was in a hurry, but then just sat there waiting, like he was meditating or something.

"I don't know, Daphna. Just keep burning."

"You don't know? It was like, two hours ago."

"Look, Daphna, I'm too tired to remember insignificant details, okay? Just keep burning!"

"Don't yell at me, Dexter."

"Then stop interrogating me!"

"Interrogating you? Is there something I should be interrogating you about?"

"No, Daphna."

"Maybe I should interrogate you," Daphna pressed. Now that Dex mentioned it, she would like some things explained. "How about

I interrogate you about how you learned to beat up an entire gang when you've never been in a fight in your entire life."

Dex stood up and flung the bundle he'd been trying to hand Daphna into the fire. "How about I interrogate you?" he challenged, stepping toward his sister.

Daphna stood up and leveled a cool gaze at her brother. They were nearly nose to nose. Dexter wasn't going to get a rise out of her with the stupid new way he'd been looking at her when he got mad, or by crowding her either.

"Do not yell at me, Dexter," she said again, this time through clenched teeth. "And get out of my face."

Dex, realizing he was about to lose it, stepped away. "Fine," he snarled, "but how about you tell me something. How about you tell me how you really got that office door open. How about that? How about you tell me how you went home and wrote a note to Latty and then got back to Dad's room in, like, ten seconds flat."

Daphna cut her eyes at Dex, but he could see she'd been put on the defensive.

"I told you," she snapped, "the door was

unlocked, and I ran."

"Right," Dex said. "Then why don't you just keep your questions to yourself, and I'll keep mine to myself."

"Fine."

"Fine."

Having reached this accord, Dex went back to handing over bundles, which he did with overt hostility. Daphna snatched each one from him and jammed them into the fireplace as soon as there was room. When individual boxes were empty, Dex cut them up to be burned along with the pads.

The twins worked this way for several more hours, taking only a short break for sandwiches. Slowly, very slowly, the number of boxes began to dwindle. Not another word passed between them all the while.

Eventually, the twins' tempers fizzled. Both started thinking about Latty, and both had similar thoughts. They wondered what it meant that she was Adem Tarik, that they'd lived under the same roof with her, that she'd been, for all intents and purposes, their mother.

Daphna continued to seethe about the

betrayal. All she could think about was finding a way to lash out at Latty. *There can't be anything wrong with getting back at people who've intentionally hurt you*, she thought—*not if you're in the right, not if you want justice!* An image of Wren's and Teal's strangling blue faces floated across her mind's eye. It was all the convincing she needed.

Dex's primary feelings were confusion and dismay. He cast his mind back over life with Latty. Beyond her constant fussing, beyond her meddling in his and Daphna's every affair, the only thing he could see was what looked for all the world like genuine love and concern. As far as he could tell, she couldn't have cared for them more had they'd been her own flesh and blood.

How could the world be so phony? he wondered. His father, who'd always appeared to care little or nothing for them, was actually full of love—and now Latty turned out to be—what, he didn't know. But she killed their mother. What kind of world was it where no one was what they appeared to be? Dex had refused to give any real thought to the possibility that the book they'd found really belonged to God. But, now that he considered the matter, if God really did create the world, what was he thinking?' Why would he make a place where people can murder your mother when she's only trying to do good? Why would he make a place where people can travel halfway around the globe to deceive you, hurt you, try to kill you—just because you were born to certain parents?

And, Dex thought, his confusion slowly transforming into dark resentment, *what kind of God makes a world where your life has to suck because you can't read because your eyes weren't wired to your brain right?*

Even these thoughts petered out for the twins, who finally let their minds go blank. It wasn't exactly sleep, but it helped. There was something mesmerizing about the repetitive work involved in all the burning, and the flicking tongues of fire devouring the pads were hypnotic, too.

It took nearly six hours, but finally the last bundle was burned. The twins looked at each other warily when they'd finished, exchanged grudging nods for their accomplishment, then grabbed their overnight bags and staggered toward their rooms. The sun was already starting to go down.

Daphna sank into her bed. She opened her bag, took out Asterius Rash's Ledger and put it on her lap. In her current state, it was nearly impossible to read, especially after having stayed up all night squinting at Emmet's weird writing in her sleeping bag, but she needed to learn as much as she could. Events were spiraling out of control, and the only thing comforting her now was the incredible potential of the Ledger.

So far, she'd only been able to make those two words work. She had to keep trying new ones. If she didn't come up with some more subtle skills, Dex was going to catch on to her, for sure. Daphna didn't feel badly about lying to her brother anymore, not with the way he'd been acting.

She opened the book and chose a Word at random. It took a moment to make it out, but when the letters finally came into focus, she said it out loud. It sounded Chinese. Nothing happened.

Daphna was about to try it again, but a crude voice outside her slightly open window distracted her.

"Shut up!" it hissed.

Antin.

With energy she didn't think she still had, Daphna lunged to her light switch, flipped it off, then crawled on her hands and knees over to the window, still holding the Ledger. Antin was outside, laying into one of his gang.

"I'm not gonna tell you again," he warned, "the guy snuck up on us in the dark. He's a coward!"

It took a second for Daphna to realize he was talking about Dex.

"I'm telling you, Antin," a boy protested, "I was looking right at him when his sister went ape. He said something, and then the next thing I knew, he was gone. Then I saw Poly go down. All of the sudden he was just lyin' there bleeding."

"Don't think I don't know what you're doing!" Antin railed. "You all panicked. You freaked. It's that simple. And the next time you hand me that load, you're the one who's gonna disappear. Got it? When the rest of those wimps get better, I'm gonna kill them. Now I'm telling you, we're gonna find out what the big mystery is all about right—"

Daphna didn't hear the end of Antin's rant.

With her face aflame, she got to her feet and stormed out of the room. The fact that Antin and who knew how many of his goons were about to invade her home was suddenly the furthest thing from her mind. Daphna was running by the time she reached the kitchen. She tore open the basement door and practically flew down the steps. Only a lucky grab at the banister halfway down saved her from winding up on her face at the bottom.

Dex, sitting at his desk, was too stunned by his sister's kamikaze attack on the stairwell to put the *Book of Nonsense* away. He'd been leaning over it, but was now looking wide-eyed at Daphna, who was draped over the railing, her face twitching with rage.

"*I KNEW IT!*" she finally managed to scream. "*I KNEW IT!* That's why you ran ahead of me with that can. What an idiot I am! No wonder you soaked it in lighter fluid! Let's finish the job for the Council," she mocked. "We're the only one's left to do it, Daphna! You thought I'd talk you out of it, huh? *YOU NEVER INTENDED TO DESTROY IT!* As soon as you looked inside it in Dad's room—!" Daphna went suddenly silent. Dex hadn't said a word or moved a muscle.

"But," she said, losing steam and thoroughly confused, "you can't read. How—when you can't see the—Wait a minute! I showed you the book 'cause the words were changing. They were moving around. You can read it, can't you? The moving words look steady to you, don't they? You learned how to make yourself invisible, and that's how you beat up all those boys, and you learned a way to make the delivery man stay when you told him to!"

Dex smiled in a disturbingly satisfied way. He nodded.

Daphna's fury redoubled. *"YOU'RE A LIAR!"* she wailed. *"YOU'RE A LIAR, DEXTER WAX!"*

Dex still wouldn't speak, but his smirk was getting wider and wider by the second.

"What!" Daphna demanded. "Why are you looking at me like that?"

"Because you learned how to teleport, and that's how you got into that office, and that's how you got home to leave that note so quickly."

Daphna, poised to unleash an even more howling attack, went pale.

"That's ridiculous," she snarled, but it was

a lame protest. How could he know? "What are you, some kind of mind-reader now?"

Dex laughed. "No, I'm a palm reader."

Baffled, Daphna looked down at her hand. It was still clutching the Ledger. She sighed, defeated and finally aware of what a massive hypocrite she was.

"Emmet destroyed it, eh?" Dex said. "I guess we're both idiots, huh?"

Brother and sister regarded one another cautiously now, unsure how to proceed. They were deadlocked. They'd both lied. They'd both acted selfishly, possibly jeopardizing everything they were trying to accomplish.

"Dex," Daphna said when the staring contest wore her down. It didn't take much. "I'm glad you know. I'm glad you did the same thing. I'm sorry, but—"

"But what?"

"I'm beginning to think it doesn't matter what we do, good or bad. In a way, it's like we have no choice anyway."

"What?" That made no sense to Dexter, and he was far too sleep-deprived to puzzle it out.

"It's like Emmet said to me," Daphna explained, "if Time is endless, we'll live a trillion times, and we'll do everything: good and bad and in-between. It doesn't really make a difference when we do which. It's like, if I make the right choice now, it just means I'll make the wrong one later. It's almost totally random. So, like I said, it's just the same as having no choice at all."

"That's a really touching apology, Daphna," Dex muttered, but his thoughts went immediately to his own insights. If that were true, and he'd understood correctly, he wouldn't have to worry about whether he'd gone too far with that board.

"You don't need a trillion lives to see how random the world is," he said, "you only need one. Just look at us. One kid gets born with everything and the other one gets screw—"

A loud creak overhead made Dex look up at the ceiling. Daphna snapped her eyes up, too. The floors creaked again.

"Oh, no!" Daphna whispered. They'd left the front door open to keep the living room from overheating from the fire. "It's Antin!" she mouthed. How could she possibly have forgotten?

Dex jumped to his feet. "Can you get these

books out of here?"

Daphna nodded. "Good idea. I'll put them in Dad's room at The R & R," she said, then closed her eyes and uttered an odd sounding Word. Daphna opened them again, only to find she was still in the basement. She repeated the Word, but still nothing happened.

"What's going on?" Dex whispered. The sound of feet walking stealthily overhead was getting louder because more people were up there now.

"It's not working!" Daphna hissed, nearly frenzied. "I'm too tired. I can't say it right!" She tried three more times, but each time the Word sounded different. "Let's hide under the stairs!" she whispered. There was a storage closet there with a door that you had to push to pop open. There was no knob, but it was still obviously a door.

"No," Dex said, trying to stay calm. He'd have to handle it again. And why not? It was easy last time. He'd be lying to himself if he didn't admit it was fun. Dex spoke the Word that made him invisible, then moved confidently toward the steps.

"Dex," Daphna called.

He turned. "What? I'll take care of them."

"I can see you."

"Ahhh, the Candle Twins!" cooed a syrupy voice from the top of the steps. "It's sooo nice to see you!" It was Antin. Three of his flunkies were standing behind him, all looking much less excited than their leader about the reunion. One had a black eye, and the other two had casts on their arms. Antin looked fine, though. Dex backed carefully down the steps. He tried his Word again and looked at Daphna. She shook her head.

"Girls!" Antin snapped at his gang when they didn't immediately come down behind him.

They obeyed reluctantly, limping, until all four boys stood facing the twins, who'd retreated to the rear of Dex's room. Dex and Daphna's obvious exhaustion and increasingly worried expressions must have been reassuring because the boys gradually took on their usual menacing scowls.

"Man," one of them said looking around, "get a load of this dump. This is worse than your place, Antiny. You were wrong. He ain't a chicken, he's a pig."

Antin snorted, mildly amused.

Despite the gravity of the situation, Daphna looked around. It was true. There were piles of dirty clothes heaped across the floor along with a vast assortment of what could only be described as junk. It looked like Dex had taken apart everything in his room that could be taken apart and then scattered the guts around like seed on a lawn.

"I told you it was a total fluke what happened," Antin said. "But you ain't seen nothin' yet." He plunged his hand into his pocket. The twins both feared the lighter, but this time Antin produced a knife. Expertly, he flipped it around in his hand until a long jagged blade was pointing directly at them.

"So, where were we?" he asked, smiling with a mouthful of sharp teeth. Everything about him was sharp. His eyes, as usual, flicked around, and also as usual, he kept checking back over his shoulder every few seconds. "Let's see, oh yeah, you guys were just about to tell me what Emmet was after when we were so rudely interrupted."

The three boys behind Antin, their confidence now completely restored, stepped forward, kicking away the litter, snickering.

"What's the matter, your tongues disappear?" one of them joked.

"Heel here says you can make yourself disappear," Antin said to Dexter. "Can you do that?"

Dex shook his head.

"No, I didn't think so," Antin laughed. "But I'm gonna show you how if you don't tell me what I want to know."

"Hey, maybe it's got something to do with them books," suggested another boy. He was short and wide, with arms that hung too far down the length of his legs.

Dex realized Daphna was still holding the books. Her knuckles were white around the spine of the Ledger.

Antin moved toward the twins now. He could see they were immobilized with fear, so he didn't even bother brandishing the knife.

"What's up with the books," he asked, but got no response. Standing right between them now, he said, "You guys look tired. I'm gonna to count to three, and if I don't get the truth, the whole truth and nothing but the truth, I'm gonna help you get some serious sleep."

"The mattress!"

Dex and Daphna called this out at exactly the same time.

"What mattress?" Antin demanded.

"In my dad's room," Daphna said, her senses returning at least in part. "That's what Emmet was after. It's full of money."

"Show me."

"Upstairs," said Dex.

"Show me."

Dex swallowed dryly, then led Antin upstairs as the other boys herded Daphna along behind. When the group entered Milton's room, Antin said, "If this ain't for real—Eyeballs, check it out."

Eyeballs, a wiry boy with purple hair and bulging eyes, ripped the sheets and covers off the bed. When he noticed the zipper on the far side, he moved around and squatted to open it. Then he screamed.

"What? What!" Antin shouted. In a sudden, terrifying motion, he whipped the blade to Dex's throat.

"There must be a million bucks in here!" Eyeballs yowled. No one was absolutely sure what he'd said, though, because his head was halfway into the opening. But then a bundle of bills came flying. It landed at Antin's feet.

It was like a piñata had been broken at a toddler's unsupervised birthday party. Antin and his hobbled cronies hurled themselves over the bed. Money went flying.

It took longer than it should have, but eventually Dex and Daphna realized they'd been forgotten. Slowly, they inched out of the room. Without running—neither had the energy anyway—they slipped carefully through the living room and, clasping their books to their chests, stumbled out through the still open front door and into the evening's dwindling light.

still not a bad man

Though the twins were nearly out on their feet, both saw him the moment they lurched onto their porch. A man in a rumpled black suit, tall and thin, with a day's worth of stubble on his slender face, was standing behind a tree across the street. He swiveled sideways and pressed himself behind the trunk when he realized they were looking his way.

Dex and Daphna exchanged a droopy-eyed glance they both understood to mean, *Now what? We don't care.* Wordlessly, they agreed to pretend they hadn't seen anything and hurried off.

They couldn't pretend for long. The man, who must have realized he'd been seen, began blatantly following them. He wasn't chasing them, though, which was fortunate since there was no way either of the twins could outrun him. They couldn't outrun their father right now.

The man simply walked down the road

behind them, calmly, like he just happened to be taking a stroll exactly where they were going. Of course, that was impossible for many reasons, not the least of which was neither Dex nor Daphna had the slightest idea where they were headed.

Being followed so openly grew increasingly unnerving. The twins began looking back every few seconds, like Antin. Since they lacked the energy to run for it, they began making sudden, random turns around the Village streets and doubling back whenever it seemed least likely.

The man was undeterred. He took each and every turn they did. He cut between houses, crossed yards and circled garages right behind them, though he continued to make no effort to catch up. The twins' heads bowed lower and lower as they trudged on. Their steps slowed; their knees wobbled; their chests heaved. Still, they didn't stop. They moved by instinct alone.

Instinct, and enough weaving through the neighborhood, eventually brought them in sight of The R & R. Dex and Daphna, both of whom were considering just turning around and letting the man kill them if that's what he really wanted to do, stumbled toward the entrance. They staggered through the automatic doors and dragged themselves down the hall. Falling all over each other, they pitched themselves into their father's room.

Milton was sleeping. Daphna called her dad's name several times, and she even shuffled over to shake him by the shoulder, but he wouldn't wake up. He slept soundly, his face flush with a healthy, ruddy glow.

Dex had immediately dumped himself onto the couch, so Daphna joined him, and the two slumped into each other, breathing heavily and staring indifferently up at the TV, which was showing a muted news talk show. They felt nothing except bone-deep exhaustion. Neither was the slightest bit curious about their stalker, though they both knew he'd be walking in the door at any moment.

Two pairs of speckled green eyes began to close. Sleep, precious, golden, glorious sleep was finally coming, but sure enough, just before the twins passed out, the door opened and the man walked in.

Dex and Daphna sat up and looked at him with blank, utterly indifferent stares. The man had olive skin and twitchy fingers. He looked at the twins, but only for a moment. Then he turned to their father.

"Mr. Milton Wax?" he demanded, but Milton didn't respond. "Mr. Milton Wax!" he repeated, raising his voice. "You will explain at once your involvement with my grandfather, and you will return his papers to me this very instant!"

"He won't wake up," said Daphna. "He's on medication."

"And he's kind of messed up in the head," Dex added, not caring how it sounded.

The man strode to the bedside and shook Milton by the shoulder, just as Daphna had. As predicted, Milton didn't wake up, though he did shift around and mutter, "Adem Tarik—Adem Tarik—I—I—" His voice was so ragged that it was becoming difficult to make the words out. The man seemed to understand, though. He drew back, looking alarmed. "I am not bad man," Milton croaked, "I—I—am—"

"Who is this 'Adem Tarik'!" the man demanded.

"No idea," Dex lied. "He made it up. He says that name all the time."

"We told you," Daphna repeated, "he's got psychological problems. He's got a—disorder."

The man sighed, mightily. He looked, the twins suddenly noticed, rather exhausted himself. He walked across the room and sat down in what had been Latty's chair and put his head in his hands.

"You're Fikret Cihan," Dex said. "You own the Coffee House."

The man looked up, surprised. "Yes, how do you know this?"

"I was the one who sent that e-mail," Dex explained, "the one that was all jumbled up. It was an accident."

Cihan looked at him, amazed and appalled. "It was nothing?" he said, almost pleading. "Random typing, you say?"

"Adem Tarik—" Milton crackled, "Adem Tarik—I—I—am—"

"I see now," said Cihan, massaging his nose. "It was one lunatic meeting another." He chuckled briefly, sounding slightly mad himself.

"But, why were you following us?" Daphna asked. "Why are you here? You must have been traveling all day and night."

Cihan ran a hand through his short black hair. "My grandfather," he explained, "spent the last sixty years of his life copying a book, a book full of nonsense and rubbish. My God! Is that the book right there?" It was sitting on Milton's food tray, on top of the Ledger.

"Ah," said Dex, "I don't know."

Cihan rose and took the book without asking permission, then began flipping through it with a mournful look on his face. Dex couldn't even pretend to have the wherewithal to stop him.

"Did your father give this to you?" Cihan asked, his voice taking on a threatening edge.

"Ah, yeah," Dex said. "He told me it was worthless. I like old books, so—"

"I—I—Adem—"

Cihan looked at Milton and heaved another defeated sigh. He turned to the twins again but didn't hand the book back. Dex and Daphna looked at each other, nervously.

"Your father came into my Coffee House," he said, "asking about this Adem Tarik, and my grandfather gave him this book. It was like a miracle after all these years! There was never a sign such a thing would ever be. How long had

I hoped to spend time with my grandfather! I was overjoyed when your father left, but things did not go the way I'd hoped."

"What do you mean?" asked Daphna.

"He was beside himself when he realized your father had not taken away the copies," Cihan explained. "I was too excited by this miracle to remember them, but your father, he left me his card. My grandfather forced me to mail every page at once, and at great expense.

"After, he got weak. I think he only stayed alive to make those copies. He died the morning I received your message, and since it was just like that book and those copies, it made me suspicious. I thought perhaps your father did know my grandfather, and that the message was in code. My family once took quite seriously the idea that the book was in a code of some kind. Many years were wasted in hopes of interpreting it. I flew all the way here to retrieve the book and notebooks and demand your father tell me what he knows. But now I see I have wasted my time."

Dex and Daphna both thought Cihan was about to hand the book back. Dex even put his hand out, but it didn't happen.

"I've got some bad news for you," Daphna said. Cihan looked at her with an expression that seemed to say he expected no other kind.

"All the copies," she said, "we sort of burned them."

"We thought they might make Dad crazier," Dex put in.

Cihan's shoulders sank further, and he dropped his head into his hands again. He stayed that way for long time, long enough for Dex and Daphna to silently urge each other to figure out how to get the book back. Before either could think of a way, Cihan got to his feet.

"Fine. Good," he said. When he saw the confused look on the twins' faces, he elaborated. "You've done me a favor," he explained. "Who knows, I may have become obsessed myself. I could never have destroyed those papers myself. Here, please keep this, too," he added, handing the book back to Dexter. "Destroy it if you like. I don't care."

"Ah, thanks," Dex said. He took the book back, gripping it with both hands.

Cihan shook his head again. "Every day, people come to my Coffee House asking for me to help them make sense of their lives," he said.

"For generations, my family has survived on such hopes, and I once believed that the riddles of the Universe could be solved. But the truth is that our lives are incomprehensible intersections of unfathomable events and meaningless coincidences. I've been arrogant and foolish to think I could decipher the pattern of even my own insignificant destiny. Let me give you a piece of advice, children," he added. "Thinking is suffering."

"Tarik—Adem—I—I—" Milton droned.

The twins could see this was a deeply troubled person, but they couldn't exactly disagree with his pronouncement.

It took a moment, but a word jumped out at Dex. "You said coincidences," he said. "Do you mean my father coming into your Coffee House and getting that book?"

"Indeed," said Cihan. "But I will not seek to understand why my grandfather chose your father after so many years when so many thousands of people passed through our doors."

"But it must have something to do with Adem Tarik, right?" Dex said. "Hearing my father ask about him must've meant something to him."

"This is impossible."

"Why do you say that?" Daphna asked.

"My grandfather was deaf. He'd been so for many years."

"Oh."

Cihan looked at Daphna, apparently expecting further questions. When none came, he said, "Remember what I told you: thinking is suffering. I bid you farewell." With head down, Cihan strode from the room. It sounded like he ran into someone in the hall. "Excuse me, Ma'am," was the last thing the twins heard him say. Then he was gone.

"Adem Tarik—I—I—" Milton croaked.

The twins stared at their father. They'd learned so much since they'd first sat right where they were now, listening to the same words just after they'd arrived at the R & R. But, then again, they'd learned so little.

"Dex," Daphna said after a few minutes, "I don't get it."

"Me neither," Dex mumbled in reply. "I give up."

But Daphna had the notion something critical had just been revealed. "Dad went into the Coffee House," she said, trying to grasp the sequence of events as she now understood them.

"Then he asked that guy about Adem Tarik, right?"

"Right," Dex agreed, though he was hearing Daphna more than listening to her. What he was thinking about was sleep.

"And then his grandfather flips out and forces the book on Dad, right?"

"Right."

Almost on cue, Milton croaked, "Adem Tarik—Adem Tarik—I am—I—"

"But he just said his grandfather was deaf," Daphna pressed. "So he couldn't've heard Dad ask about anything. That's what we assumed happened, I guess. I mean, why wouldn't we?"

"And?" Now Dexter was getting plain annoyed. Why wasn't Daphna letting him pass out?

"Dexter," Daphna insisted. "The old guy saw Dad, then he gave him the book. He saw Dad, then he gave him Adem Tarik's book. And Dad was actually there to get it, whether he knew it or not."

"It makes no sense," Dexter protested, "not unless he thought Dad was actually—"

Without warning, Milton sat bolt upright in his bed, his eyes shocked wide. "I—I am—" he shouted in a crystal clear, metallic voice, "*I—I AM—ADEM TARIK!*"

The twins' blood froze.

Their father turned his head back and forth, looking around the room like he'd never seen it before.

"*I am Adem Tarik!*" he roared in a voice resonating with profound amazement and relief. Then he hopped out of the bed with no sign of pain whatsoever. The twins sat stupefied as their father walked around the room stretching out his back and flexing his arms and legs. His posture was perfect. He looked as agile as a man of twenty, and his speckled brown eyes glowed with lightning sparks of energy.

"*I AM ADEM TARIK!*" he declared to the mirror on a dresser. "My, oh my, oh my, oh my! All these years, trying to remember! My, oh my, oh my!" He bent over to touch his toes and noticed the twins on the couch, staring at him like imbeciles. "Who are you?" he asked.

"All—all this time—you were looking for—yourself," Daphna stuttered in a baleful, mousy voice. "You—you were never searching for Mom. You kept going to Turkey all those years because you found the book sixty years ago and took it to that man and made him copy it for you. It was in the back of your mind all the time after the accident, and—and—it starting coming back when we were going to turn thirteen!"

Though Daphna wasn't aware of it, her voice was growing in strength as she spoke. "That's why you always talked about it being such a big birthday! You'd been planning all along to get it back when you had kids who turned thirteen! It's just like the doctor said!" She was shouting now.

"That's why the book showed up just when Rash and everyone else came for us! There were no coincidences in anything that's happened! Fikret Cihan's grandfather recognized you when he saw you and gave you back your book!"

Milton, Adem Tarik, regarded Daphna with a curious look. It seemed both admiring and scornful. Then he nodded, looking wholly pleased. "And who might you be, young lady?" he asked.

"I—I'm—Daphna," Daphna whispered, cut to the heart.

"And you, young man?"

"Dexter. You're our father."

"*I HAVE CHILDREN?*" Milton cried. "Living children?"

"Yes," Dexter snarled. "We didn't die like the ones you had with Mrs. Tapi and Mrs. Kunyan and Mrs. Deucalion. You married them all, but you ditched them when their babies died."

"My goodness," Milton said, smiling. His face had lost its wrinkles. He looked like he was getting younger and healthier right before their eyes.

"You two know quite a lot about me. That's wonderful," he added. "Please, do tell me more. You say you're thirteen now? And I see you've got my book! Probably still useless, though, no? What am I doing here?"

"I'll tell you more," Dexter growled. "You killed our mother."

"Oh, thank goodness!" Milton sighed. He crossed back to his bed and sat on its edge.

"The last thing I remember," he said, "was trying to shove her and that assistant of hers over a ledge in my caves. The caves! I got hit in the head, didn't I? Oh, how absurd! No matter! I killed them both." When Milton noticed the horrified way in which the twins were looking at him, his expression changed. He tried to look friendly.

"Look, children," he said, "you must understand. I'm not a bad man. I have a plan."

"You didn't kill—" Daphna started to say, but Dex shot her a dire look.

Why should they tell him he didn't kill Latty? he thought. Why should they tell him anything? And Latty! What about Latty?

"Anyway," Milton said, getting back to his feet, "I'm sure I seem like some kind of monster to you. I shouldn't be acting so callous. She was your mother after all. I'm sorry for your loss. But if you'll allow me, I'd like to explain why what I did had to be done. I want to share my plan with you, the most ambitious plan ever conceived! When you understand, you'll thank me, I promise you."

This speech was met by icy glares from the twins, so Milton said, "I see you aren't interested at this time. Please, take care of that book. It's easily damaged, and someday it might be of great use to you. In the meantime, if you'll allow me, I'd like to fetch some other materials that might be of more immediate benefit. You may already know about the First Tongue. I want you to speak it."

Daphna spat on the floor at her father's feet. "That's what I think of your grand plan!" she cried. "I know what you told those poor kids who trusted you! You told them they'd be making Heaven on Earth! Well, if your kind of Heaven includes murdering people, you can go to Hell!"

Milton, Adem Tarik, looked amused by this outburst. He seemed ready to respond, but Daphna didn't give him the chance.

"And guess what!" she shouted. "We know all about the copies. We burned every last one of them! And another thing—we don't need you! We're already learning the First Tongue, and *WE KNOW YOU CAN'T—!*"

"And soon, we'll master it!" Dex interrupted, emboldened by his sister's audacity, but alarmed that she kept almost giving away information they might be wise to keep to themselves. There was no reason on earth to tell their father they knew he needed them.

"And then you better hide under the biggest rock in the universe," Dex shouted, "because we're going to make you wish you were never born!"

In response to the blazing eyes of his just-discovered children, Adem Tarik bowed, but while his body language was of one justly defeated, a sparkle of absolute pleasure shone in his eyes.

"Fair enough," he said, "I see I am of no use here, though you did not express my aspirations quite correctly. Bear in mind, children, that words matter, even the smallest among them. I wish you the best of luck in all your endeavors." Then, like Fikret Cihan had just a few minutes earlier, he walked out through the door.

Dexter and Daphna turned to each other yet again in total disbelief. "L—L—Latty," Daphna whined. "She—she knew the truth all along. She told us she saw him trying to save her, but the truth is she saw him pushing her! She—She—"

"She took advantage of him forgetting who he was so she could stay with us as his assistant," Dex said. The house of cards that was their previous understanding collapsed in a heap in his mind. "She was protecting us," he whispered. "It's just like Ruby said, remember? Keep your friends close, but your enemies closer."

"But not too close. That's why she encouraged him to be a scout, to travel around and stay away from us until she learned his stupid plan! And that's why she doesn't like Evelyn, because if Dad married her, she wouldn't be able to look after us."

"That's why she got so scared he'd remember! That's why she took off. If he finds out she didn't fall, and that she knows the truth, he'll kill her for sure. She—she—"

"Loves us," Daphna choked.

"Everything makes sense now, Daphna. He was in great shape before the accident, until he forgot who he was. Now he remembers, and it's coming back. Who knows how old he really is."

"That voice—it's horrible, Dex. You were right all along! Dad never cared about us at all!"

"If I was right," Dex groaned, "it was for the wrong reasons. Have two stupider people ever walked the face of the earth? He's been telling us he was Adem Tarik over and over for days! All that stuff he was saying in his sleep, that he was failing, that he'd done something wrong. He was failing to carry out his great and wonderful plan."

"Latty!" the twins cried in unison. "What have we done?"

Part II

The Library

a bit of a situation

"Daphna? Dexter?" Evelyn asked after peeking into the room. "What's wrong? Where is your father?"

"Adem—Tarik—" Daphna stammered, "Dad—"

"What's that, honey?"

"Tongue," whispered Dex, his eyes fluttering. "Himself—looking for—himself." He laughed crazily.

"Did he go out by himself? Never mind, you two look positively traumatized!" With practiced calm, Evelyn maneuvered the twins onto their cots.

"I thought something like this might happen," she said softly, helping them into their sleeping bags, "after all you poor kids have been through."

Neither Dex nor Daphna offered the slightest resistance to Evelyn's bony but assured hands, and they were deep asleep before she even finished tucking them in. When they were settled, Evelyn looked down at them with intense concern. Then she hurried from the room.

It was well past noon the next day when the twins were woken by Evelyn softly calling their names. They'd been profoundly unconscious for nearly fifteen hours, and both felt immeasurably better for it. They got up, stretched and smiled at each other, thrilled to feel functional again. Bagels and apples sat piled on a tray, so they attacked it. But then they saw Evelyn watching them with an uncomfortable smile. They'd slept in their clothes. And their father's bed was empty.

Like the proverbial piano hurtling down a flight of stairs, reality clobbered them. For just a moment, a brief, sweet moment, they'd been nothing more than two kids waking up revived after running themselves ragged. But now, once again, they were two key players knee deep in a mystery seemingly as old as time.

"What's wrong?" Daphna asked. She wasn't too concerned. Whatever Evelyn thought was wrong, she couldn't even begin to know the first part of it.

"Kids," Evelyn said, "I tried to wake you earlier, but I couldn't manage to rouse either of you. I'm afraid we've got a bit of a situation."

"What kind of situation?" Dex asked. He hadn't been overly worried either, but Evelyn's sympathetic expression was setting off all kinds of alarms in his head.

"Well—" said Evelyn. Her skinny fingers were interlocked nervously, and her always fidgety looking arms and legs seemed even more so as she apparently tried to figure out what to say.

"Well what?" Daphna pressed, getting nervous now.

"It's your father," Evelyn said. "It seems he's gone missing."

Dex and Daphna looked to each other, unsure what reaction was called for from children to such news, at least from children who'd learned only hours earlier that their father murdered their mother when they were only a few months old. The nervous glance they exchanged must have looked appropriately distressed, because Evelyn's smile grew even more sympathetic.

"Now, I'm sure this will all turn out to be

nothing," Evelyn assured the twins, "but to be on the safe side, I've spoken with our resident social worker—"

"Social worker?"

"—and I called the police."

"The *police*?" If Dex and Daphna hadn't appeared quite upset enough before, they did now.

"It was the proper thing to do," Evelyn explained, "but it doesn't mean we should jump to any conclusions. Here's the thing, though, kids," she added, looking pained. "The situation is slightly more complicated."

"What do you mean?" Daphna asked. She was beginning to fear that Evelyn was about to tell them she knew everything.

"Well," Evelyn answered, "the police went by your house late last night. It seems your housekeeper, Latty, cleared out all of her belongings. She's gone, too. And—"

The twins winced. Evelyn didn't know what was going on, but they both knew what she was going to say next.

"And they found money scattered around your dad's room. It was apparently hidden in his mattress—"

It had been, of course, but neither Dex nor Daphna said so. In fact, they didn't say anything at all.

"Do you have any idea why your father and Latty might have had to go somewhere," Evelyn asked, "perhaps together, in a big hurry, with a lot of money?"

The twins shook their heads.

"I understand the bookscouting business sometimes requires things like that," Evelyn said. "I'm so sorry to bring up difficult memories, kids, but what has me so worried is—Well, I know the last time Milton took off on such short notice was with Latty and your mom, just after you were born, and—of course you know what happened in Turkey—the earthquake in those caves. Your father told me about it when we all met flying to Portland from New York."

Evelyn paused to see how the twins were taking this. Then she said, "Latty gave me the impression the other day that he was going to retire, just like your mother had back then. The similarities disturb me. Do you think this might have something to do with rare books?"

The books!

Dex and Daphna wheeled around, looking frantically about the room. But they were right there, Asterius Rash's collection of Words of Power and the ancient, ravaged *Book of Nonsense*, sitting innocently atop a dresser like a couple of harmless library loaners.

Daphna exhaled. "Oh, thank God," she said, but then she realized Evelyn was looking wide-eyed at the books.

Now they'd done it.

"I found those last night," Evelyn said. "Do they have something to do with—?" But she stopped short. Dexter had interrupted her.

Daphna hadn't heard what he'd said, so she turned to her brother—but he was smiling at Evelyn, who now appeared stunned. It took a moment, but Daphna realized Eveyln was frozen. Her lips were still forming her next word. She looked like one of those street performers who can stand in awkward positions without moving for longer than you can ever stand around to watch.

"Nothing like a good night's sleep," Daphna sighed.

"No kidding," Dex agreed, looking at Evelyn's misted eyes. "What are we going to do?" he asked. "I have no idea how long she'll stay like that."

"We've got to find a way to stall," said Daphna. "We need to learn more Words of Power. Maybe we can make Evelyn forget about us or something. If we don't, we're gonna get sent to a foster home."

"A foster home?"

"Why else would she talk to a social worker?" Daphna said. "We have no parents, Dex! I can't believe it! Dad is Adem Tarik! He's thousands of years old! Older than Mom was!" Everything the twins had discovered the previous night came flooding back to Daphna, threatening to overwhelm her.

"He killed Mom!" she shouted. "Latty is gone!" Daphna had another memory, but this one put a glint of pleasure in her eye. "I told Dad to go to Hell, didn't I?"

"Yeah," said Dex, "right after he told us we'd thank him for killing Mom if we let him explain his stupid plan to make Heaven on Earth. You were awesome."

"You told him we were going to make him wish he was never born. That was awesome, too. And if it's the last thing I do in this lifetime, I swear that's exactly what's going to happen. But first things first," Daphna said. "We're going to have to get at least some of that money back from Antin and his psychos. Otherwise, how are we going to buy food? I repeat, Dexter, we have no parents. This is not good. This is really not good."

This time the words sunk in for Dexter. It was true. He had no parents. Not that he ever really did with a mother dead his whole life and a father who'd been absent both mentally and physically most of the time. But in that life, his mother died in an earthquake and his father was just busy and distracted all the time tracking down rare books. Dex resented that life, of course, but it suddenly seemed a whole lot better than what he had now.

The thought that things couldn't get any worse crossed his mind, but Dex was looking at Evelyn again and suddenly realized why her sympathetic expression was so irksome. It was the same cheesy, trying-way-too-hard-to-say-I-feel-your-pain look worn by every social worker, every counselor and every Vice Principal who'd ever made him talk to them about his lifetime of academic failure.

"This is worse than not good, Daphna," Dex

concluded. "It's me who's going to Hell, and in less than a week."

"What do you mean?" Daphna asked.

"Well, it's Heaven for you, of course."

"School!" Daphna cried. "I forgot all about it!"

Like father, like son

After a hushed but heated discussion, the twins switched their father's light off, closed his door and simply walked out of the R & R. Dex had at first resisted the idea, but he couldn't come up with a better plan. Daphna didn't seem troubled at all that Evelyn might be stuck for a long time before anyone found her. As they walked home, she kept saying that it was the best and quickest solution, and that if he didn't like it, then the next time around they'd handle things better.

Dex was starting to get annoyed with all of Daphna's talk about Infinite Time and living trillions of lives, but he'd finally agreed to abandon Evelyn because the one thing he did understand, and he understood it well, was that life between this Beginninglessness and Endlessness was nothing but a crapshoot. He'd been shot with crap all his life.

Standing there looking at Evelyn's foggy eyes, all he could think about was how horrible everything was turning out and how he'd so pathetically let himself begin to think lately that things were looking up. What a joke he and Daphna had been. They'd actually thought they knew what they were involved in. Two dumb kids is all they were, whether or not they were thirteen.

They'd been nothing but pawns—worse, pawns of pawns!—from the first second they'd been sucked into this ordeal. They were dealing with people who'd been living for centuries! Evelyn could fend for herself. If it was someone else's turn to get shot with crap—so be it. Next time it would probably be him again. And besides, the deliveryman he'd frozen yesterday didn't stay that way very long at all.

"We better get started," Daphna said the moment they got home. "I say it's a matter of hours before someone starts harassing us for one reason or another. We've got to find some more Words of Power we can use with no practice, and we've got to come up with them *now*. Crash course."

Then, as if to prove her point about harassment, the phone rang. Though it was the same ring they'd heard all their lives, it sounded somehow ominous. The twins stared at it until voicemail picked up.

"Let's read in our rooms," Dex suggested, "so we don't bug each other saying stuff out loud."

"Good idea," said Daphna. "I just can't believe you can read that book. Are the pages still changing?"

Dex hadn't thought of that. It would be just perfect if they'd stopped. If so, whether or not the book actually belonged to God wouldn't matter in the least. It would be useless to him. He'd have to depend on his sister, and he knew he couldn't handle that.

Dex opened the book fearing the worst, but to his relief, saw that indeed, he could still read it. The words must still be moving. His mood lifted immediately at the sight of actual, discernible letters. It was exhilarating to look at a word and not have to guess what it said. He was more than willing to start this "crash course" now. Maybe he could find something that would enable him to read for good.

If the universe was as truly random as it seemed, how could he continue to be the unluckiest person in the world? If there were a God, he would have to be personally, actively messing things up for him if his luck never changed. Wasn't the definition of 'luck' that it changed? Of course, Daphna would probably say something like eventually everyone had to live a life of all bad luck. It would be just his luck if this one were his.

They were agreed, so the twins went off to their rooms and hunkered down.

Daphna, sitting at her orderly white desk, opened to the first page of the Ledger. She'd already gotten two words to work: she could choke people, and she could teleport. But she'd tried a whole lot of other words with no success at all. Of course, she was rested now.

Daphna chose a Word and pronounced it as slowly and clearly as she could. When nothing happened, she repeated it. She tried three more times, and when still nothing happened, she moved on to the next.

Daphna fully expected the process to be difficult, so when the next Word failed after three attempts, she moved on again. This new Word failed as well, but Daphna didn't lose heart. She forged ahead, trying Word after Word, working her way methodically into the heart of the Ledger.

Dex swept an arm over the top of his desk, clearing CD's, odd-shaped rocks, aborted drawings and the random innards of dozens of old mechanical devices. He set the book down and sat in front of it with a serious, almost studious look on his face. It was an expression he wouldn't have recognized.

Ready, Dex turned to the first page of the *Book of Nonsense*, figuring it was probably different than the last time he looked at it. This was going to be difficult.

Finding any Words from the First Tongue was obviously a matter of chance, thanks to his mother's quick thinking who knew how many thousands of years ago. Yes, he'd seen two Words there already, but the vast majority could be anything. The only option was to try every one and see what happened. Dex, focused and intense, leaned down over the page.

He sounded out the first one. Nothing doing.

Wild, violent stress flooded Dex's system. Despite the fact he expected failure at all times, when it came, it always threatened to annihilate him. Lately, he'd been dealing with frustration well, so he forced himself to let it pass. It was way too early to quit.

Dex tried the second word, and when nothing happened, he managed to press on.

"Check this out!"

"Ah!" Dex clutched his chest. His sister was . suddenly standing next to him. Despite having no success whatsoever, he'd been absorbed in the book for over an hour, but not too absorbed to hear the basement door opening and someone coming down the steps.

"Sorry!" Daphna apologized. "Sorry. I've got that teleport Word working again."

"Obviously," Dex gasped, patting his heart.

"I went back to the R & R," Daphna explained, "to check on Evelyn. She was running around looking for us, but that's not what I want to tell you. Check this out. Wait, first, look over there, across the room."

When Dex looked at his mess of a bed, Daphna uttered a bizarre Word that sounded like a mouthful of t's and z's.

Dex blinked, waiting for—he didn't know what. He half expected the bed to start levitating or maybe fall away through a hole into alternate dimensions.

"Well?" he said, scanning the drifts and

shoals of junk on the floor for something more subtle.

"Look at me," commanded a man's low voice.

"Ahhh!" Dex, this time nearly crippled with fright, scrambled out of his chair and stumbled backwards across the room. Daphna was gone, and in her place stood the twins' father, Milton Wax. Bushy browed, gray and slightly stooped, he looked the way he always had, at least up until last night.

"No!" Milton cried, looking aghast at having caused his son such panic. "It's me, Daphna!"

"Who—Wha—?" Dex was backed up against the wall, calculating the odds of successfully charging his father, knocking him down and making a break for the steps. He couldn't process what was just said. Something about Daphna? But then Milton repeated the bizarre Word, and suddenly Daphna stood in his place again.

Dex, thoroughly flummoxed, was left staring.

"Isn't it incredible?" Daphna gushed, sounding like herself again. "It was a total accident. See, I went over to the R & R when I couldn't get any new Words to work, to take a break. When I got back, I tried this one Word, and I guess I was thinking about Dad. Actually, I was thinking about how when we told him we already knew the First Tongue, and all about his phony plan to make Heaven on Earth, he said something weird, like—I'm not exactly sure, but the gist of it was—"

"He said we didn't quite express his aspirations correctly and that even the smallest words matter."

"How do you do that?" Daphna asked.

Dex shrugged.

"Anyway," Daphna said, "I was thinking about that, and about who he really is and what his plan might actually be. And then I was wishing he could just be Dad again, the way he was, even if he wasn't the greatest father in the history of the world. Anyway, I happened to look in my mirror when I was thinking of him and saw that I looked just like him. I think I can look like anyone! It doesn't last very long, though. I turned back after, like, five minutes. Sorry for scaring you again."

Dex, his chest still seizing from the second shock, let out a slow breath.

"You're going to give me a heart-attack," he complained, walking back to his desk. But he was amazed. In fact, he was too amazed even for jealousy. It was absolutely incredible.

"Show me how," he said.

"Well," Daphna offered, "think of some-one and then just say this—" She repeated the Word, this time thinking about herself to avoid changing again.

Dex tried it, but the neutral look on his sister's face told him he hadn't transmogrified into Muhammad Ali.

"Try it again," Daphna suggested. Dex tried it again, but got the same non-result, and the third time was no better.

"Hmm," Daphna mused. She knew very well that her brother's darkening expression meant this little tutoring session was about to be terminated. "Here, try the one that lets me teleport," she said, risking making things worse. Daphna shared the Word, a long vowelly one that sounded somehow Scandinavian.

Dex mimicked it as best he could, to no avail. "Forget it," he said, turning away.

"Did you find anything new?" Daphna asked, but she cringed as soon as the words escaped her lips.

"No," Dex said shortly, "and I must've tried five hundred words."

"But you don't know which are from the First Tongue, right? None of them could be." Again, Daphna cringed. She couldn't annoy Dex more if she tried. "Wait a minute," she said, "you froze Evelyn, and you made yourself invisible in the ABC—try that again."

Dex, controlling the urge to trash his room for the millionth time in his life, spoke the Word for Invisibility. He vanished.

"It worked!" Daphna cheered, amazed to see her brother dematerialize. Actually, she didn't see it. It happened too quickly. "Come back," she said.

Dexter repeated the Word, and suddenly there he was, looking considerably less sour.

Daphna tried the Word, but she didn't disappear. "Did I say it right?" she asked.

"Yeah," said Dex. "I think so."

Daphna tired it again, but again failed to disappear. "I was right," she concluded.

"About what?"

"Think about it. The kids on the Council studied the First Tongue for years! The Words are very difficult to pronounce, remember? I've tried a ton of them and only gotten a few to work, and they don't work for very long. We've just gotten lucky so far. We're different, so we've gotten lucky with different Words. This means we're not going to be able to learn much, Dex, not without a heck of a lot more than six days practice. Hey, I just had another thought—"

"What?" Dexter asked.

"What if the First Tongue can't be learned out loud? What if you have to read Words of Power even to have a chance to use them?"

"That would figure," Dex sighed, "but you must be right because that would be another reason the kids had to learn Words of Power out of the *Book of Nonsense* themselves."

"But why can't Dad learn it?" Daphna asked. "I still don't understand. What if he's pretending? And I threatened him!"

"No," said Dex. "I don't think he can. If he could, why would he have needed the kids? And why would his plan ever have gotten messed up?"

"But he had the *Book of Nonsense*," Daphna replied. "He could have taught it to himself.

Dad's not blind, Dex."

A strange, furrowed look was drawing over Dexter's face.

What?" Daphna asked. "You just figured something out. What is it?"

"I'm positive Adem Tarik can't speak the First Tongue," Dex declared, "and he never will, either."

"What? Why?"

"He can't learn Words of Power," Dex explained, "because he can't read them. He has whatever I have, Daphna—at least when it comes to the First Tongue."

"But—" Daphna said. "Is that possible?"

"I don't know if it's possible," Dexter replied. "I only know it's true."

"Okay," Daphna said. "That's really good, Dex. Just let me see if I can understand everything."

"Okay."

"The *Book of Nonsense*—where it came from doesn't really matter," Daphna said. "Anyway, Dad—Adem Tarik, I mean. I can't call him Dad anymore, either. He somehow finds it a few thousand years ago. Even though he can't read it himself, he somehow knows what it is. He recruits some genius kids—"

"Thirty-six—"

"Right. And tells them they'll learn the First Tongue and make Heaven on Earth."

"Or something like that—"

"Right. Anyway, Rash and Ruby start a war among the kids and everything goes haywire. Mom charms the book so it'll change forever and then it gets lost. So Adem Tarik has no book and no genius kids."

"Keep going," Dexter urged.

"Everyone searches for the book, but it's Dad who actually finds it. Only it's not much use changing all the time, even if he could read it like you can. So he finds this Fiker guy—"

"Fikret Cihan—"

"He finds this Fikret Cihan guy's grandfather and makes him spend his whole life copying it while he works on a new plan, which is to have new kids learn the First Tongue, his own kids this time—"

"Wait, Daphna," Dex said, "like you just said, he wanted the kids to learn the First Tongue. Now he wants us to. He said so last night. It can't be the right thing to do!"

"But—" The undeniable logic in this gave Daphna pause, but she'd committed herself to learning as many Words of Power as she could. After a moment, she saw why it was still the thing to do.

"But he probably thinks we don't know he can't speak it himself," she said. "Oh, gosh, I almost told him, didn't I? He probably figures he can control us by scaring us. Oh, man," Daphna snarled, "he's in for a serious surprise. I don't care how long it takes, I'm going to master it all and wipe him out."

"So that's why I can't read," Dex whispered. He didn't hear his sister's last comment or her vicious tone. His mind was suddenly somewhere far away. He didn't even realize he'd spoken out loud.

Daphna paused a moment, thinking she ought to acknowledge that this discovery might be important for her brother, but before she could think of what to say, the sound of sirens and the screeching of tires sent both twins into immediate distress.

They stood motionless, barely breathing, hoping the sounds would fade away. They did, but only to be replaced by car doors slamming, and then, moments later, heavy pounding on the front door upstairs.

Like father, like daughter

"Kids! Kids!" It was Evelyn. "I've got the police here with me! Kids! Are you in there?"

The twins looked helplessly at one another as the pounding on the door continued. Finally, Daphna said something, and the next thing Dex knew, he was looking at his father again. He nodded, spoke a Word and vanished.

Daphna had no idea what she was going to do, but she hurried up the steps, assuming her brother was behind her. She passed through the kitchen, crossed the living room to the front door and opened it.

"Milton!" Evelyn cried. Two uniformed officers stood beside her. Daphna didn't acknowledge them at first because her attention had been drawn to the squad car parked outside. In the back seat sat a sullen boy in handcuffs. It was one of Antin's goons. Eyeballs, they'd called him.

"Milton!" Evelyn said again, "what in the world is going on?"

"Um," said Daphna, turning back to her, "I guess there's been a bit of a misunderstanding."

"My name is Officer Richards," said one of the cops. He had deeply in-set eyes and a farmer's sun-baked skin. "This is my partner, Officer Madden." Officer Madden was thick shouldered, middle aged and intense.

When Daphna didn't respond with anything but a nervous smile, Richards said, "We'd like to come in, sir, and ask you a few questions if you don't mind."

"Ah, yes," Daphna hurriedly replied. "Sure. Come in." She felt certain it was obvious to everyone she wasn't her father, but how could it be? Daphna turned and led them all inside, remembering just in time to limp. Everyone took seats.

"Milton," Evelyn said yet again, "What is going on? You disappeared from the Home last night! We've been worried sick. The kids looked shell-shocked, and—this is all so strange—I went to talk to them this morning, and, I don't know, they must have run out. Seeing you here makes me worried this all has something to do with that horrible tragedy in the park with Daphna's reading group.

And we know Latty is gone, and now the police—I called them again when the kids disappeared, and on our way here we were sent to pick up this boy, Eyeball, or whatever he calls himself, who seems to have gotten a hold of part of your money. The mattress—"

"I'm really sorry," Daphna said. "I can explain."

But she couldn't explain. Frantic thoughts were leaping around her head. She could only manage to stare at Evelyn, who was staring back, expectantly. Everyone in the room was staring expectantly, leaning forward, waiting for her to speak. But Daphna simply couldn't think of anything to say.

The tension grew oppressive. No one even moved. It was like they were all trying to make her crack.

Someone else talk! Daphna nearly screamed.

"They're frozen," said Dex's disembodied voice. He reappeared in the middle of the room.

Daphna nearly disintegrated with relief. She hadn't heard Dex say his Word.

"That's why they're all just staring at me like that!" she cried. "Why didn't you say something sooner?"

"I was trying to think of something," Dex snapped. "I thought you knew what you were doing."

"How am I supposed to know what I'm doing, Dexter? Why is it always up to me?"

"Who says it's always up to you?"

"Look, just forget it. What am I going to say? They're not going to stay frozen for very long. And these are cops, Dexter."

"Thanks for pointing that—Wait a second," said Dex, "they busted that Eyeballs kid out there, so they know we got robbed, right? Tell them the whole gang broke in here yesterday and held us up with knives, which is the truth, anyway. Tell them—tell them we called Dad and Latty at the R & R after the gang left, and they rushed home to us—And, and—"

"And when he—I mean I," Daphna said, "when I got home, I told you and Daphna to go right back to the R & R where you'd be safe in case the goons came back. Then Latty and I went searching for them all night. That's perfect!"

The group in the room was beginning to make small movements. The cops were twitching. Evelyn was shifting in her chair.

"Okay, let's do it," Daphna said. "They're

coming out of it."

Dex whispered two Words. The first made him vanish, the second brought the room back to life.

"Milton?" Evelyn said.

Daphna, very calmly, began sharing the story she and Dex had just concocted. Halfway through, she realized she'd have to explain Latty's absence, but an idea came to her right away.

She explained that Latty had gotten herself one of those fancy recreational vehicles to travel the country, and the four of them were going to take a trip together while Milton finished recuperating. Latty was already living in it to get used to it, and that was why her stuff was out of the house. Afterward, she was going to retire and continue to travel on her own. After all, Milton was retiring too. She really wouldn't be needed anymore.

It seemed that this was going over pretty well, which gave Daphna confidence. In fact, Evelyn couldn't conceal a twinkle of pleasure in her eyes at this last bit of news.

"My goodness," Evelyn said, "I—this is all so—"

"I'm sorry if the kids ran out on you," Daphna interrupted. "That was rude, but they ran back here to check on us. I decided to send Latty and the kids off on a trip without me so things could get worked out here safely. They'll be back before school starts next week. They were still a little shaken."

Daphna paused to swallow. She looked around the room. Everyone still seemed to believe her. But then Evelyn looked confused.

"There were some books," she said. "The twins seemed very agitated—"

"Oh, gifts," Daphna explained. "They just had their thirteenth birthday. The books are rare, but nothing too valuable." Daphna held her breath, but Evelyn looked reasonably satisfied. It was hard to believe how well she was doing. All of this was coming to her freely. It was like she just needed help opening the tap, but once open, the lies flowed freely.

"Can we get in touch with the kids?" Madden asked.

"They promised to call every few days," Daphna replied. "But otherwise, I'm not exactly sure where they'll be."

"I see."

And that was it. They bought it all.

The officers were somewhat concerned about not being able to take the twins' statements, but Richards said it might not even be necessary. Eyeballs had been seen in the Village spending huge sums of money in the same stores from which he usually shoplifted.

A suspicious shopowner called the police, and when they picked him up, he had not only piles of cash, but also an antique-style silver bookmark engraved with the initials MAW, for Milton Adam Wax. He'd claimed Milton gave it to him, along with the money. It seemed like an open and shut case.

"He's holding out on the names of his buddies," said Madden, "but he won't last. The amount of money he had, breaking into your house and taking it with a weapon—that'll land him in McLaren down in Salem, which might encourage him to think about ways of shortening his stay. We'll get all the boys, and we'll get your money back, eventually. By the way, about how much did they take?"

"Uh, um, well—" Daphna didn't know what she should say, and worse, she was starting to tingle all over. She was going to turn back into herself.

"No need to take a wild guess," said Richards. He stood up, took a card from his breast pocket and handed it to Daphna. "Why don't you take some time to figure that out, and give me a call when you think you know. We may need you to come down and give a statement, and we'll probably need to talk to the kids when they get back. And you might consider a more secure location for your cash. Perhaps a safe."

"Yes, I'll do that," Daphna said, willing everyone to get going already.

Officer Madden stood up. "Thank you for your time," he said. Evelyn got up, too.

"No problem, Officers. Thanks so much for coming over—" Daphna opened the door, and to her immense relief, the policemen walked outside.

Evelyn, however, stopped on the threshold and turned back. She was shaking her head, looking both pleased and baffled that things had so unexpectedly turned out so well.

"Milton," she said, "how's your hip?"

"Oh," said Daphna. The tingling was intensifying, and something about the way Evelyn was looking at her made her nervous. Was she changing back right then and there?

"Ah, it's great, really," Daphna said. "I'm so happy with it. Thanks for all your help, but I think I won't stay over at the Home—"

"That's fine, Milton. I'll take care of the paperwork."

"I should probably rest after driving around all night. You understand—"

"I can't believe you did that," Evelyn scolded. Then she actually giggled. "What were you going to do in your condition? Still, I'm impressed with the superhero routine. You know I've always considered you a good friend, even if you haven't been the best communicator."

"Ah—" Daphna was beginning to sweat. Should she run for the bathroom? Was Dex going to help? Then she realized what was going on. Evelyn was flirting with her.

"I just want you to know that I'm here for you if you need me," Evelyn said. "It will be tough for you without Latty. Teenagers aren't easy to manage. If you need anything, call me."

"Um—thanks," Daphna said. An idea came to mind, so she put her hand on Evelyn's arm and said, "I really think we—I mean I really think I need a few days alone, to think, like totally by myself, after everything that's happened." She was tingling like crazy. She was going to have to run for it if this didn't work right away.

"I understand, like totally," Evelyn teased. She put her free hand on Daphna's hand. Then, before Daphna knew what hit her, Evelyn leaned forward and planted an awkward kiss on her cheek.

Suddenly flushing like a schoolgirl, Evelyn turned and hurried off. Had she looked back for a final good-bye, she'd have seen a stunned Daphna Wax standing in the doorway with a hand at her cheek.

Daphna remained where she was, too flustered to realize she'd become herself again. She didn't even hear the heavy thud behind her. It was Dex, collapsing on the floor in hysterics. The sound of cackling came from the air where he lay.

the good life

"Oh, ha, ha, ha," Daphna said, returning to her senses and quickly closing the door. "Come back, Dexter."

Dex reappeared. "First Emmet, then Antin, and now Evelyn," he sniggered. "You're one hot chick." Dex felt a surge of ill will at having been forced to see his sister this way again—as someone's potential girlfriend rather than just a girl. Of course, in this situation, she was a man, which was absurd.

But regardless, from the moment Antin called her good-looking the other day, he'd been bothered about it. Just the fact that Daphna thought she could flirt with someone as dangerous as Emmet or Antin galled him.

Of course, she hadn't pulled it off with Antin, but still, watching the little romantic scene with Evelyn unfold had angered him to the point of irrationality. He'd plainly seen how distressed his sister was getting, yet he didn't step in.

"What's wrong with you, Dexter!" Daphna demanded. "If Evelyn would've seen me change back, we'd've been doomed. She would've freaked out! But I'm sure that would've been worth a good chuckle."

As ridiculous as it was, Daphna couldn't help but feel a twinge of pride at having turned Evelyn's affections to their advantage, even if she hadn't accomplished it as herself. The disaster with Antin had cast some major doubt over her recently discovered flirting skills.

Dex didn't respond to his sister's railing because he'd realized something. When Antin had knocked her nearly silly in the burned out bookstore, he hadn't interfered then either, and it wasn't because he was being restrained. He hadn't even tried.

Now Dex knew why: secretly, he'd been pleased. He couldn't face it at the time, but there it was. Dex felt horrible about it now— Daphna had been trying to save their lives! He also finally understood what an idiot he'd been for almost letting Evelyn find them out.

But, he wasn't going to dwell on guilty feelings. How could Daphna blame him anyway? He was just doing whatever he was doing in this life, right? Dex wondered if maybe people weren't even responsible for reactions they didn't intend. Maybe thoughts crossed people's minds as randomly as words crossed the pages of the *Book of Nonsense*. If you lived a trillion lives, what thought wouldn't you have?

"All right, all right," Dex said, getting up. "Keep your hair on. I wasn't going to let her see you change back. You seem to enjoy flirting, anyway."

"Fine, whatever, Dexter," Daphna retorted. "I imagine if she'd seen me change back, you would've solved the situation in a way you'd've enjoyed more, like by bashing her in the head with something."

"Yeah, that was my plan exactly," Dex snapped, but he'd been stung. He didn't know Daphna had seen how elated he'd been after thrashing Antin and all his thugs. It did get them out of the ABC, didn't it? He hadn't enjoyed hurting anyone. Maybe he'd only enjoyed their trying to get out of his way.

"Anyway," Daphna said, "my flirting probably bought us a week of privacy. If we're lucky. Shall we spend the whole time bickering?"

"I guess not," Dex said. "I guess we better

get busy. But man, that Evelyn lady. Is she pathetic or what?"

"She's lonely. Don't be such a jerk."

"Got a crush, do you? You two are soul mates, you know. Maybe she'll bring you that gift we saw in her files for Dad."

"Shut up, Dexter! Look, there are things we need to do."

"I know, I know," Dex conceded. Enough was enough. "We'd better get back to our books."

"There's that," Daphna agreed, "but don't you think we better figure out a way to get the rest of that money back before the cops do? Who knows how long it'll take for them to give it back if they find it. And what are they gonna think if they find out how much it really is? It looked like hundreds of thousands of dollars! That's probably money Dad—Adem Tarik—I don't know what to call him! It's probably money he collected over who knows how long. They're going to have questions, Dexter.

"And then there's Latty! Don't you think we should at least try to find her and tell her what's going on? The poor woman probably is running cross country, looking for a place to hide! After all she's done for us! We've been totally un-grateful. I feel worse than I did about the way I treated the Dwarves—I mean the Council!"

As usual, Dex realized, he hadn't thought everything out. As usual, his sister had. "Okay," he said. "What should we do first?"

"Well, I guess it makes sense for me to do some scouting. I'll teleport to the police station to see if they know any more than Evelyn told us. I wish I could be invisible, too. Then, it'd be easy. But still, if I can look like anyone—" Daphna made up her mind. "I think you should hit the books, or book, again. It's too bad you can't read the Ledger, but still, you could find more Words in the *Book of Nonsense.*"

"Okay," Dex agreed, trying not to sound as pessimistic as he felt.

"Right, then." And with that, Daphna spoke a Word, and she was gone.

Dex took in a breath and slowly let it out. The inevitable frustrations awaiting him were daunting, but he forced himself to slouch downstairs and sit at his desk. The word he'd last been trying was gone, so he picked a new one at random. Of course, nothing happened when he tried it. The phone rang. Dex stood up, paced around the room until it went silent, then sat down again. He tried the next word. Nothing. He went on to the next. Nothing. The next, nothing. Nothing. Nothing. Nothing.

For nearly an hour, Dex kept at it, but soon enough, his stamina waned. He began getting up more frequently to kick debris around his floor. The phone kept interrupting, too. Gradually, the breaks got longer and longer. Dex took a nap. He built some weird gadgets out of spare parts under his bed. He watched TV. He ate lunch. He took another nap.

Dexter's third nap developed into a full-fledged slumber, and he slept right into the late evening. When he finally jolted awake, he lurched off his bed, realizing he'd lost several hours of valuable time. One more try, he decided, lurching sleepily back to the desk. He sat down, chose a word and said it.

Nothing.

"That's it," he hissed, standing up. With a forced calmness, Dex took up the old book. *To hell with it*, he thought, *the Council wanted it destroyed anyway*. He got a good grip on each cover and prepared to pull it to pieces.

"Dexter! What are you doing?"

Dex dropped the book and fell into his chair, scared to death again. "*STOP DOING THAT!*" he roared.

"I'm sorry!" Daphna said. "I'm sorry. Look." She dropped a heavy, bulging garbage bag onto the floor. Then she grabbed a handful of plastic from the bottom and overturned the whole thing. Out tumbled bundles and bundles of cash.

Dex rushed over and picked some up. "How did you do it?" He wasn't sure whether he was relieved or annoyed. He was both.

"It was in the ABC."

"You're kidding."

Daphna described her afternoon. She'd first teleported to the police station disguised as a stranger. Inside, she'd hung around for almost two hours hoping to overhear something, though she had to go into the bathroom every ten minutes or so to keep from changing back into herself, which made her sure she was going to miss something.

Finally, just as she was about to give up, three cops came in dragging along what looked like the rest of Antin's flunkies, though not

Antin himself. A couple of them were crying, and they were all pleading not to be sent to jail.

"They didn't look so tough anymore," Daphna commented. She'd walked along behind them until they were hauled past a barrier she couldn't cross, but she managed to hear one of them whisper to another, "Just, whatever you do, man, don't mention that bookstore. Give 'em all kinds of places if you gotta. He'll mangle us with worse than broken boards."

"Wow," Dex said. He couldn't help but smile at the image of those jerks reduced to tears. He bet more than one of them was wetting himself then.

"So I went to the ABC," Daphna explained. "Antin was in there, underneath, in the dark, sitting on top of all the money."

"Sitting on top of it?"

"Yeah. He was just sitting there talking to himself about how he was going to throttle all those morons, how he'd told them to lay low, not go spending money all over the place like a bunch of imbeciles. Some of the time he paced around, ranting and raving about his birthday and being hungry. He was probably looking over his shoulder every two seconds. He's crazy, Dex. He's way worse than Emmet ever was."

"So what did you do?" Dex wanted to ask whether she'd made out with him to get the money, but he restrained himself.

"I just sat in the dark and listened," Daphna said. "After—well, I don't really know how long it was—but eventually, he stormed out, probably to get food. So anyway, I just grabbed the bag and teleported back here."

"And it came with you—"

"Yeah, what do you mean?"

"If you're holding on to something, it teleports with you."

"Yeah! Maybe I could take you!"

"That's what I was think—" The phone rang just then. "It's been doing that all day," Dex groaned. "Probably Evelyn looking for another kiss."

"I take it things didn't go so well here," Daphna said. "But it's no big deal. We just have to keep at it. I'm wiped out again, but we still have five whole days left."

"We have as long as we want," Dex corrected. Why that didn't occur to him until just then, he had no idea.

"What do you mean? School starts on Monday."

"School starts when we go to school, Daphna. Think about it. Who's here to make us go?"

"Dexter," Daphna said sharply, "we have to go to school. We have to make it look like our lives are totally normal for as long as we can. Otherwise, everyone will be on to us, and who knows where we'll end up."

"Yeah, I guess so," Dex groused. That was obviously true.

Daphna was relieved this didn't develop into another massive argument. "I'm starving," she abruptly announced. "I skipped lunch."

Dexter was hungry too, so the twins headed upstairs. When they reached the kitchen, they both smelled something delicious, which was odd since neither of them had prepared anything. The smell wasn't coming from the kitchen, so they wandered around until Dex opened the front door. There on the doorstep was a steaming tureen of soup. Next to it was a basket containing nuts and chocolates. Dex brought them inside.

"What in the world?" Daphna asked.

"There's a note in the basket," Dex said,

heading right to the kitchen table. Eat first and ask questions later was his thinking.

Daphna took the folded note. *Dear Milton,* she read, *I know things have been awfully rough on you and the kids lately. I respect your need to be alone, but that doesn't mean you have to be hungry! I'm betting Latty did most of the cooking, so I thought I'd help ease the transition with my Skordalia. Hope you like garlic! Bon appetit. Love, Evelyn.*

"Hey," Dex said with a mouthful of soup. "Potatoes! This is delicious!"

Daphna served herself some soup and tried it. "Yum!" she agreed. "Walnuts, too." Then she turned thoughtful for a moment. "You know, Dex," she said, "maybe we've been looking at this situation all wrong."

"No doubt. If you'd've let her kiss you on the lips, who knows what we might've gotten."

"Funny, Dexter. But I mean it. Think about it. We're rich, totally free, and now we have our own cook! This is what you call the good life."

The phone rang again just then.

"Evelyn," Dex said.

The twins waited it out, then dove back into their soup. The pair ate with relish, and fifteen minutes later, they sat back, satisfied. The phone rang again, and they ignored it again. But when it stopped, something occurred to Dexter.

"Why would Evelyn keep calling if she respects Dad's need to be alone?" he asked.

"She wouldn't," Daphna said, reaching quickly for the phone. She keyed in the voice-mail code, and the twins both listened in.

black spider, brown cow

Beeeep. Message one: no message. *Beeeep.* Message two: no message. *Beeeep.* Message three: no message. *Beeeep.* Message four: no message. It wasn't until message seventeen when an urgent but familiar whisper came on.

"Kids, this is Latty. I don't know what else to do but leave a message. I've been calling all day. Please listen to this and then erase it right away. You might have reasons not to answer the phone, but I beg you to find a way to let me know you are safe. I have to know you're okay, or I'll lose my nerve completely.

"I know your father, Adem Tarik, is gone. I'm following him. He came home last night and found the money gone. I saw this from outside his bedroom window. I assume you moved it, and that makes me slightly less anxious about you right now. If you need anything, anything at all, buy it. Use that web delivery service

I use for groceries.

"Tarik left and went right to the airport. He used a credit card to buy a ticket for a flight to Turkey that left this morning. I did the same. I'm sitting about ten rows behind him right now. I'm using one of those phones built into the seats. I left you a note explaining things as best I could. It's taped under the kitchen table. Please read it right away and then tear it up. I am truly sorry for anything I wrote that pains you.

"As for what you should do while I try to discover what he wants, I can only say make your lives as ordinary as possible until I can get home. You know I love you both. I'll call again when I learn something. Erase this message right away."

Beeeep.

Daphna hung up, then immediately got to her knees and peered underneath the table-top. There was a piece of paper taped to it. She pulled it free with a trembling hand. Dex had taken his seat again and was looking at her expectantly. Daphna read:

> I was watching the house—I had been since I got your note.

I know you understand what is going on. I followed behind that man who followed you to the rest home and listened at the door. He nearly ran me over on his way out. I heard what happened next, of course.

It was the scene from my worst nightmare all these years—your father remembering he was Adem Tarik. You can be sure I was ready to intervene, but only if I had to. When Tarik left, I ducked into a closet in the hall, then followed him.

He practically cartwheeled home. I held my breath the whole way, hoping that even if he remembered where he'd lived as Milton Wax, he wouldn't remember me. I guess he didn't, though he wandered all over the house looking at this and that.

Thank goodness I removed

every trace of my presence in his life. After a while, I guess he became exhausted. Right now, he's sleeping in his bed, so I'm taking the opportunity to write this note—just in case things go drastically wrong. I'm going to sneak in and tape it under the kitchen table if I can.

I'm sorry if my disappearing so completely caused you any shock. It felt to me like I was abandoning my own children. Let me try to explain what I've been doing since this all began.

I know now, of course, that your father came home from his trip with that book. If only he hadn't returned early, while I was still out shopping—though I understand he went directly to the bookstore with you, Daphna. But there's no use in regretting what can't be changed. I didn't find out about the book until later.

First you have to understand that I have been hiding all these years—hiding right under Adem Tarik's nose, but hiding nonetheless.

All I have concerned myself with was making sure you two were safe. If my constant hovering was difficult for you, I am sorry. You were all I had. Your mother, my best friend, told me her secrets, her mission to find the book, her pain at giving it up, her boundless love for you that made her willing to do it. I was able to fulfill my promise to watch over you as you grew up, but everything is in jeopardy now.

It was when your father told you, Daphna, to go help at that bookstore that it all started. He mentioned the name "Mr. Rash," and I nearly fainted. I'm sure you didn't notice, but I had to leave the room. Later that night, your father told me about the book he'd sold, and I feared the worst.

That, kids, is why I left you alone on your birthday morning. I went to try to get the book myself. Only, my nerve failed. I knew about Asterius Rash and couldn't face him. And that is why—oh, gosh—please don't be too upset by this, that is why I wrote that note to you from your mother.

I knew you poor kids would find it searching for your birthday gifts. I hoped by telling you just enough about the book and its history, you might manage to get it while I watched over your father, whose returning memories worried me a great deal more than even Asterius Rash. (I saw subtle signs of it well before he went to Turkey and found the book.)

I know this put you in grave peril, and I know now what must have really happened in the park. Your reading group! Of course, I knew nothing about that until it was too late. I don't know whether you have the book or not. If so, you must destroy it.

All I can say is I hope you understand how hard I've been working behind the scenes. The guilt I felt for having endangered you and the stress of seeing your father's memory returning almost did me in. I did everything I could possibly think of to stop it.

You must know that I saw him push your mother into the crevasse when the caves began to collapse. He tried to push me, too. Our best hope lies in the fact that he thinks he succeeded. He can't know I'm alive, or he'll try to kill me immediately. Then there would be no one left but you to stand in his way of getting whatever it is he wants.

There I was, nearly losing my mind, trying to decide if I should stay with your father in the hospital and then at the Home to keep working on blocking his memory, or get away from him in case I failed.

Finally, I decided to rely on you two again. Of course, I was terrified for you. If you are angry with me, I understand, but there is something special about you both. I have always, always known it. And I swear to God that I will not knowingly put you in harm's way again, for as long as I live. I better go hide this letter now.

"That's it," Daphna said, offering nothing further in the way of a reaction.

"At least now we know why Dad didn't believe

we found a note from Mom in the mattress."

Daphna nodded. After a moment of tense silence, she took the note Latty had forged out of her pocket for the last time. She tore both notes to shreds, then tossed them in the trash. Then she got the phone again, erased the voice-mail and recorded a new out-going message to replace her father's, thinking that ought to be enough to show Latty they were safe. Then she sat down at the table and joined her brother in staring at nothing.

The twins remained that way until Daphna finally said, "That note—from Mom—I—It felt like some kind of connection to her. It helped. Now there's nothing."

Dex felt as disheartened as his sister sound-ed. He hadn't been able to read the note, of course, but he was feeling cheated, too. "We've got to destroy the books," he said, trying to get back to the issue at hand.

"But Latty doesn't know about the Ledger," Daphna protested, "or that the *Book of Nonsense* is showing us some Words of Power again. I mean, isn't everything different now? Wasn't the Council's big fear Rash anyway? No one ever thought Adem Tarik was the real puppet master. I know he wants us to learn the First Tongue, but would you really feel safe burning the books and just waiting around to see what he has in store for us?"

"No," Dex admitted, "I wouldn't. But still—"

"Me neither," Daphna said, "and don't you want to make him pay for what he did to Mom, what he's done to us? He's ruined our lives, Dexter."

"I don't know," was Dex's response. Part of him really did, but another part of him was sure that going after Adem Tarik would be a very big mistake.

Daphna could see which way her brother was leaning. "How about this," she proposed, "let's study hard for the next five days—I'm going to bed now, but I'll get up early and start again. Then, when school starts, we'll decide for sure what to do."

"Okay," Dex agreed. He had no real hope of finding any more Words of Power, but he supposed there was no reason to make a hasty decision. He felt badly for having almost torn up the book without Daphna's consent. "I'm going to bed, too," he declared. He was also tired, even after all the naps.

The twins stacked their dishes in the sink, both fully aware of the dismal mood that had settled over them. There was no point in discussing things any further, so they headed off to their rooms and went to sleep.

The next few days were grueling. Daphna poured over the pages of Rash's journal, pronouncing, proclaiming, shouting the stubborn Words until her voice grew hoarse. Though nothing worked, her efforts never flagged.

Daphna had known for a long time that studying hard paid off in the end. Besides, being so completely engrossed helped her ignore the gnawing disappointment that Latty had forged that letter from her mom, and that she'd put their lives at so great a risk—the woman who wouldn't let them cross the street alone until they were ten years old!

The only breaks Daphna took from her studies were for meals. She and Dex ordered what they needed for breakfasts and lunches from Latty's web service. Dinner was delivered too, but by Evelyn.

Like clockwork, something new and delicious appeared on their doorstep every evening: a bean soup called Fassolatha, a lentil soup called Fakes, even oysters one night. And there were always fruits and nuts and deserts, some kind of chocolate or honey dripped pastry. The notes that explained each meal were spritzed with jasmine or cinnamon or other scents the twins couldn't name. It was embarrassing, but Eveyln never tried to come in.

The twins didn't discuss their progress with the books, though it was obvious enough to Daphna from her brother's moping that he was faring poorly, too. She considered telling him how lousy she was doing, but decided he'd think she was lying to make him feel better.

Anyway, she needed to maintain focus on her own problems. Odds were it was going to be up to her to find new Words of Power. She kept at it, putting in as many hours as her eyes would tolerate.

Despite her resolve, on the third day, Friday, Daphna began to wear down. For a change of pace, and because it seemed prudent, she took some time to teleport around town again. Her first stop was the R & R, to check up on Evelyn, who she found talking to a colleague about Milton Wax and his children and all the ordeals they were going through.

The next stop was the ABC, where she

found Antin holed up, pacing around like a wild dog, muttering about cops and thieves and informants and birthdays and bad fast food. He'd chilled Daphna by muttering something about her and Dexter, but she couldn't quite make it out. It wasn't affectionate, that was for sure.

After returning home, Daphna took up the Ledger again. She studied it diligently, reading Word after Word with renewed concentration. But it didn't matter. She continued to fail with each and every one.

It was late Saturday night when Daphna's luck finally changed, though she'd never have known were she not terrified of spiders. It was black and hairy and as big as a quarter, and it crawled up the leg of her desk and right out onto the Ledger.

Daphna had just called out a long throaty Word when it crossed into her field of vision. As usual, her muscles tensed up, and she teetered a bit in her chair, sweaty and shaking. When it headed down the center of the binding toward her lap, she felt faint.

Daphna tried to scream for her brother but could only mouth his name. Helpless, all she could muster in her own defense was a pathetic, silent order for the thing to go away.

Incredibly, the spider did exactly that. It reversed course, climbed off the book and then began descending one of the rear legs of the desk. Daphna was too rattled to make a connection between her thought and the spider's actions, but when it started climbing back up, she ordered it away again—and it obeyed again.

Uncertain, but curious, Daphna commanded it to go out her open window. Immediately, the spider climbed down to the floor, crossed her carpet and walked up her bedroom wall. She had to repeat her Word four times, but it did go out the window. When it was gone, Daphna beamed.

Dexter didn't last long at his studies. He continued his on again, off again approach, but as each day passed, it was more off than on. When he ate with Daphna, he could just tell she was learning tons of Words of Power. She was probably keeping them to herself so he wouldn't get jealous and quit trying to help. Dex didn't want to hear any more of her annoying pep-talks, so he just kept his mouth shut about his complete failure, not that she probably didn't assume it anyway.

Between meals he listened to the radio. He built stuff out of junk. He laid around. Even the sheer joy of being able to read couldn't overcome the disappointment that compounded with every useless word he tried. They were probably all the best Words of Power, too. He was probably reading them wrong. Still, Dex didn't give up completely, and finally, like his sister, he was rewarded.

Despite sleeping in Sunday morning, Dex woke up groggy to the sounds of a song he hated on his talking clock radio. He punched it off. Then, before pessimism got the best of him, he grabbed the *Book of Nonsense* off the heap of junk on his bedside table where he'd tossed it before falling asleep.

Slightly bleary-eyed, Dex looked over the first page. It was the only one he looked at anymore since it was different every time. He chose a word at random, a long, goofy Pig-Latinish word that struck him as funny when he said it. Nothing happened of course, so he tried the next one, a word that sounded Spanish. When nothing happened, he moved on once again, or tried to.

Upon reading the next word, Dex did something bizarre. He started singing that song he hated. He stopped quickly, then threw the book on the floor. Enough was enough—he was going stir-crazy. He had to get out of there for a while.

Dexter grabbed a hunk of cash from the pile on his floor and took himself to breakfast. Then he went to a movie. Afterward, instead of sneaking into a second show like he enjoyed doing, he went out and paid again, just for the joy of peeling money off the wad. Then he took himself out to lunch. Why not? He wasn't spending that much money, and there was such pleasure in knowing he didn't have to be the slightest bit concerned one way or the other. When he was done with lunch, Dex went out for ice cream.

That's where it happened, all because he didn't realize he'd been unconsciously repeating that funny Pig-Latin word under his breath all day long.

Dex loved ice cream, but for several reasons rarely went into the local shop. For one thing, Pops always hung out there. For another, the nasty old man who owned the place wouldn't tell him about all the new flavors when descriptions were clearly written on the label cards. Choosing by the look of the ice cream was usually a disaster, and Dex didn't dare ask for tastes of every one.

Of course, he could always just order a boring flavor like chocolate or vanilla, but having to do that made him feel like a loser when they weren't what he wanted. But Dex was riding high after his day of being rich and lazy. He wanted to try some exotic new ice cream flavor, and he was going to get one.

"Speak up, boy," the old man snarled two seconds after Dex stepped inside the store. "I don't brook mumblers!"

Dex was momentarily confused. He hadn't said anything, but then he realized he had. It was that funny word. No other customers were there, so Dex decided to pretend he hadn't heard anything.

"What new flavors do you have?" he asked, bracing for more surliness. None came. Instead, the old man pointed to each new flavor and described them rather politely. Dex supposed it was possible the old crab could've suddenly decided to become friendly, but enough incredible things had happened lately to make him attuned to more unusual possibilities. The old guy's eyes did look a touch hazy.

Dex repeated the strange Word and then asked about the flavors again. The old man, looking dazed, repeated the entire list without the least sign of annoyance.

"Do you recommend anything?" Dex asked. The old man screwed up his face at this. His eyes had cleared, and he looked annoyed, so Dex repeated his Word one more time, then asked his question again.

"Brown Cow's the way to go in my book," the old man said. The mist was back in the eyes. He sounded almost pleasant.

Dex, thrilled, ordered and paid for a triple scoop of Brown Cow. When he sat down to eat it, he noticed immediately that the clarity in the old man's eyes had returned, as had his crabby disposition. It seemed further experiments were in order, but a group of girls filed in just then. They were giggling and chatting at a hundred miles an hour. Dex shrank a bit in his chair. They were Pops from school—all hip, all great looking, all totally oblivious to his existence on the face of the earth. They made him almost as nervous as the Pop boys.

The girls ordered milkshakes, and while waiting, they continued to chitchat. Two of them walked over to look at the ice cream cakes in the display freezer just behind Dex.

"Only a few more hours until Wren's party," one of them said.

"I know," the other answered. "It's gonna be the best thing ever. A cleaning party!"

"Shhh! Don't say that out loud."

"Why?"

"True. At least something good came out of Wren's sister making her wash her sheets all the time."

"What a witch. So, anyway, when's it gonna be?"

"During the New Pop Initiation. Lucky they stock up so well there, 'cause that stuff has totally been recalled. Oh, shakes are up!"

The girls hurried to the counter before they got yelled at.

Dex had forgotten all about Daphna's surprise invitation. Too much had happened since then, but he got to wondering about it now.

Wren and Teal had lied to Daphna about being at summer camp so they wouldn't have to hang out with her. And as far as he could tell, for two years they'd been using her at school to cheat from. So the apology Daphna claimed they made must've been just to make sure they could keep using her this year. How could Daphna not have figured that out herself?

She may be one of the smartest kids in the school, thought Dexter, *but she's also one of the dumbest*. Dex tried to remember the way the invitation had been given. Daphna had acted nonchalant, like it was no big deal. And Wren— she'd looked sort of, well, afraid.

Suddenly, Dex understood. Daphna had done something to them that day. She'd somehow forced them to invite her. And now she was somehow forcing them to make her a Pop! That must be what this initiation thing was.

So this is what she's planning to do with the First Tongue, he thought, bitterly. *Well, isn't that just grand*. How could they even consider burning the books when there were Pop parties to attend? How stupid of him.

The girls were leaving, so Dex waited until they were gone before heading out himself. He hadn't the slightest idea what a "cleaning party" was, but what did a nobody like him know about Pop girls? Maybe they sat around brushing each other's fur coats like monkeys picking nits. He had much more pressing concerns, anyway. School started tomorrow, but for the first time in Dexter's life, the thought wasn't crippling. Not at all. He might even enjoy it this year.

Dex celebrated his new attitude by taking himself to a third movie. Then he sauntered home, all the while whispering his funny Word like it was the name of his new best friend.

the cleaning party

The moment Daphna opened her eyes Sunday morning, she remembered Wren's party. Despite not having thought about it for even one second since getting the invitation, it came back, unbidden, and it immediately elbowed all other concerns out of her head.

She'd been invited to a Pop party! Yes, it was true she'd nearly choked Wren and Teal to death in the park for what they'd done to her, pretending to be her friends, lying to her about their summer plans, lying to her for two years— but she didn't tell them they had to invite her to a party! The only explanation was that either they were really scared of her, or they actually were sorry, and either way they wanted to make it up to her. What was the difference really?

Daphna leapt out of bed, showered and then walked tentatively down to Dex's room. Finding him gone was a relief because she didn't have to explain what she was doing.

She grabbed some cash and then teleported

to the Village's beauty salon for a full treatment: she had her bob reshaped, a manicure, a pedicure, and even a massage. It took all morning.

Afterwards, Daphna teleported to every department store downtown and wound up buying ten outfits and a ton of accessories. She had no experience whatsoever shopping for stylish clothes, but the nicest saleswomen helped her with everything. Daphna had no idea they did that.

Unfortunately, the saleswomen didn't live with her, so once home, Daphna couldn't decide which was the best of the bunch. Consequently, she anguished over the options until early evening. Finally, she settled on black slacks, a white blouse with a patterned collar and a long sweater jacket.

Daphna was just confirming her decision in the mirror when she heard Dex come in the back door. Avoiding her brother seemed advisable just then, so she prepared to teleport outside.

"Daphna!" Dex called before she got the chance. "There's another message from Latty!"

Daphna sighed and headed to the kitchen, girding herself to endure a taunting. But Dex didn't look the least bit surprised by her appearance.

"She said they're in Ankara, the capital of Turkey," he explained. "Dad, Adem Tarik, he's been spending all this time in banks setting up some kind of account and buying some property in Eastern Turkey, in the mountains, right where those caves are. And there's been some small earthquakes in the region. They've been happening on and off for months. Latty knows we're okay from your message, so she sounded happy even though she still has no idea what he's doing. We should probably change the message after every time she calls."

"Yeah," Daphna said, "good idea." This was disturbing news, but not enough for her to worry about just then. Far more disturbing was Dex's silence about the fact that she was wearing lipstick.

Daphna suddenly felt ridiculous for having spent an entire day worrying about how she looked. But how else was she supposed to go to a Pop party? If Dexter would just laugh at her or something, it'd be much easier because she could storm off in a huff. For lack of anything else to say or do, she picked up the phone and recorded another out-going message. Then she put it down.

Still at a loss for what to say, Daphna said only, "Um—"

"Better get to that party," Dex finally said. "Otherwise, what's the point of learning the First Tongue?" He'd tried to sound sarcastic, but not overly so. But now he regretted saying anything at all. If Daphna would clear out, he'd have total freedom to experiment with his new Word.

"Dexter," Daphna retorted, pleased he'd finally gotten it out, "if you think I made them invite me to this party, you're wrong. I admit I scared Wren and Teal. I learned a Word from Emmet that chokes people. They totally deserved it. But I didn't tell them they had to be my friends. And besides, I didn't even know about this party until Wren caught us outside that restaurant. And Dex, Latty told us to go on with our normal lives as best we could."

Actually, Latty had said that again on the message Dex just listened to, but he didn't mention it. "Whatever, Daphna," he said, "but I guess your normal life is over. They're initiating you tonight."

"They're what?" Daphna was stunned. Dex told her then what he'd overheard in the ice-cream shop, and she couldn't help flushing with embarrassment and excitement. Could it be true?

"I didn't know they actually initiated people," she said. "I mean, I know they have to start calling you a Pop and all, but—Wow."

"And it's a 'cleaning party,' whatever that's supposed to mean. They said something about Wren's sister and washing sheets. Oh and something about something being recalled. I don't know. Maybe you guys will be dusting the mansion all night. Sounds like a blast."

"That would be weird," said Daphna. "Wren has two maids."

"Whatever," Dex said, "I'm just telling you what I heard. They said everyone will be talking about it all year."

"Huh. Well—I guess I better go then."

"Right. Have fun."

Daphna walked out of the house, too anxious to wonder at her brother's rather mild reaction to all of this. The party didn't start for another half an hour, and Wren lived only a few minutes away, but she needed some time to prepare herself mentally. It was almost overwhelming to think she was going to become a Pop.

As she walked, Daphna wondered if she'd have to say anything in front of everyone. Would she have to answer questions, like Miss America? A vision of what her eighth grade year might be like came to her. Surely, she'd learn just how all the Pops manage to look and talk the way they do, the way they get boys to do their bidding and keep the non-Pop girls in their place, all without seeming to try. She could afford anything they could now!

Maybe being a Pop isn't the greatest thing to aspire to in life, Daphna thought. *But then again,* she told herself, *I'm going to be a Pop in one of my lives, so why not this one?*

As splendid images of Popdom sashayed past her mind's eye, all of Daphna's troubles obediently backed away. Adem Tarik didn't seem interested in them, anyway. Latty was keeping an eye on him, so why worry about it until they had to? Let him buy half of Turkey for all she cared. Maybe it was even possible, Daphna thought, that she wouldn't have to use the First Tongue after being initiated.

Dizzied by the promise of her new life, Daphna continued walking with no particular direction around the Village. Eventually, she noticed the clock on top of the local wine shop. Somehow it had gotten to be just past seven.

After a deep breath and a check of her hair and clothes in the wine shop's window, Daphna headed over to Wren's street and began climbing the hill leading to her beautiful three-story brick and stone house. It was by far the largest and nicest home in Multnomah Village. Wren's parents were divorced. Her dad lived in another state, and her mom was a semi-famous actress who was always overseas somewhere shooting movies in glamorous Mediterranean locales. That left Wren's older sister in charge, and Wren's older sister apparently didn't take that job very seriously. As far as Daphna could tell, Wren could do pretty much whatever she wanted.

When she approached the house, Daphna could see that lots of girls were already there. They were sitting on the various stone sculptures in the front yard, sipping multi-colored drinks and watching fountains burble.

Daphna's school had over five hundred girls, but only 21 of them were official Pops. It looked like they were all there, actually. For a moment, the sight of them made Daphna stop short, horrified by the thought that every single one of them knew how she'd been used by Wren and Teal. But if that were true, why would they all be there? The initiation obviously wasn't a secret if Dex heard some of them talking about it.

And if she'd scared Wren and Teal into this, she hadn't scared them all. Those two were the most popular, but it wasn't like they could just tell everyone else who was going to be a Pop. Everyone must have agreed.

This eased Daphna's mind, but then she panicked about being late. Was that uncool since everyone was already there? Pops were always late for class, but this obviously wasn't school. Daphna approached the glittering white picket fence that ran around Wren's property, fearing the worst, but Wren and Teal jumped up and ran to greet her. They grabbed her by the elbows the second she stepped through the gate and led her to a little stone bench shaped like a unicorn.

"Daphna!" Teal sighed. She and Wren were both wearing pink baseball hats with little rhinestones all over them. Hats were their thing.

"Thank goodness you made it!" said Teal. "We were thinking of calling to remind you, but we didn't have—"

"We didn't have any doubt you'd remember," Wren said. "But we were worried anyway 'cause we didn't want to miss the chance to show you that we're really sorry. We want to start fresh."

"We've got a surprise for you."

"For me? What is it?" Daphna asked, hoping to sound startled and pleased. Should she apologize for choking them? But they couldn't really know she'd been the cause of it.

"Can't tell you yet," Teal answered with a conspiratorial smile. "We're gonna watch a movie first." She stood up and shouted, "Movie time!"

Everyone in the yard got up and headed inside straight away. Daphna joined the crowd with some trepidation, but her fears vanished when virtually every single girl said hi to her on the way in. Even Branwen said hi, and she was a notorious snob, even among the Pops themselves.

By the time everyone was seated in Wren's gorgeous basement theater, Daphna was electric with anticipation. She wanted to hop up on the professional quality mini stage in the front of the room and dance for joy, but of course she sat down quietly with everyone else when the lights went off.

Someone pressed a button somewhere, and a screen slid down from above the back of the stage. When it stopped, someone behind Daphna said, "I'm just glad these seats are soft. My butt was starting to kill me out there."

This struck Daphna as odd. She'd gotten there after seven, but not long after. Did the party actually start at six? She was pretty sure Wren said seven, but she didn't have a memory for details like Dex. How long could they have been sitting out there?

The movie was coming on, so Daphna put the issue out of mind. It was a cheesy old black and white horror movie about a girl who gets infected by alien spore from a meteorite then goes on to infect everyone in her school, turning them into flesh eating zombies who infect everyone else in town. It was idiotic in the extreme, but maybe it was the Pops' favorite movie. Maybe they liked it because it was so bad.

This explanation satisfied Daphna, and her

excitement welled. In a matter of hours, she'd be a Pop! She felt as if she were standing in the brightest, most beautiful field of flowers looking up into a perfect blue sky of possibilities.

But as the movie went on, something began to gnaw at Daphna. A tiny black speck appeared in her perfect sky. She couldn't immediately identify what was bothering her about this story, but it flustered her enough to get up to find a restroom so she could think clearly. It seemed like everyone looked at her as she made her way to the aisle, and with alarm.

When she whispered 'bathroom' someone pointed to a door in the back. She went through into a laundry nook with a marble-tiled half-bath. Daphna splashed cold water on her face, but it didn't help. She decided to let it go and stepped back into the laundry nook—then stopped.

There, laying sideways on the laundry machine was a detergent, a brand that gave her pause. It had been in the news recently. Daphna wracked her memory. Yes! It had been recalled. Dex said something about that. It had been recalled because it caused a horrible rash. Daphna opened a cabinet next to the washer and saw dozens of boxes of the same product. They were all empty. Finally, she got it, and the now massive black shape in her sky revealed itself for what it was: a falling anvil—and it hit her in the head. Daphna understood everything.

She was being set up.

In less than an hour she'd built an entirely new life for herself, all based on an invitation to a party thrown by people who were hateful. Why was it so important to be among them? Daphna despised them. She admitted that now. She'd always despised them. It's just that despising them seemed totally unrelated to her wish to join them.

Standing there with tears cascading down her face, Daphna figured how it all must have gotten planned. Wren and Teal, after getting over their fright at being choked in the park, probably laughed it off. Why would they think Daphna had what would have to be supernatural powers? The very idea would've seemed absurd. They probably decided it was some kind of fluke—allergies or asthma maybe. One of them probably said she was diseased and made the connection to their movie. Then the other no doubt said, *Hey, wouldn't it be the best if we—?* And so, here they were, waiting for Daphna's final humiliaiton.

Wait a minute, Daphna thought, *here we are*.

The tears dried up at once. It was no comfort now to think that with an endless number of lives, this humiliation would eventually happen to each and every girl sitting in the dark with her. *If it has to happen to me, too,* Daphna thought, *it didn't necessarily have to happen now*. She was perfectly free to do whatever she could to make sure it didn't.

Let the next Daphna get covered in rashes, she fumed. There was still plenty of time left in the film, so Daphna hurried back into the theater. She didn't fail to notice the looks of relief on the faces she passed going back to her seat. She got right to work.

She whispered her new Word and willed the girl in front of her to go for a drink of soda. It took almost fifteen minutes, and the girl only got up and walked away for a moment before returning to her seat somewhat confused. It was a start, though. It took twenty minutes to get a girl in the front row to go to the restroom, but she went all the way in.

Daphna could tell the Word was weak, at

least the way she was using it. For the duration of the movie, she worked on making girls scratch their heads or brush their shoulders, and with each attempt, it got a little bit easier.

By the time the lights came back on and the screen was raised, Daphna was reasonably sure she could handle whatever they had in store for her.

"Okay, everybody!" a voice boomed from speakers overhead. It was Teal. She and Wren had made their way up onto the little stage. They wereleaning over a microphone on a stand they'd pulled out from the wings, and they were positively glowing now in little black berets.

"We have a surprise for Daphna," Teal announced.

We really do look alike, Daphna thought. And then, once again, despite everything, *she's the pretty version.*

All atwitter now, everyone turned to look for the guest of honor. Daphna realized instantly that they all knew what was coming. The reason they'd gotten uncomfortable outside was that they'd all been there for some time before she came, planning, envisioning how hilarious it was going to be. Well, it was going to be hilarious all right. Daphna stood up, and everyone began clapping.

"Come on down!" Teal called out with the enthusiasm of a game show host. Daphna obliged, having noticed the way Teal's eyes had flicked upward momentarily. She felt completely calm, almost numb, as she worked her way to the aisle in the center of the room. Things seemed to be moving in slow-motion as she approached the stage, but Daphna maintained her presence-of-mind.

Once on the steps, she flicked her own eyes upward. The bucket was there—a trash can, actually. It was suspended from the rigging right above the microphone but behind the proscenium, so it wasn't visible from the seats. A thin dark cord ran from the barrel back over the lights and then behind a curtain covering the back wall, where no doubt someone stood, hiding, waiting for the cue to yank it.

Wren and Teal reached for Daphna and maneuvered her between them.

"It's not every year we initiate someone before school starts," Teal announced, "but this year, we'd be crazy not to. I nominate Daphna Wax. Will anyone second?"

"I second! I second!" shouted various girls from around the room. Then everyone was shouting it. They could barely contain themselves.

Daphna cast a cold eye over all the smirking faces. Only Branwen's was missing.

"Okay," Wren called out, "now we need to make it official with a vote. We need three unanimous 'Yea' votes to swear in a new Pop. Do we have one?"

"Yea!" the crowd yelled, and as it did so, Wren and Teal both took a large step away from Daphna on either side.

"Do I hear two?" Teal shouted. She was too far away from the microphone to use it. She and Wren took another step.

"Yea!" the crowd roared.

"Do I hear three?"

The girls rushed offstage. The crowd didn't respond at first. They wanted to savor the moment, so there was a collective pause. And into that pause, Daphna, standing alone, spoke her new favorite Word into the microphone. Then she said, quickly, "Bran, be still."

"YEA!" everyone screamed. Then—nothing happened.

The Pops turned to one another. They

looked to Wren and Teal, both of whom were leaning in from the wings and glaring at the black curtain backstage.

Daphna took the microphone and cleared her throat. Everyone looked at her with mouths agape.

"I am so honored," Daphna said. "This is the best day of my life, of all my lives." Then she added, "But it's not perfect yet." Daphna turned round to look backstage. She pronounced her Word, then said, "Bran, come out here. Wren and Teal, would you join me, too?"

Branwen came out and did exactly that. So did Wren and Teal. All three of them had misty eyes.

All other eyes were devouring the developing scene, which is exactly how Daphna hoped it would go.

"I'll be right back," she said.

Then she turned and walked casually backstage, briefly recalling the similar way her father's eyes had looked after his first encounter with Asterius Rash behind another curtain. *Rash,* she thought. *Perfect.*

Daphna found the edge of the fabric, slipped behind it and located the cord. It was wrapped around a hook mounted on the wall. With deliberate care, Daphna unwrapped the cord and let it be pulled up and away.

Seconds later—she didn't look—there was a tremendous splash, like a tidal wave crashing on a dock. Dead silence ensued for just an instant, then came three horrified screams.

And after that—laughter. Gales of hilarious, jeering laughter.

The slow-motion was even slower now. Daphna had entered some sort of dream world. She walked along the edge of the backstage area until she discovered an entrance to the main floor of the house. Light as air, she walked through a series of luxurious sitting rooms until she found her way to the front door.

She let herself out.

study buddy

When Daphna left, Dexter went down to his room to think about how he might best practice his new Word. He didn't want to try it out on anyone in public again for fear of being noticed, but there didn't seem to be any other way. He wished someone was there with him, someone other than Daphna, of course. He needed what his goofy third grade teacher always called a "Study Buddy."

She had another expression she used all the time, too, especially with Dex because he often told her he wished he didn't have to go to school: Be careful what you wish for. Dex had never really understood the expression. That is, until about a second after he remembered it.

Which was when Antin, blackened by soot from head to toe like a coal miner, appeared on the basement steps. Daphna must've left the door unlocked.

Despite the urge to panic, Dex remained sitting at his desk. He sensed a golden opportunity, never mind that his life was probably at stake. It helped that Antin looked dead on his feet. On the other hand, his eyes were even more crazed and jumpy than they'd been the last time he paid a house call to the Wax's.

"Gimme my money," Antin spat, flicking open his knife and glancing quickly back over his shoulder. "Figures you'd just leave it sitting there in the open. Should've come here right away, but I figured you'd have cops crawling all over the place. Should've known you were too stupid—What did you say?"

"I said, put the knife away," Dex ordered. Actually, he'd spoken his new Word, and as forcefully as he could. Antin blinked, looked down at his blade, then back at Dexter. Then he looked over his shoulder and snapped the knife shut, just like that.

Dex grinned—his first try! But then Antin shook his head as if to clear cobwebs and the blade shot out again. He stepped forward.

Dex nervously repeated his Word. Then he repeated the order. Antin screwed up his eyes and closed the knife again, but just as quickly opened it and took another step forward. Dex stood up and backed away. He called out his

Word several times and shouted, "Put it away!" Antin finally obeyed again, but once again, only for a few seconds.

A harrowing tug-of-war ensued in which the blade went in and out, and an increasingly frustrated Antin came closer and closer to Dexter.

Soon enough, Dex was up against the wall.

"I got no idea what game you're playing," Antin growled, "but I promise you, I can't be played. You've ruined my life," he said after looking over his shoulder, "so I'm gonna ruin yours."

Antin looked Dexter in the eye then and leaned forward with the knife.

Dex screamed.

Antin stopped.

The tip of the knife rested against Dex's shoulder, but did not penetrate. It wasn't moving, Dex realized, and neither was Antin. He'd been frozen. Dex had involuntarily called out the Word he'd used to freeze Evelyn.

He sighed, slipping around Antin after pushing the blade carefully aside. He knew what he was going to do now, so he pulled his chair across the room and sat down to wait.

Antin remained frozen for a few minutes,

which was fortunate because Dex needed some time to recover. It didn't matter that he'd been that close to Antin's knife before. The experience wasn't something you got used to. He took some slow, deep breaths until his heartbeat slowed.

And so Dex was ready when, like an unpaused character in a video game, Antin came to life. Outraged to find his victim gone, he wheeled round, and at the sight of Dex sitting calmly in his chair, he charged. Dex spoke his new Word right away, then ordered Antin to stop. It worked, and for slightly longer this time. When it wore off, Antin came at Dex again, his face contorted with furious incomprehension. Dex stopped him again, and six times after that before the knife got too close. At that point, Dex froze Antin again.

Not bad, Dex thought to himself. He was getting better.

With Antin immobilized, Dex walked back across the room and set up a second chair. Then he sat down to wait. It took fifteen minutes this time, but eventually Antin turned and charged. Dex stopped him nine times, and on each occasion, for almost half a minute. When the knife got close, Dex froze Antin yet again and went back to the other chair.

This process went on for well over an hour: Antin charging, stopping, freezing; charging, stopping, freezing, all the while growing nearly apoplectic with rage and confusion. His teeth were bared and his body shook with each new attempt to get at Dexter.

With each round, Dex found himself growing in confidence. The Word was somehow feeling more and more comfortable, like a baseball glove getting broken in.

Finally, like a beaten fighter, Antin gave up. Glaze-eyed, he dropped his switchblade and slumped into one of the chairs. Dexter was astonished with himself. Never before in his life, in any situation, had he ever felt—he didn't even know a word for it—mastery? The only thing was, now that he'd won, Dex had no idea what to do.

What do winners do? he wondered, tossing the switchblade into the trash. On second thought, he picked the knife back up and tossed it into the mess in his closet under the stairs. Antin remained slouched in the chair, utterly undone.

"Ahh—" Dex said after clicking the door shut, "So—um—"

"I can't be played!" Antin snapped, though it came across like a feeble strike from a defanged snake. His voice was strained to the breaking point. The pleasant thought occurred to Dex that Antin might very well cry, like the rest of his gang at the police station.

"I'm gonna kill you," Antin said, still sagging in his chair. "I wasn't gonna kill you before, but I'm gonna kill you now, and then I'm going to burn down this house."

"Wow," Dex replied, feeling smug. "Didn't your parents ever tell you it's rude to kill people and burn down their houses?" Another thought occurred to him then. If he suggested that Antin have a little accident in his pants, the victory would be complete.

"My parents are dead."

"I—I'm sorry about that," Dex said. He'd been taken completely off guard. Antin looked at Dex, but didn't reply.

"My mom's dead, too," Dex added without deciding to. "My dad killed her."

"You're kidding," said Antin. He was curious, plain and simple. "Wait a minute, your father?"

he said. "That freaky old book dude?"

"He pushed her over a cliff in some cave," Dex explained. "I was like, two months old or something. I didn't know, though. I just found out the other day."

"Well, well, well," said Antin.

"What happened to yours?" Dex asked, aware that he was suddenly trembling.

Antin shot a glance over his shoulder, then answered. "My dad left my mom before I was ever born," he said. "He never cared about her, not even for one second. He was a thief. Got killed in prison."

"Oh," Dex said, awkwardly. "He didn't kill your mom, did he?"

"Nah. My mom had to work, like, four crappy jobs or something to try to support me 'cause she never went to school. She got really sick working in some foodpacking plant, in the refrigerators. She couldn't afford a doctor or to miss work, so she died. I don't remember it, though. They shipped me to a foster home after that. They were pretty nice, but I was a jerk so they booted me out. I got sent to another one— to some tough guy who said he didn't mind me being a jerk. That turned out to be 'cause it gave him an excuse to beat on me all the time."

"I—I—" was Dexter's only response.

Antin took an uncharacteristically long look over his shoulder. Dex could tell he hadn't meant to say so much. A strange air was in the room. Dexter had never had a conversation like this with anyone, not even Latty, though she'd tried about ten million times to get him to talk to her. He did when he was little of course, but even then he'd been careful to avoid the real depths of his frustrations. But just now, everything he'd ever been frustrated about seemed slightly shabby.

Dex wanted the conversation to continue, but he didn't know how to keep it going. Antin was just sitting there now, looking down at his knees. Finally, he jerked his head up and glared at Dexter. His pupils were tiny black balls of anger again.

"What's going on?" he demanded. "Why did I tell you that?"

Dex didn't know why. Antin's eyes were clear. Dex said his Word, then asked, "Did you get away from that guy? I mean, are you in another foster home now?"

Antin, his eyes softened into a haze, said, "I

moved on after I burned his house down about a year ago."

"Oh."

"He busted me up when I was a jerk, but most of the time he did it for no reason, whenever I wasn't expecting it, just for fun, to keep me on my toes. Once he threw a telephone book at my head when I was sleeping. Your dad ever beat you?"

"Um—no," Dex admitted. "He was never around."

"Lucky you, then."

"I—I guess," Dex answered. He couldn't tell if Antin was sharing this additional information because he wanted to, or because Dex's Word was still holding sway. His eyes already seemed clear again.

"So—" Dex fumbled, "you burned down the house to get revenge?"

"Sort of. Mostly, I was sick of waiting to get hit. First I tried doing stuff to tick him off on purpose, you know, so I could always know when it was coming. But then I realized that was stupid."

"Ah—well—yeah," Dex stuttered. He was pretty sure Antin was talking under his own power now. Dex desperately wanted it to stay this way, but his brain seemed incapable of finding appropriate things to say. "Have you been just, like, living around town since then?" he managed.

"Here and there—wherever."

"But you don't have a job or anything, right?"

"Been stealing stuff, small time things, money from kids around here. The cops haven't been able to do too much, but I just turned eighteen. That's why I'm taking this money and leaving town for good. I've been looking for something big for a long time now, something to get me gone."

"Do you believe in God?"

Dex heard these words come out of his mouth, but he hadn't been thinking about God, and even if he had, he'd have kept such an embarrassing question to himself. Dex felt his face burn with shame. What was the matter with him? He'd better order Antin to forget the entire conversation and get rid of him once and for all.

"There is no God," said Antin, jolting Dex before he got the chance to use his Word.

The casual certainty of Antin's reply was even more shocking to Dex then his having asked the question in the first place. "How— how do you know?" he asked.

Antin stood up and started walking around the room with a cryptic smile on his blackened face. He never stopped checking back over his shoulder all the while.

"You know what's funny?" he said. "Those first people I lived with, the ones that weren't so bad, they always tried to talk to me about God. I told 'em God was dead, which I guess was one of the things that really made 'em mad. When I did bad stuff, they'd always say I might be able to fool them, but God knows everything. He knows everything that ever was or ever would be. So I said, if he knows all the bad stuff that's gonna happen and doesn't do anything about it, then he can go to Hell. That didn't go over too good."

"Yeah, I'd expect not—"

"My mom was real religious," Antin said. "That's about the only thing I remember about her, how much she believed God was watching over us. She told me so every night before she put me to bed and made me thank him for all the good things in our life, even though we didn't have jack.

"If there's a God, then he just kicked back and watched while our life got ruined and she got dead. If there's a God, then he's kickin' back right now while kids are gettin' starved to death and locked in closets and whipped with belts— or whatever. You name it, and I know a kid it happened to. You wanna believe in a God like that, Wax? Innocent kids!"

Dex opened his mouth to say, he didn't know what, but Antin didn't wait.

"You know what else those people tried to tell me?" he said, getting worked up. "They said messed up things happen to people who did something to deserve it. You ever notice the only people who tell you that crap are people that messed up things never happen to? I told them they must've pissed God off big-time to deserve getting me. That was when they kicked me out. My old case worker always said that God works in mysterious ways, and we can't understand his plans for us. I finally told him— it was a couple of weeks after my new 'dad' hit me with a golf club when I was watching TV—I said, 'Good, then Antin works in mysterious ways, too.'

"The next day I torched the place and took off. If God's plans involve crooks getting everything and lyin' and cheatin' and killin' and stealin', then so do mine! 'Course I don't really believe that. It don't make sense. God wouldn't be God if he was all screwed up like that. That's how come I know ain't there. That's how come I say, you do what you gotta do to get by."

"I—ah—" Dex fumbled. The ferocity of Antin's speech had rendered him nearly mute. He was amazed Antin had anything at all to say on the subject. He'd clearly thought about it a lot. Antin was obviously not what he appeared to be. Was anyone? Antin was crazy all right, and dangerous, too. But he wasn't— evil. Daphna had tried to say as much about Emmet.

Dex felt like pieces of his mind were coming loose and sliding, like the little rocks that fall down a slope before the whole landslide. Then a question came to mind.

"What if—" Dex asked, "what if God just, you know, has something against you, personally? What if he just picks certain people out to kind of, I don't know, mess with?"

"Sure," Antin sneered, "he must really hate

all those kids who look like skeletons on those commercials in Africa. That makes a lot of sense. If there's a God, Wax, he's a screw-up. That would explain why he made a screwed-up world. But I still say there is no God. Or, here's another idea: maybe he woke up one day and saw what a piece of crap he made and got depressed and knocked himself off."

Dexter shuddered as a thought struck him. "Or—or—maybe somebody killed him," he croaked, looking at the *Book of Nonsense* sitting just a few feet away on his desk. Had God been killed for it? Was that even possible? Could Adem Tarik—his father—have killed God for that book?

"Maybe," said Antin. The idea seemed to impress him slightly. Then he shook his head.

"Why don't you tell me what the hell's going on here," he demanded, turning to face Dexter. "Why can't I kill you and go? Why don't I want to anymore?"

"Look, Antin," said Dex. His brain was actually hurting. He wanted to be alone.

"What?"

Dex got up and took a large bundle of cash out of the bag on the floor. Then he walked over and handed it to Antin. He whispered his Word one more time and said, "This is more than enough money for you to start over. I'm gonna tell my dad not to press charges. He'll listen, I promise. Go and get yourself a place to live and then go back to school or get a job or something. And you don't need to be on edge all the time. No one's gonna hit you any more, not if you get it together."

Antin blinked. Then he put the stack of bills inside his shirt and walked up the basement steps.

He left without looking back.

school daze

In the morning, Dex and Daphna met in the kitchen. Daphna was dressed reasonably in slacks and a light sweater, though she hadn't made more than a token effort with her hair, and none at all with make-up. She was pretty sure she'd never do that again, at least not to fit in with a bunch of brainless, stuck-up, prima-donna piranhas.

Dex's decision to wear his usual shredded jeans and oversized sweatshirt was no surprise, but to Daphna it suddenly seemed almost like some kind of statement about not being phony—almost, that is. She'd never go that far. *It's one thing to be yourself*, she thought, *but if yourself is a slob, a little fitting in wouldn't kill you.*

Neither of the twins were in the mood to talk while they ate cold cereal. Both were still too wrapped up in the events of the previous night.

Daphna had no idea what to expect at school. Would she be treated like a hero? An outcast? She suspected what had happened was far too bizarre and confusing for anyone to understand, so she wasn't too worried about having her new talents discovered.

Dex, for his part, was trying to maintain the optimism that had kept him up half the night. After his incredible success with Antin, he'd been certain he could somehow make school manageable. But now that the reality of it was so close, he was losing confidence. A familiar, nauseating pool of revulsion was rising in his stomach with each passing minute.

He did notice his sister seemed out of sorts. That was odd, of course, since going back to school for her had to be what it's like for a fish to get thrown back into water. But he didn't ask questions. Dex didn't want to know about the party. He'd made sure to be in his room when she finally came home last night. Daphna could now be the Queen of all Pops for all he cared.

Neither of the twins spoke until they were putting their dishes into the sink. That's when the phone rang.

"Should we get it?" Daphna asked.

"No," said Dex. "You can if you want. I don't think I could talk to her right now."

"Me neither. We don't have time anyway, and besides, it could be Evelyn or the cops. They must think we're home by now."

When the ringing stopped, the twins waited for a few minutes, then each picked up a phone. Daphna keyed in the voicemail code. It was Latty, and her message was brief.

"Kids, it's me again. I just want to keep you informed. This is all very strange. I have no idea what it means, but Tarik's got a whole fleet of trucks out there already, in the mountains. He's purchased several libraries and is having thousands and thousands of old books hauled out there, though there've been some delays because of another small earthquake. Like I said, I have no idea what's going on, but I'm going to try to get out there and see what's what.

"Oh, gosh, speaking of books, today's the first day of school isn't it? Maybe you're already there. I'm so sorry I'm not home to make lunches and see you off! Just keep letting me know you're okay. I'll call as soon as I learn more. Love you both."

This bit of news wasn't nearly interesting enough to deflect the twins' immediate concerns. They grabbed their bags and headed out the door.

Daphna, as she always did, took the direct route and walked as swiftly as she could.

Dex, as he always did, veered off to make his journey as long as possible.

On the first day of both sixth and seventh grade, Daphna walked to school brimming with excitement, wondering about what her teachers would be like and what she'd be learning.

This year, such thoughts were furthermost from her mind. She brimmed only with anxiety. Lots of other neighborhood kids walked to school too, and all Daphna could think about as she fell in among a crowd was that everyone was watching her. She paced forward with her head down so she wouldn't know one way or the other.

Of course when she checked, no one was looking at her, but maybe that meant something worse. None of the Pops were there—they didn't walk—but everyone knew how fast gossip flew among the kids at her school.

For all Daphna knew, everyone had heard something about what happened by then. She had no idea how she was going to play it when someone confronted her. Cool? Smug and superior? Confused and amazed?

Half a block to go. The ugly, low-slung school building was in sight. Daphna pressed on, trying to force herself to focus on ordinary thoughts. She'd go in, pick up her schedule, find her homeroom and head right there. Simple.

But a group of kids was just behind her now as she approached the school's front steps. Daphna tried not to look back. They were chatting about this and that, something about vacation being a rip off because it was way too short.

"What'd you do all summer?" one of them asked.

"Nothing."

"What'd you do?"

"Nothing."

"Eighth grade, man. We're gonna clean—"

Daphna, halfway up the steps by then, wheeled around with eyes ablaze. The group—it was five kids, all in her grade—stopped in their tracks and nearly fell back down the steps.

"What did you say?" Daphna hissed, leaning down at them. No one responded at first.

"What did you say!" Daphna demanded.

The boy who'd last spoken looked around nervously. Then he shrugged and said, "I said—I was saying, we're eighth graders now, so we're gonna clean up around here."

"Oh. Ahh—right, then. Sorry."

"What's your damage?" sneered a girl in the group. Suddenly they were all glaring up at her.

Daphna, flushing with embarrassment, had no choice. She couldn't start off this way. She spoke the necessary Word and told all five kids to forget the whole conversation.

Then, noting how quickly and totally the glaze came over their eyes, Daphna added, "By the way, the Pops are out this year. They're totally un-cool." Then she turned and rushed up the steps and into the school.

She knew exactly how she was going to play things now.

Being tardy to school was imperative for Dex because latecomers weren't allowed into their homerooms once Silent Sustained Reading started. Instead, stragglers were herded into the cafeteria where, since most of them didn't have their novels with them, they wound up doing homework. It was much easier to doodle on worksheets than it was to sit and stare cross-eyed at squirming words for forty minutes. Walking out of his way also let him avoid all the other kids who walked.

When he reached campus, Dex veered around the main pathway and cut through the staff parking lot. Halfway across, he came to an abrupt halt. He was being ridiculous. What was the point of wasting another year of his life? He still couldn't read normal books, and nothing he'd learned so far in the *Book of Nonsense* could change that. It would make much more sense to keep searching it for something that would just get rid of the problem once and for all. Dex turned to sneak away.

"Dexter Wax?"

Dex froze. Someone had called his name through the passenger window of a slowly moving car, a police car, which stopped beside him. "Are you Dexter Wax?" It was Officer Richards.

"Ah, yeah. How did you know?"

"We were just looking at pictures of you and your sister in the office."

"Oh," Dex said, afraid to learn what this meant. "My dad said we'd probably be hearing from you," he said, "but I'm gonna be tardy, so—"

"We came to take statements from you kids this morning," said Madden, "but we just got a few tips about where the redhead might be. We'll be back later to—What's that? I didn't quite hear what you said."

"Why don't I get in the car so we can talk?"

"Why don't you get in the car so we can talk?" both officers suggested at the same time.

Dex got into the back seat. "My father has decided not to press charges," he said. "You can let Antin go."

Officer Richards turned to Officer Madden. "His father isn't pressing charges," he said. "Captain's gonna freak."

"Nah, he'll go forward anyway," answered Richards. "The gang's going to pieces at McLaren, which is why we're starting to get leads out of them."

"Let's go talk to the Captain," said Dex. "And let's have the gang brought up to the station—top speed, okay? That way we can all have a talk."

"Let's go talk to the Captain," said Richards. "I'll call and have the gang brought up to the station—top speed," said Madden. "That way we can all have a talk." He put the car in gear and pulled out of the lot.

Dex ducked down so some kids coming in late didn't see him in the back of a cop car, smiling.

Daphna walked straight to the office avoiding eye contact with everyone in the jostling halls. She listened as best as she could to all the conversations percolating around her but didn't hear the slightest mention of the party. She didn't know what to expect, but she expected something, and right away. It should've been front page news.

Standing in line in the office, still trying to puzzle things out, Daphna realized two Pops were waiting directly in front of her. She wished she could be invisible, but it turned out not to be necessary. The girls were looking forward, oblivious of her presence. Of course, it was always as if they couldn't see non-Pops, anyway, unless they needed to use one, that is.

"When will they be back?" one of them whispered. Her name was Robin.

"Not sure," whispered the other girl, Jarita.

"They both broke out in hives head-to-toe. You saw it; they looked like a couple of swollen beets! But we better just shut up about the whole thing before somebody—What? Daphna? Ah—did you say something?"

"What happened at the party?" Daphna asked, looking into the two sets of suddenly fogged-over eyes.

Robin blinked at Daphna, then said, "Wren and Teal and Bran—the stain remover stuff fell on them instead of you. You were right there, but no one knows what happened. You said something, or you whispered something. Some people said you just mouthed something, and then Bran came out, and then you went backstage, and then it fell."

"And everyone laughed," Daphna said.

"Yeah, everyone laughed," Jarita confirmed. "It was the funniest thing I've ever seen in my entire life."

"Those three finally got what they deserved," said Robin. "It was a thing of beauty."

"Really?" Daphna said, "But, then, why aren't you telling people about it? Why isn't everyone talking about it?"

"'Cause after it happened," Jarita explained,

"Wren talked to us. She was all red and everyone was pointing and laughing. But she said if this gets out, it's a stain on all of us. It's a stain on being a Pop, and when one of us gets humiliated, all of us get humiliated."

"She said Pops are Pops only because everyone who isn't a Pop thinks so," Robin continued, "and if people find out that some loser like you can take some of us down, then everyone will think they can. It'd be like dominoes. It didn't seem so funny after that. So no one's gonna breathe a word about it."

"What about me?" Daphna asked. "What's to stop me from telling the whole world?"

"Mud," said Jarita.

"What?"

"Teal said you covered her in soap, but we're gonna cover you in mud. You know, ruin your reputation so no one will believe anything you ever say for the rest of your life."

"Is that so?" Daphna snapped. "Turn around now and forget we had this conversation. Oh, one more thing. You're not Pops anymore. The Pops are out. Totally uncool."

"I just hope they don't try to talk to us," Robin said when she and Jarita turned back around. "I'm done with them. I'm so done with the whole Pop thing."

"Totally," Jarita agreed. "It's so last year."

"Captain, this is Dexter Wax. He wants to talk to you."

"What's that, young man?"

"I said my father won't be pressing charges against Antin or his gang. You can forget all about them. I think I can straighten them out myself."

"Right then. But I've got cops out there hauling him in. Found him at the bus station."

"That radio, on your desk. Can I talk to those cops?"

"Sure. You can talk to every cop out there."

"Really? Great. Can you set it up?—Thanks— Okay—"

"What's that, Captain? Didn't read that clearly."

"To the cops who got Antin, let him go. Forget about him totally. Go about your business. All the other cops out there who know anything about this, forget about it. Get rid of all the paperwork on this case. Ten-Four."

A woman stuck her head into the office just

then. "Captain—those boys you wanted are here," she said. "They're in the holding tank."

"We'll be right there," said Dex.

There were still a few minutes before the late bell, so Daphna got to as many kids as she could. She was as efficient as possible. A touch on the shoulder, the whisper of a Word. Daphna felt like an avenging angel, alighting here and there, making a Pop-free world. The only problem was there were too many kids at her school. It would be nearly impossible to get to everyone. Just as the bell rang, Daphna slipped into her homeroom. She'd never come that close to being tardy before.

The annoying signal that morning announcements were about to begin blared from the intercom next to the door. Daphna sat back and let the atmosphere soak into her at last. Being in school was the next best thing to being in a bookstore.

"Good morning students and staff, this is Principal Francisco Isidoro. Hola and welcome back one and all!

"Here is this year's first Daily Dose of Wisdom: In the Jewish tradition, there is a story that describes how a man offered to become Jewish only if the famous Rabbi Hillel could teach him everything he needed to know about the religion in the time he could stand on one foot. Instead of sending the man away for this absurd request, Rabbi Hillel said this: 'What you find hateful do not do to another. Everything else is commentary.' This is, of course, the Golden Rule. Treat others as you would have them treat you.

"This year we will be studying all kinds of subjects from Geography to Biology to Poetry to Art to Technology—and so much more. But keep this in mind: all you learn will be meaningless if it does not make you a better person. I hope you use today well. I hope you use this year well. Just remember, what you do is always up to you."

Daphna normally paid close attention to the Daily Doses, but she hadn't been able to listen closely to this one with so much on her mind. She'd heard the last line, though, probably because it was always the last line. *Just remember, what you do is always up to you.*

Not always, Daphna thought. Her hand shot into the air.

"Yes, Daphna? I'm sorry, I didn't hear that?"

"I know it's SSR, but I think they need me down at the office."

"I know it's SSR, dear, but I think they need you down at the office."

"Ah, hello? Is it on? Okay. Um, hola everyone, this is Daphna Wax. Please pardon the interruption, but we are going to have an extra Daily Dose of Wisdom."

Daphna cleared her throat and clearly pronounced her Word. Then she plowed ahead.

"This year, everyone will treat everyone as an equal. No one will care how expensive each other's clothes are or where each other lives. No one will pick on anyone or call anyone ugly or nerdy. No one will cheat. We will all smile at each other. Those of you in sixth grade, and you seventh graders who are still twelve, well, I hope you're listening too, but I guess it really will be up to you.

"Oh yeah, Dexter, sorry about this. I'll undo you later. And I'll explain. Okay, Bye."

"Well, Dexter, the gang's all here."

Dex hadn't known what a "holding tank" was. He'd half expected to find the boys in an empty aquarium, but it was just a cell, although seeing one in real life made his pulse race for a few moments. The sullen boys, slouching on benches, leaning against walls and sitting on the floor, looked up at him apathetically when he came in. But when they realized who he was, every one of them leapt to their feet and rushed to the bars. Dex backed away, but he wasn't under attack.

"Tell 'em! Tell 'em Antin made us do it!" everyone pleaded all at once. "Tell 'em we didn't even want to come into your house! Tell 'em!"

"Quiet!" Dex called out, but his voice was lost in the shouting.

"Tell 'em it was Antin!"

"Tell 'em we don't know where he is!"

"Tell 'em!"

"I said *QUIET!*" Dex roared. "I'm here to help you!" This, finally, got everyone's undivided attention.

"Sheesh," Dex sighed. Then, before they could start up again, he spoke his Word. All eyes misted over.

"Okay," he said, "you are all free to go. You

will all quit being followers and jerks. You will all go back to your families, or find somewhere you can be safe. You will all go back to school and do the best you can not to screw up the rest of your lives."

Nods all around. Dex turned to the Captain, who opened the cell. The boys filed out, and Dex followed them into the lobby of the station. The crowd drew highly concerned looks of surprise from the officers there. Dex realized this was all more complicated than it seemed at first. People dealt with other people—if you got to one, you needed to get to them all. Then he saw the answer on the main secretary's desk.

"Is that a p.a. system, Captain?"

"Sure is."

"I'll need to use that for a second. In the meantime, can you go get me all the money you confiscated from the gang? Then I'll need to talk to the people down in Salem."

"Will do."

seventh period

Why not? Dex thought. He was letting Officer Richards drive him back to school. Maybe it was going to spoil the most spectacular morning of his life, but he doubted it. What was there to be afraid of now? Granted, it wasn't like him to go back willingly when there was no more reason to, but if he could handle school, Dex thought his confidence would be complete.

Who knows, he might even be ready to take on Adem Tarik, not that he was in a hurry even to think about that. If nothing else, he should find Daphna. She'd go ape if she realized he wasn't there. He ought to tell her what he'd done.

Dex was ecstatic. An entire station of cops, totally bent to his will! An entire gang of delinquents changed their lives in a heartbeat! They would be good kids now, and Dex had a pretty good feeling the change would last. The more he thought about it all, the more excited he became. His muscles were actually twitching. His eyes felt like they were vibrating, making the traffic through the police cruiser's windshield almost seem to shimmer. The power he possessed was nearly inconceivable.

Dex changed his mind. Daphna could wait. They almost never saw each other during the day, anyway. He had an idea, so he leaned over and shared it with Officer Richards, who was, of course, fully agreeable.

Richards made a U-turn just a few blocks from school, and within fifteen minutes, they were touring the Portland underworld. Dexter wanted to meet the worst criminals who weren't in jail.

It was frightening at first, walking casually into litter-strewn alleys and filthy, run-down apartments, especially because the men they were seeking in them looked even more hostile than their surroundings. Some of them looked downright murderous. At the sight of Richards, every one of them tried to flee. Of course they ignored the Officer's orders to freeze, but not Dex's.

Normally, had he seen any one of these people coming toward him, Dex would've run the other way, but he quickly conquered the impulse. Their first "visit" was with a six-foot giant wearing a spiked collar, who at Dex's order, approached them like a first-grader caught running in the halls. Dex watched the hatred in the man's eyes soften into a milky white cloud of agreeability as the Word took hold.

After that, it was a breeze. When Dexter and Richards walked away from him, as was the case when they walked away from each successive "visit," they left a hardened criminal scratching his head, trying to remember who they'd just talked to and feeling a strange and irresistible urge to start living an honest life.

In the afternoon, after a fast-food lunch, Richards drove Dex around the West Hills. It was like they'd entered another world. Now they were waltzing into fancy homes to talk to attractive men and women in tailored clothes.

On their way into the first gigantic house built into the side of a hill overlooking the city, Richards explained that though these offenders were clean cut and well-spoken, they were every bit as dangerous as those they met in the morning, if not more so. A few of them were personally just as violent, but most didn't commit crimes with their own hands. They were much more likely to pay criminals in the dangerous parts of town to do their dirty work, which made them hard to catch and even harder to convict.

He needn't have worried. Dex would never again assume anyone was what they appeared to be, not after everything he'd been through.

Dexter was more than happy to straighten out this type as well. It was too easy not to. After they visited a half dozen residences, Richards whisked Dex downtown to a series of high-rise buildings. They rode up plush elevators and invited themselves into the offices of men and women who ran companies that exploited thousands of people or poisoned the environment or cheated their customers. Dex's presentations were brief, but persuasive.

As the day wore on, the energy coursing through Dexter's body increased until he felt near to bursting. It took a long time, but he finally realized what it was: he was having fun again. Only this time, and maybe for the first time, he was having fun doing something good. It was a simple but startling realization. The only things he'd ever really considered fun before were things he knew were in one way or another wrong, like skipping school or spying on Daphna's first meeting with Rash, a million years ago now.

On the way to a CEO's lavish penthouse apartment, Dex turned to Richards and asked, "Do you believe in God?"

"I believe I do God's work everyday," was the Officer's reply.

This struck Dexter as significant. Didn't people mean by "God's work" exactly the work God never did?

There is no God, he thought on his way out of the penthouse. *Maybe there never was a God, or maybe Adem Tarik killed him, but either way, he isn't doing his own job.* Then Dex thought: *I am.*

As Officer Richards conducted him from place to place, Dex became so taken with the notion that he nearly forgot about school altogether. He didn't get dropped back off until nearly 2:30, and he had to have the siren turned on to get him there by then.

Before he hopped out of the car, Dex made sure to tell Richards to forget everything they'd done. The Officer nodded, and as he drove off, Dexter watched him for a few seconds. Then he hurried through the parking lot, thinking he could make seventh period if he hustled. His plan was to show himself that school wouldn't get the better of him this year, then he'd find Daphna and tell her what was up.

Out of habit, Dex circled behind the building and headed to the rear entrance, where there were never any adults. But the moment he hauled open one of the red metal doors, he realized he was going to have to go all the way through the building to the front office to get his schedule card, which would make it nearly impossible to find his class on time.

Then Dex sensed something wasn't right. He let the door slam shut without stepping inside and looked around. Something was off. A few cars were parked in the mini-lot there. Kids were playing football in gym class out on the fields beyond. They seemed to be having a great time, which was slightly odd. Usually at least one kid was complaining or sulking or picking on someone loudly. But that wasn't it. What was missing?

The Slackers! Dex realized—the dozen or so kids who hung out behind the dumpsters, skipping class all day long—not a single one was there. *Maybe the office finally got a clue,* Dex thought. He heaved open the doors again and headed that way.

The bell ending sixth period rang just as Dex entered the main hall. There was no way to avoid being late now, so he stopped and turned, thinking it better just to leave, but someone touched him on the shoulder and said, "Hi Dexter."

Dex spun to see who could possibly have said hello to him, but whoever it was had moved down the hall and gotten swallowed in a crowd. This was far stranger than a harmonious PE class or AWOL slackers. No one ever said hello to him.

"Hey, Dexter," someone else said passing by.

Dex turned again, but again couldn't identify the source of the greeting. Was there some sort of practical joke going on? He looked around for Daphna, but he didn't really expect to find her.

"If you need help with anything this year," said a boy who actually stopped before hurrying off, "you can ask me."

Dexter was flabbergasted. That was a Pop. And now he noticed that the Pops weren't all in a pack. They were scattered around, and all talking to people they'd normally rather spit on. Something bizarre was going on, and now Dex wanted to get to the bottom of it.

He rushed forward, noticing yet another strange phenomenon: people got out of his way. There wasn't the usual mob scene going on. The older kids, who usually threw their weight around, were circulating slowly, calmly exchanging books at their lockers. Everyone was smiling like it was the last day of school rather than the first.

Only the sixth graders weren't looking thrilled. They looked nervous, but not completely petrified like they usually did, which had to be a direct result of the seventh and eighth graders not stampeding them.

Dex was stopped four more times. It wasn't until the bell rang that he was finally able to get free and hurry down to the office. No one was there but the school's main secretary, Mrs. Kodama, who was talking into a headset, working on a computer and filing some papers all at once. That was normal. What wasn't normal was that the blue chairs were empty.

The blue chairs were for troublemakers who had to wait to get detentions from the Vice

Principal. It being the first day of school did not explain the absence of miscreants.

"Can I help you?"

Dex had been staring at the chairs but now looked up at Mrs. Kodama, who must've asked him that several times, even though she wasn't looking at him. She didn't sound too irritated, though.

"Ah, yeah," said Dex, ready to use his Word to help Mrs. Kodama overlook the fact he was nearly six hours late. "I need my schedule card. I know I'm a little—"

"Sure, honey." Mrs. Kodama didn't even ask him for a note. Instead, she flipped through a box on her desk while resuming her phone conversation. Dex couldn't understand why things were so strange with everyone. But then Mrs. Kodama handed him a yellow card, looking him in the eye when she did so.

That's when Dex finally understood.

"No! I don't believe it!" Dex cried. "Not again!"

"What's that, honey?"

"Can you tell me what class Daphna Wax is in right now?"

"Certainly. Let's see—here she is! A-13, with

Mr. Guillermo."

"Thanks."

"Not at all! Have a great day!"

Dexter stalked down A hall. He had no idea what he was going to do, and that made him even angrier because he had Shop this period, the one class he always relied on to salvage his GPA. He stopped in front of Mr. Guillermo's door and glared in the little vertical window. Dex was pretty sure the same guy used to teach at their elementary school. Some sort of animated discussion was already going on inside.

Daphna was right in the middle of it, of course, talking while waving a ballpoint pen in the air. The seat behind her was empty, but there was no way to get in without drawing attention to himself. He had to wait for someone to come out. It took nearly fifteen minutes, but a student in the back of the room finally got up and headed for the door with a bright orange hall pass in hand.

With a Word, Dex turned himself invisible, and when the student came out, he slipped through the open door and sat down behind his sister. Then he hissed, "I know what you're up to."

"Dexter?" Daphna cried. She looked to her left and right, then behind her, confused and alarmed.

"Excuse me, Daphna? Is something wrong?"

"Sorry!" Daphna apologized, turning back around, crimson-faced. "I'm really sorry. Go on, Mr. Guillermo. This is a really interesting discussion."

And it was. The course was an elective called World Religions. At lunch, when Daphna remembered it was one of the options she didn't choose at the end of last year, she went to the office and had her schedule changed. She thought the class would be the perfect opportunity to look deeper into the history of the *Book of Nonsense*, and it would be ideal if she could get credit for doing the research. They'd been talking so far about how Mr. G would be open to pursuing whatever interests the students had.

Mr. Guillermo smiled warmly at Daphna over his half-glasses, then turned his attention to Tory, the girl sitting next to her. "Perhaps then this isn't the best choice of classes for you," he said.

Daphna tried not to nod. Tory was the only one in the room not smiling or misty-eyed, which meant she must have come in late and missed the announcements, and she'd been hogging most of the conversation.

"Remember," Mr. Guillermo was saying, "this is an elective."

"*Daaaphna*," Dexter whispered a few times. It was hilarious to watch her cock her head and get all agitated trying to figure out what was going on. But that got boring quickly, so he looked around the room. It was exactly as he expected: everyone had fogged over eyes, except maybe the girl next to Daphna who wouldn't shut up.

Everyone else looked engaged and thoughtful, but through a thin film that made them look ever so slightly somewhere else at the same time. *Did she do the whole school?* he wondered bitterly. She obviously knew the same Word he did, or one that did the same thing. Couldn't anything in the world be his alone?

"I know what's going on," he snarled as anger surged through him again. He made no attempt to keep his voice low this time. "I know what you've done, Daphna."

Daphna suddenly turned all the way around

in her chair. To Dex it seemed like she was looking right at him. In a way she was, because she'd finally figured out what was going on.

She smiled, shrugged and whispered, "Good for you." Then she turned around.

Daphna hadn't planned to conceal anything from Dexter this time. She had too much to worry about. How he'd figured her out again, she had no idea, but what did it matter? It wasn't like things wouldn't be much better for him at school, too. It wasn't like he wouldn't benefit from her taking revenge against Adem Tarik, which she was going to do as soon as she was confident enough.

Still, Daphna felt a twinge of guilt. She turned round again and whispered, "I'll explain after—" but then she realized that if Dexter had heard her announcement this morning, he wouldn't be sitting there hissing at her. "You've been skipping school!" she cried.

Now it was Dexter's turn to shrug, invisible though he was.

"Daphna?"

"Oh, sorry! Sorry, Mr. Guillermo. Go on."

"Yes, Tory? You were saying?"

"I'm just saying there's no point in studying

other religions when there's only one right one. We should just study the Bible!"

"I'm only worried that someone saw you!" Daphna whispered over her shoulder. "What if Evelyn finds out? What if the cops find out?"

"Tory thinks every word in the Bible is true," said a student in the back, but very politely.

"Well, it is!" Tory declared.

"Don't worry about the cops," Dex muttered.

"What do you mean don't worry about the cops?"

"Listen, kids," Mr. Guillermo was saying. He'd taken his glasses off. "Hold on—Daphna, would you mind? Honestly—"

"I'm so sorry!" Daphna blushed. She'd never been asked to stop disrupting before. She'd never been so out of touch with class discussion, either. Before Dex had come in, she was right there, scribbling down notes. She was the only one in the room who had a notebook out! But now, two minutes with her brother and he was already dragging her down to his level. Still, she had to know what he meant about the cops.

"Thank you for your attention," said Mr. Guillermo, putting his glasses back on. "Now," he continued, "this is great discussion. Really. We won't shy away from any of it. In this class, you are free to have and express any opinion you want about these issues. You're all, what, thirteen now? I think we can assume a certain level of maturity. It's time you engaged in some serious intellectual and philosophical investigations. It's time for us to follow Socrates's advice. It's time for us to get to know ourselves."

"I'm not thirteen!" Tory announced. "I skipped two grades!"

"Dexter—what about the cops? Did you forget what could—*Thirteen*?"

"What's that Daphna?" asked Mr. Guillermo.

"Did you say something about us being thirteen?"

"Yes, I did. Though it seems I was wrong about Tory. I'm sorry about that, Tory. No offense intended."

"That's okay."

That explained why her eyes were clear, Daphna realized. But Tory was suddenly of no concern. "Why is that such an important age?" Daphna asked. "What's the big deal about it?"

"What a great question!" Mr. Guillermo beamed.

Daphna sat up a bit. Dex rolled his eyes, but he did want to hear the answer, even though he had no idea what the class was talking about.

"Let's look at that for a moment," said Mr. Guillermo, removing his glasses. "Did you know that, worldwide, a vast number of cultures have a ritual that formally marks the transformation of a child into an adult, from someone who depends on the community to someone who can contribute to it? You'd be amazed how many of them have that ritual at age thirteen." He put his glasses on again.

"But, it's just a number, thirteen, right?" Daphna asked. "I mean, couldn't it be twelve or fourteen or something?"

"Or eleven!" Tory insisted.

"It's puberty!" someone called out from the back of the room. Half the class tried but failed to suppress giggles at the mere mention of the word.

Mr. Guillermo was not embarrassed. In fact, he seemed even more pleased. "Yes," he said. "That's the traditional thinking, and it certainly makes sense. That is the age where most children begin to look like young adults. But there's something else—"

"What is it?" Daphna nearly shouted when Mr. Guillermo's pause grew a split second too long for her to bear.

The class all turned to look at Daphna, who yet again went red in the face. "I mean, sorry, I'm just very interested."

"I encourage your enthusiasm!" Mr. Guillermo replied with enthusiasm of his own. He put his glasses back on and said, "I was going to say that we can look at the physical development of people, but also the emotional development, and—this is where it gets interesting—the moral development."

"What does that mean?"

"Well, to be brief, some psychologists believe that a child is incapable of exercising free will, that is, making truly free choices in life, until they are able to understand right and wrong. This ability doesn't seem to be completely formed in most people until the age of thirteen. So, it makes good sense to think that one becomes an adult not when one starts to look like one, but when one starts to think like one."

This was fascinating. The twins both sensed it explained something about why the First Tongue had no affect on children under thirteen, but they both needed time to think about it.

Mr. Guillermo switched back to his more general discussion. "You have to be willing to listen," he said, taking his glasses off again. "You have to be willing to think and to consider what we discuss. If your mind is closed to possibilities—I don't mean to be rude—but choose another class. I will bring up things that will challenge what you might believe. I like to look at even the most "out there" beliefs because they shed—"

"You mean like God was murdered?"

Everyone looked around to see who'd spoken. It was Dexter, who felt the burn of everyone's attention when it was directed in his vicinity, though of course no one could see him. He wished he'd kept his mouth shut.

"His son was murdered!" Tory declared. "Everyone knows that!"

When her brother didn't saying anything else, Daphna weighed in, though she found it difficult to keep her composure. *Did Dexter think their father murdered God?*

"No," Daphna managed, turning to Tory, "I—I think some people think God was killed, *The* God."

"That's horrible!"

"Please, Tory, calm down," said Mr. Guillermo. He'd been looking perplexed in Dex's direction, but now he focused his attention on Daphna.

"Well," he said, "that's not something I'd planned on discussing. But there certainly are philosophers who've claimed that God is dead. More than philosophers suggested as much after World War II. How could God have allowed millions of innocent people to be murdered? But God being *murdered*? I don't know about that. I'm fascinated, though. Do you recall where you came across this idea?"

"Ah, no," said Daphna.

"Perhaps you might do some research for us."

"Um, sure." Thankfully, someone else in the room said something then, and the discussion went off in another direction.

"Dex, what was that all about? Do you think Adem Tarik killed God?"

"I know he did."

"How? What have you been doing all day?"

"*BUT IT IS TRUE! EVERY WORD!*" This was Tory again, startling the twins, who'd lost the thread of the conversation.

"Oh—well. Let's see. All right then," Mr. Guillermo said, taking his glasses off again. "No offense, Tory, dear—I don't mean to pick on you—but your example is perfect. Many people believe that every word in the Bible is literally true, right? Okay. Well I dare say many of the people who believe that haven't read it."

At this, the whole class seemed to turn as one to look at Tory, who turned a shade of purple.

"I'm not talking about Tory," Mr. Guillermo insisted. "Allow me to go on. When people actually read the Bible, they realize there are things that make it rather difficult to believe every word is true."

"Dexter," Daphna whispered again, "what is wrong with you? Answer me!"

"Like what?" someone asked.

"Well, sometimes there are completely contradictory statements."

"What does that mean?"

"If it said the walls were blue and then it said the walls were yellow—"

"Oh, I get it."

"So for example—who is familiar with the story of Adam and Eve? Good. So, how were they created?"

"Dexter, talk to me—please!"

"God made Adam, but he got lonely so God put him to sleep and took one of his ribs out and made Eve."

"Good, Tory. That's one of the stories."

"What do you mean?"

"There are two creation stories in the Bible. The other one simply says that God created man and woman together. So, can both be true?"

"Dexter!"

"What are you saying?" Tory roared. "Are you saying none of it's true? Are you saying there were no Adam and Eve? No Garden of Eden? This is the worst class in the world!"

"I heard there are these dudes looking for the Garden," a boy said from the rear of the room. "They think it's in Israel or something."

"Yes," said Mr. Guillermo, ignoring Tory now. "Some people believe every word in the Bible is true—so if it says in Genesis that there was an actual Garden of Eden, then it's got to be somewhere. We'll look at a range of beliefs, from not a word of the Bible is true to every single word is literally true."

"Dexter!"

"Shut up, Daphna! I'm trying to listen!"

"In between those two extremes are people who believe that the major events described in the Bible are based in reality: the Garden, the Flood, certain wars, but that the actual truth of the events has been lost or altered over time. I think last year you read about how some experts think *The Iliad* and *The Odyssey* evolved from real life events, right? I think, in the case of the Garden of Eden, some people want to find it so they can learn the true story."

"That's it Dexter. If you don't tell me what happened right now, I swear I'll—I'll—"

"People have been looking for it forever," Mr. Guillermo added. "Some do think it was in the territory of ancient Israel, but some think it was located in Egypt or Iraq."

"I dare you to try—"

"Others think it was actually in the mountains of Eastern Turkey, and still others—"

"*WHAT?*"

This was Dex and Daphna, shouting out together.

Mr. Guillermo, startled by the strange double voice, dropped his smile momentarily and frowned at Daphna.

"Did—did you say," Daphna sputtered—Dex had gone quiet—"Did you say Eastern—*Turkey*?"

"Why, yes," Mr. Guillermo replied, once more putting his glasses on. But before he could get another word out, the final bell rang.

major big news

As the thirty plus students filed out of the room, Mr. Guillermo asked Daphna to stay behind a moment. She was mortified at the thought of being held back and "spoken to," but he only wanted to chat.

"You seem to have a genuine interest in all of this," Mr. Guillermo commented. He took his glasses off and set them on his desk. "I love to see that!" he said. "And so I thought maybe, since we'll be doing independent research projects on our own personal interests, that you might want to get a head start. Daphna, a paper about why the age of thirteen is so often chosen for rites-of-passage would be fascinating. Of course, the murder of God might be even more so! Or how about something on the search for lost religious relics? Who wouldn't want to read that?"

Tory, Dex almost said, standing behind his sister.

"Actually," Daphna ventured, "I'm kind of

interested in this whole Garden of Eden thing—about where people think it is."

"Really!" Mr. Guillermo said. He searched for his glasses among the files and papers on the desk. It took a few seconds before he had them. "Well," he said, putting them on, "that's fascinating too, of course."

"I'm especially interested in Turkey," Daphna said.

"Great!" said Mr. Guillermo. "Wonderful!"

"Would you know anything about—" Daphna said, "I mean, does anyone believe that there were books in the Garden of Eden? Maybe a lot of books?"

"I've never heard anything like that before," Mr. Guillermo replied, "but what a neat idea! By the way, Daphna, are you feeling all right? Your voice, in class, it sounded a bit—What's that?"

"Let's just forget all about my behavior in class today, okay? I'm really a very attentive student."

"Let's just forget all about your behavior in class today, okay? You're really a very attentive student."

Dex and Daphna walked out of school together, which was a first.

"Dex," Daphna blurted as soon as her brother reappeared, "this stuff about the Garden of Eden—remember what Tarik told the kids they were doing? Making Heaven on Earth! Wasn't the Garden of Eden basically Heaven on Earth?"

"Yeah," Dex agreed. "But he said that wasn't exactly it. We got that from Ruby and Rash, right? The Garden of Eden—that's Paradise, which is another word for Heaven, isn't it? Maybe that's what he really told the kids. Maybe he really wants Paradise on earth. Maybe he's been searching for it all this time."

"But what did he need to train all those kids for? Why does he want us to learn the First Tongue? And we think he has dyslexia, right—or whatever you have—when it comes to Words of Power?? How does that fit in? And Dex, everything seems like it happened right there. It's like he's always known where it was. And what kind of Paradise do you get with murder?"

"I don't know," Dex admitted. "Maybe he knows it's near there, but he won't actually know unless something happens, something he needs the First Tongue for, which would explain why he needs help."

"We need to figure it out Dex!" Daphna insisted. "We've got to do some serious—Ah—Hi—"

The twins hadn't noticed that a group of kids walking nearby had approached while they were talking. The kids, several of whom were Pops, or former Pops, seemed to want to chat. Daphna, reveling at the sight of such snobs hanging out with "regular" kids, tried to engage in small talk with everyone, but she couldn't concentrate very well on the job. Dex didn't try at all. Small talk was not his forte. Finally, the twins turned toward their own street and found themselves alone.

"Outstanding work, Daphna," Dex sneered. "If you can't join 'em, beat 'em—is that it?"

"Look Dexter," Daphna retorted, "I found a Word that let's me—I don't know how to put it actually—it let's me—"

"Bend wills."

"Exactly! So what's wrong with getting practice and making school a nicer place at the same time? It doesn't matter what we do anyway, Dexter. I keep telling you. We're all—"

"I know, I know," Dex interrupted, "we're going to live trillions of lives. I know."

"Fine," said Daphna. "My point is that I need to get really good before—Wait a second, how did you know, anyway? Their eyes?"

"I can do it, too."

"You're kidding!" Daphna looked genuinely excited by this news, which made Dexter feel suddenly much less hostile.

"That's great!" she added. "Dex, the two of us, if we get really good, we can take care of Adem Tarik and get Latty home and start living a normal life again! I feel like I'm really pretty good right—Wait! The cops! That's why you said we don't have to worry about them. What did you do?"

"Richards found me," Dex explained. "It's all taken care of. Antin and his gang, too. I've got the rest of the money in my backpack."

"Dex, that's great! That's really, really great." Daphna was being totally sincere, Dex could tell.

"Let's hurry up then," she urged. "We're almost home. We need to do some research. Let's surf the web for something about books in the Gar—" Daphna stopped short, having rounded into view of their house. There was an Anne & Anthony Show news van sitting in their driveway. Instinctively, the twins reversed course and hurried back out of sight.

"What's this all about?" Daphna asked. Then her jaw clenched. "You didn't do something to call attention to yourself, did you?"

"No!" Dexter snapped. "I have no idea what it's about! Maybe they're wondering why our school got turned into Mr. Rogers' Neighborhood today!"

"It really doesn't matter what it's about," Daphna conceded. "We just need to go over there and make them leave and forget all about us. Then no one will bother us for as long as we want. We'll practice until we're experts, and then we'll nail Adem Tarik before he knows what hit him."

"Yeah, I agree," Dex said, "but I want to know what's up. Don't you?"

"Well, let's just go over there and make them tell us. I'm sure I can do it, no problem."

"I can, too."

Daphna nodded, ignoring the challenge in her brother's tone. The twins moved toward the house again, but stopped when they noticed the other car parked in front.

"It's Evelyn," Daphna said.

"Oh," Dex said, "no big deal. We'll get rid of her, too." He stepped forward, but stopped when Daphna didn't follow. "What?"

"I guess I'd just feel badly about—bending Evelyn again—I mean, after all she's done for us."

"Okay," Dex agreed. She had done a lot. "You be Dad again, and I'll be invisible. We'll find out what she's scheming and try to get rid of her the regular way. If anything goes wrong, I'll freeze everyone so we can talk about another plan."

"You better mean that this time," Daphna warned.

"Yeah, yeah, I promise."

It was agreed. Dex vanished and fell in behind Daphna, who was already Milton Wax. When they opened the door to their house, Evelyn and two men stood up from the couch. A third remained sitting, talking on a cell phone. A TV camera was on the floor.

"Milton!" cried Evelyn, exactly the way she had the last time she'd been there, "I'm—I'm so sorry to be in here without you. I was also bringing over a casserole—it's in the fridge. The door wasn't locked so I figured you'd be right back. I—Oh, I hope you don't mind. We've only been here for a few minutes."

"What's going on?" Daphna asked, thinking they really had to pay better attention to locking the door.

"Please don't be mad, Milton," said Evelyn. "It's just that, I was thinking, you've been through so much, you and the kids, and how courageous you've all been, and, well, I was being interviewed at the Home about everything that happened there, and I suddenly thought you would make a much better story! I thought, if the kids got excited about it, it might help them deal with everything. You know, make them feel recognized for getting through it all. They deserve some attention! Oh, this is Emil. He's a reporter, or an intern actually. That's James, his boss. And this is Edwin, the camera man."

"Hello," Daphna offered to the room at large. She was too surprised by all of this to think of an appropriate way to respond. This was really nice of Evelyn.

Of course the idea of being on TV was enticing, but it was out of the question. For one thing, Milton would never want that kind of attention, and besides, there was way too much going on. Edwin shook Daphna's hand while all of this ran through her head. Emil smiled. James nodded slightly from the couch as he listened to his phone.

"I don't know about this," Daphna said, trying to respond the way her father would, at least when he was their father. "It really wasn't such a big deal."

"Not from what Ms. Idun here tells me," Emil replied. "Your kids—twins, right?—survived a grisly multiple murder scenario in the woods, then fended off a knife attack by a renegade gang of juvenile delinquents in their own house? And then you went chasing after them just after an assault? Sounds like a big deal to me. Are the kids coming home from school soon? This is pure human interest, and local, too. Ann & Anthony's viewers will eat it up!"

"Forget it," growled a gruff voice from the couch. Everyone turned. It was James, putting his phone away. He sighed with world-weariness and got up from the couch.

"Is something wrong?" Emil asked.

"I'd say something's wrong. I'd say something is very wrong," James snarled. "Valuable time has been wasted. Professionals have been prevented from performing important services to the community."

"I—I don't understand," Evelyn stuttered.

"I just got off the phone with an Officer Madden."

"Yes? He was here with another fellow, Officer Richards. Did I mention that?"

"You did mention that, and I spoke with him, too."

"And you say something is wrong?"

James sighed again. "Neither one of them knows anything about you or some gang of kids breaking in here."

"But—that's impossible!" Evelyn protested, tossing her long arms up. "There must be some sort of confusion! Am I going crazy? Tell them Milton!"

Before Daphna could decide how to handle this new development, James laid into Evelyn.

"Tell me if this sounds like confusion," he demanded. "They know about this thing in the woods—that's old news—but they didn't pick up a kid named 'Eyeballs'; they have no confiscated money; and they don't have any other kids in custody on charges even remotely close to what you've made up.

"Listen lady," he said, cruelly, "we are very busy people. We don't appreciate being used to help you land a husband, and it will be over my dead body that we'll broadcast your fantasies to the entire city. Now, if you'll excuse us, we'll be going."

"But—!" Evelyn pleaded.

James strode angrily toward the door, but halfway there, he froze with one foot still off the floor. Emil was frozen too, though he seemed to have been that way since the moment his boss went off. Edwin had just picked up the TV camera and now stood motionless with its strap slung over a shoulder.

Daphna was relieved, though slightly perturbed that her brother seemed to enjoy waiting until the very last second before stepping in. It occurred to her that she could've just used her Word to handle things, but it didn't matter now.

"What was that all about?" she asked when her brother reappeared.

Dex explained what he'd done to Antin and his gang and told her about the rest of his day as well. Daphna was impressed.

"Well," he said, "at least we know this wasn't

anything to worry about. So now we just make them forget all about this little visit and go on their merry way. Too bad Picker's not here. He'd have been in his Paradise."

Daphna thought a moment about Picker, that poor little man whose brief contact with Rash's Ledger had led to his death. All he'd wanted was to be famous, or maybe just for everyone to know who he was, or maybe just a little respect as a person.

"Daphna," Dex said. "Let's get—"

The phone rang.

"Latty!" Daphna cried.

"Don't get it," Dex said. "Let's finish this first."

"Did I change the message last time?"

"I don't remember."

"She might get worried."

"Daphna, we'll change it later," Dex insisted. But he could see his sister had her mind made up. Frustrated, he scanned the room. It was true that everyone looked pretty firmly frozen. "Oh, all right," Dexter said. "We ought to talk to Latty at least once. Tell her not to do anything dangerous because we'll be able to take care of Adem Tarik ourselves soon."

Daphna nodded and stepped quickly past three human statues to the phone. She didn't realize it had stopped ringing until she heard the signal for voicemail.

"Missed it!" she complained. Daphna tapped in the code and listened to the message. It was brief, but alarming. "Dex!" she said after putting it down.

"What?"

"All those books," Daphna said, "thousands of them—the ones he had trucked to the mountains—he's carrying them into some caves, by himself. He's just going in and out all day long talking to himself."

"What's he saying?"

"That he's not a bad man, over and over."

"Still? He's still saying that?"

"Yeah, and something about getting back to the original plan."

"The original plan? We still don't know what that is!"

"I know. And there was another little earthquake. Maybe he'll get killed and none of this will matter. But—" Daphna didn't finish her thought, which was, *No—he's still our father*.

"I think he's crazy," Dex concluded. "I think

he's been crazy since forever, and I think the reason no one knows his stupid plan is because there is no plan because he's crazy! Did Latty say what she thought it meant?"

"No. And I don't think he's really crazy," Daphna said, "or if he is, he's still going to do something terrible. That's scary, Dex. I mean, what if there really is some kind of connection to the Garden of Eden there? We've got to do something soon!"

"You're right," Dex agreed, checking quickly on the statues. "But what do you want to do? Should we just go there and make him stop whatever he's planning?"

"I'd be scared to try that," Daphna admitted. However panicked she was, she didn't feel ready.

"Me too."

"I wish there was a way to protect people from him without getting near him. That way it wouldn't matter what he did."

At that moment, Emil began to stir, just slightly. Dex turned to re-freeze him, but an idea stuck him first. His face suddenly lit up.

Daphna saw this and looked at James. Her face lit up as well.

"Rolling!" Edwin called. Daphna and Dexter were sitting on the couch looking at the camera's red light and swallowing into dry throats. "Rolling!" Edwin repeated.

"Ah—right. Okay," said Daphna. "Hello out there. My name is Daphna Wax. This is my brother, Dexter, but I guess our names don't matter. Please listen closely because I am going to say a Word. Okay, here goes—" Daphna pronounced her Word as clearly as possible. Then she said, "Good. So, okay. Now, listen closely again. I need everyone to know this. There is a man. His name is Adem Tarik. He is evil and has plans that could affect the entire world. No one is to cooperate with him no matter what he says or does. He does not have the power to force you to do anything. He should be ignored completely, or maybe thrown in jail—"

"And while we're at it," Dex said, "all you criminals out there—give it up. You are going to start living honest lives, right now. If you are cheating anyone, stop. If you—"

"And—" Daphna put in, "people are going to start being nice. Don't judge anyone by how they look or how much money they have. Life is not a popularity contest!"

"And you need to take it easy on people who have problems, like if they have reading issues or things like that—"

"And kids who read and study a lot and who want to make something of themselves should be respected, not used—"

"And this world shouldn't be a place were people's lives stink because they have bad luck! What kind of God—"

"Dex," Daphna interrupted, snapping out of the fever she'd been drawn into.

Dex shook his head and snapped out of it, too. They'd said far more than enough.

"Okay, Edwin," Daphna said, and the red light blinked off.

The twins turned to the others in the room.

"Just make sure this gets on the news," said Dex. "The national news—no, the international news. Do whatever it takes."

"Easily done," said James. "Everyone on earth with a TV set will see this tonight."

"Wait!" Daphna shouted at Edwin, who was fitting the lens cover back on his camera. James had just made her realize a limitation of their plan. "I need to add one more thing."

A minute later, the camera rolled again.

"Sorry," Daphna said to it, "I forgot something. We need everyone who sees this to find anyone and everyone who didn't see it and ask them to call us. We'll leave a recording of our message on our voicemail. Here's the number—" Daphna gave their home phone number, but then another snag occurred to her. "And, for the people who live way out there, like in tribes, with no technology, we need people to go out in those trucks—with the speakers on top?—and broadcast the audio part of our message. After that special Word, you can translate what I said into whatever language you need. There," she said, "that should cover everyone I think."

"Good," said Dex. Daphna always thought of everything. He suddenly realized, once and for all, that he needed to appreciate that.

"You wouldn't believe the power of word-of-mouth," James said. "Within twenty four hours, you could reach literally everyone in the world this way, everyone who isn't deaf anyway."

Dex and Daphna looked at each other. "Wait!" they shouted, but neither knew exactly why this time.

"What can we do, Dex?" Daphna asked. "There are a lot of deaf people in the world."

"I don't know. Do we really need to worry about them?"

"Maybe not, but it just seems like we ought to be thorough. Everything counts, right?"

"But, if someone can't hear the First Tongue, how can we get to them?"

Daphna turned to Emil and James. "How do you reach deaf people?" she asked.

"Well, there's closed captioning," James replied. "And many newscasts feature signers. It's incredible what they can do these days. They can even sing!"

"Right!" Daphna cried. "But wait—we don't know a sign for our Word, and just reading it doesn't do anything to you."

"I know one that does!" Dex cried.

"What? How?"

"Singing! That's why I sang that stupid song that woke me up! The other day, I read this Word that sounded Spanish. Then I read the next word, which was 'sing," and I started singing! I didn't even think about it. I thought I was just losing it."

"So, if you read that Word, then you'll do

whatever you read afterward? That's perfect!"
Daphna said. "And I've got an idea that might
be even better than closed captioning." She
signaled to Edwin, who trained the camera on
her.

"And if you know anyone who's deaf," she
said, "get them to go to this website—" Daphna
gave her father's site address.

"Genius!" Dexter cried.

Edwin lowered the camera once again, but
only by an inch or two.

"We'll reach everybody," Dex said, "except,
I guess, anyone who's blind and deaf, but how
could they help Adem Tarik anyway?"

"They couldn't," Daphna promised, feeling
very satisfied with their spur-of-the-moment
planning skills. "This should buy us a little
more time to learn more about—"

"Wait!" the twins cried together, but the
red light was already on.

"Sorry!" Daphna said. "This really is the last
thing. We want anyone out there who's an ex-
pert on the Garden of Eden to call us and tell us
if you know anything about books being there.
We need a little help on that. Okay. Cut."

Edwin looked hesitantly at Daphna, unsure

whether to bother moving the camera off his shoulder.

"You can all go," Dex said, "and by the way, forget everything that happened here. Just get that tape to every network in the world. Tell 'em it's major big news, and then forget about that, too."

a little help

It took Daphna just under an hour to clear her father's webpage and insert their message. Dex remembered everything they'd said into the camera, virtually word for word, so it didn't take long to reproduce it. While Daphna worked, Dex called the pizza shop; it was one of the many speed dial numbers he had Latty set up. It arrived just as Daphna clicked the upload icon.

"There," she sighed, calling up a search engine. "Now we can get to work finding out more about the Garden of Eden. Gimme a slice." Suddenly aware that she was starving, Daphna snatched at the piece Dexter held out for her and took a ravenous bite that immediately scorched the roof of her mouth.

"Youw!" she whined, but the pain didn't register for long. She was already well into what she liked to think of as "Project Mode," the frame of mind in which she completed major assignments for school. In Project Mode, it took far more than a burned mouth to knock her off stride.

Dex, biting more carefully into a slice of his own, sat down on the chair he'd dragged into his father's office. He observed his sister's feverish work with a mix of scorn and grudging admiration. She looked possessed: eyes narrowed, shoulders hunched forward, forehead wrinkled.

"Theresatunashtuf."

"What?"

"Shorry," Daphna said. Her mouth was full and still burning, but after a painful swallow, she managed to say, "There's a ton of stuff about the Garden of Eden. I thought I'd start with just that, for some background information. But there's way too much. Here, I'll refine the search with 'location'—Wow."

"What?"

"There's a lot for that, too, but it looks manageable. Gimme another one." Daphna clicked on the first link on the list. When it came up, she skimmed it over while chewing absently on the second slice of pizza she scarcely noticed getting.

"This one says the Garden was in Mongolia.

I'm going to the next one." Daphna backtracked and followed the second link. "Well then," she said after reading it over.

"What?"

"This one says that mankind is not permitted to know the exact location of the Garden, and those who seek to find it are evil."

"That seems about right. Look at Adem Tarik."

"True, but what about us?"

"We're not seeking to find it," Dex protested. "We're trying to find out what it has to do with Tarik's plans. Besides," Dex added, "won't we find it in one of our trillions of lives anyway?"

"Good point," Daphna said. "Here's one that says it's in Africa, and that Alexander the Great was looking for it there."

"Hey!" Dex exclaimed, "maybe Adem Tarik is Alexander the Great, and he's still looking for it!"

Daphna considered the idea. "I guess we haven't tried to figure out who he really is yet," she said. "I mean, Alexander the Great wanted the world to be his, right? And I think it just about was for a while."

"And remember what Ruby told us?" Dex

said, "that throughout history some individuals learned the First Tongue pretty well and used it to gain great power over others!"

"True! How else could someone take over half the world when he's like, I don't know, twenty or something like that?"

"It's him! He's Alexander the Great! Oh, wait. Dad can't speak the First Tongue. I forgot. But maybe he trained his generals to use it!"

"Hold on," Daphna cautioned, reading through another site. "Looks like Alexander the Great isn't the only candidate. This one says there was a saint, Saint Brendan, who sailed around the Atlantic for seven years searching for Eden in the 5th Century, and speaking of boats, Columbus was supposedly searching for it, too."

"Columbus?"

"Yeah, hold on. "It says he wrote a lot about it in his journal. All that stuff about proving the world was round and finding better trade routes—it was all cover."

Dex was crestfallen. The Alexander the Great theory felt so right. "Anyone not looking for it?" he grumbled. As usual, he'd been hasty.

"Wait a minute," said Daphna. "I ought to

at least try a search for 'Adem Tarik.'" Daphna returned to the search engine and typed into it. Zero matches came up.

"Nothing," she sighed. "Not that I thought he'd have a website or anything. I'm going back. Hold on—"

"Okay."

Daphna waited a moment for the results to come back on screen. Then she scrolled down to find links she hadn't tried yet.

"Okay," she said after choosing one, "this-site says the Garden is in the Seychelles Islands in the Indian Ocean."

"The Sea Shells Islands?"

"It's not spelled like that. Here's one that says it's in the Sinai Desert. That's much closer."

"Why don't you just type 'Turkey' in there with 'Garden of Eden' and see what comes up?"

"Because," Daphna replied, slightly put out, "I'm getting background information, like I told you. It's good to do that before you dive right in because sometimes you learn stuff that gives you ideas you wouldn't have thought of, like Alexander the Great—Whoa—"

"What?" Dex asked, but only because he'd stopped listening to his sister the second her voice took on lecture tone, halfway through the word 'because' on this occasion.

"Western Missouri," Daphna read.

"Western Missouri? Someone thinks the Garden of Eden was in Western Missouri?"

"Yeah."

"I think we've gotten enough background, Daphna. No, wait, see if anyone thinks it's under the steps going down to my room."

"Ha, ha. Garden of Junk, maybe. Here's one that says the entire story is a metaphor and anyone who looks for it in real life is a flaming idiot. Wait—here's another close one: 'The Garden of Eden is now under the waters at the head of the Persian Gulf where the Tigris and Euphrates rivers flow into the sea.' Hmmm, let's see. Okay, here's another one in the same area. It says the Garden was definitely in the Mesopotamian region because that area was the birthplace of so many things: writing, organized cities, written laws, some type of agriculture, and a whole bunch of other stuff."

"And—?"

"A ha! Here's one that says Turkey, from the *Chicago Sun Times!*" Daphna clicked over and read the title to Dexter. "Garden of Eden said to be in Turkey!"

Daphna put out her hand for a third slice of pizza and munched on it as she skimmed the article. When she'd finished both the munching and skimming, she summarized for Dexter.

"Okay, in Genesis," she said, "the first book in the Bible—it says that a river rose out of Eden and divided into four heads, which it says were, hold on—here they are: the Pison, the Gihon, the Hiddekel and the Euphrates."

"And all those are in Eastern Turkey?"

"Well, not exactly, or it really would have been obvious. I guess they think one of those is the modern day Euphrates—one of the other three is a fork in it. Then there's the Tigris, and the last one is the Murat. The guy's big claim is that no rivers 'rise' in the desert. These are the only four rivers that meet in that entire region, and they just happen to rise in the mountains of Eastern Turkey. He used satellite photographs or something."

"That's it?"

"Yeah."

"No one else could have come up with that in all of history?"

"I don't know. I guess not if you need satellite

pictures. Do you think he's crazy?"

"Could be, but that wouldn't mean he's wrong, I guess."

"He's not wrong—or, if he is, then Adem Tarik is wrong too, and something tells me, he's not wrong."

"So what about all the books he's putting in the caves?"

"Right." Daphna returned once again to the search engine and typed in "Books in Garden of Eden." Nothing came up. She tried 'Garden of Eden' + 'library,' but all that got her were library websites with books about the Garden of Eden. She tried various other combinations of related words but wound up with nothing useful.

Discouraged, and growing drowsy and crampy from too much greasy pizza, Daphna finally gave up. "Dead ends, all of them," she sighed.

"Well," said Dex, "maybe someone will call after they see the news."

"The news!" It was 6:01. The twins jumped up, ran to the kitchen and turned on the TV.

They were already on. The lead story.

For a moment, the twins stared incredulously at the screen. The experience of seeing their own faces staring back at them was intoxicating. But as soon as the initial thrill wore off, it was mostly embarrassing. Dex flipped around the channels quickly. They were on all the news shows.

By 6:04, they were off.

At 6:05, the phone began to ring.

Electrified by the immediate results, Dex and Daphna waited for the voicemail to collect the information they'd asked for. When it was done, the phone rang again.

"Dex, it's working!" Daphna cheered. The second message was received, and then the phone rang again. And after that message came in, it rang again, and then it rang again and again and again and again. It rang ceaselessly for an hour, pausing only for the length of time it took for voicemail to record. The twins were gratified to see their plan working, but by the end of the hour, they were also getting a bit annoyed.

By the end of the second hour, they were more than a bit annoyed, and by the end of the third, they were going batty. They discussed playing CD's on high volume, but since Dex's screaming guitar music gave Daphna a headache, and her "easy-listening" songs made him wretch, they abandoned the idea.

They turned off the ringers on all the phones for a while, but both became irrationally worried that would somehow kill the line. Dex had the idea of putting pillows over the phones to deaden the ringing, but it was even more annoying trying to strain to hear if what sounded like a call really was a call. And it was impossible to tune the ringing out because the messages people were leaving weren't all the same length. The exact moment the phone would start ringing again was always a surprise.

At 9:30, the twins decided there was nothing to do but go to bed. They unplugged all but the kitchen phone, which was still just slightly audible in both their rooms. But that wasn't the reason neither could get to sleep. They were too wrapped up in thoughts about who was calling and what they were saying. Even more exciting was the thought of their message making its way around the world, bending people far and wide.

Dex got up at ten and flipped through the *Book of Nonsense*, but it wasn't changing. He put it back on his desk and lay down again. He didn't want to deal with it anyway.

The phone was still ringing. He could hear

it through the vent overhead. He leaned over and flipped his radio on, but it didn't help. At eleven, he turned it off. The phone was still ringing. Ringing and ringing and ringing. It wasn't until midnight, when Dex's imagination was exhausted and the quiet ringing finally blended into the background of his mind, that he finally fell asleep.

When Daphna climbed into bed, she could just barely hear the phone from the kitchen. She continued to struggle with the conflicting urges to listen and to block it out. She put her fingers in her ears. She put the pillow over her head. This kept her busy for a while, but at ten, curiosity got the best of her. She had to listen to at least one of the messages. Daphna got up and padded into the living room, but stopped before reaching the phone. It wasn't a good idea. She might mess something up and prevent the most important call from coming in.

But there was something she could do to satisfy her curiosity safely: check the website. Daphna turned and walked to the office. She didn't know what to expect when she checked the counter on the site, but it wasn't 363,3011 hits. She could hardly believe it. Daphna nearly went down to tell Dex, but thought he might actually be asleep. Instead, she went back to bed and laid there awhile, lost in thought, mercifully oblivious of the phone.

Around eleven, the sound of the phone reintruded into her consciousness, so Daphna got up and checked the computer again: the total was now well over a million. Were there that many deaf people in the world? Then she went back to bed and stared up at the ceiling. She may have fallen asleep for portions of the next few hours, but at around two, she became aware of staring at the ceiling again. She gave up on sleeping for the night.

Dex opened his eyes, momentarily unsure where he was. It was morning, and the house was eerily quiet. He jumped out of bed, realizing only then that he'd slept in his clothes, and ran up to the kitchen. Daphna, showered and dressed, was sitting at the table with the phone between her shoulder and ear, writing in a notebook. She had dark circles under her eyes again.

Daphna looked up at Dexter and said, "Been up half the night listening to these. It stopped ringing at four thirty, but only because the voicemail couldn't handle any more messages. I've been listening and deleting. I think half the lunatics on the planet called, Dex. Some of them are interesting, though. I've been jotting them down. Hold on, there are fourteen more."

Dex was glad not to have had to listen to all that. He poured himself a bowl of cereal and crunched on it groggily while Daphna continued to scribble away. Ten minutes later, she was done.

"So?" Dex asked, "What's the deal?"

"Well," Daphna said—she was still in Project Mode—"I starred the ones that seem interesting. Like I said," she explained, "most seem crazy. Things like this: 'The Garden of Eden is a story in a book. The book is the world, and we are the main characters. Or, this: 'I live in the Garden of Eden, and I have written four hundred books about my life here. Will you buy them? Credit cards accepted.'"

"I see," said Dex.

"And how 'bout: 'It's all Eve's fault Adam ate that apple. God should have thrown the book at her. Women are Evil. Look at Pandora."

"Who's Pandora?"

"It's a Greek—Never mind. I'm thinking we might not have been specific enough in our requests."

"So, what were the good ones?"

"Right. Hold on—Okay, here's one. It's a little hard to read my writing. It says the Hebrew word for 'paradise' is the same as the word for 'orchard.'"

"And an orchard is a kind of garden," Dex said.

"Right! Hey, that was good! Maybe you were right about those words being the same!"

"And that has what to do with books?"

"Don't know," Daphna said. "But someone earlier said something about the word for paradise, too. Let me find it." Daphna scanned her page. "Here," she said, "somebody named Yarmolinsky or something said the Hebrew word for 'paradise' has all three letters that make up the word for book, just out of order."

"That seems pretty weak."

"Yes, but he said that kind of thing is a really big deal in studies of ancient Hebrew because many people believed back then that the actual letters in the Bible—the Torah—had power. And that I imagine, doesn't seem so far-fetched."

"No," Dex agreed. "Go on. Now we've got a connection between paradise and book, and since garden and paradise are connected, then book and garden are too, in a way."

"Right!" Daphna said. "And how about this—well, first let's try to remember the story. Dad told it to us once. Adam and Eve were— Dex!"

"Sorry. I tuned out for a second."

"This is important."

"All right, all right. Go on."

"Anyway, Adam and Eve were allowed to eat from any tree in the Garden, except for the Tree of Knowledge. But the Snake talked Eve into doing it anyway, so she could taste the source of Wisdom and know right from wrong, like a divine being. She took a bite from an apple and offered it to Adam, who bit it, too—willingly I might add. And then God got mad and worried they'd eat from the Tree of Life and be even more divine by becoming immortal. So, anyway, he banished them."

"Yeah, I remember all that."

"Anyway, so this other caller said that the Tree of Knowledge in Hebrew is *Etz Ha-da-at*, and that the word *Etz* is also used in the term

Etz Chayim, which means 'Tree of Life, which is also the name of the handle that the Torah is rolled around. The Torah is a scroll, but that's also a kind of book."

Dex tried to gather what all this meant. "Translation?" he requested.

"Well," said Daphna, "I think the point is that more words connected to the Garden of Eden are connected to books, especially religious books."

"Okay. That much I get."

"Just saying all that out loud is helping it make more sense to me," Daphna said. "In part of some other bizarre message," she continued, "someone said that the Hebrew word for book is also the word for "volume," which could mean part of a larger work or a series of books, or in other words, lots of books."

"Hmmm." Dex had to admit that all this felt like it was leading somewhere significant. He felt like a bunch of loose strings were being pulled together in his mind, though they weren't tied up yet.

"And one more," said Daphna. "'Fruit is the product of a tree, and so are books,' which is very inter—What? You get it, don't you?" Dex had the unmistakable look of breakthrough on his face. "Tell me!"

"The Garden of Eden was a library," Dex declared, "a library full of books. And it wasn't fruit Adam and Eve weren't supposed to eat—"

"It was a book they weren't supposed to read! That's it, Dexter! That's it! The *Book of Nonsense*! It's—it's—the Tree of Knowledge! Reading it makes you kind of like a god, not because it teaches you about good and evil, or not only because of that, but because it contains the First Tongue!"

Dex felt an electric charge. They were right, he knew it. Of course, he'd had the exact same feeling about fifty times since they'd first started trying to get to the bottom of all this, and he'd been totally wrong on just about every occasion. Even so, the certainty he felt now was deep and bracing. Then something occurred to him.

"When were books invented, anyway?" he asked.

"It doesn't really matter," Daphna replied. "Maybe God destroyed all the books when he kicked Adam and Eve out, so they had to be re-invented later."

"But he didn't destroy the *Book of Nonsense*, and he obviously wouldn't have let them just take it."

"Well, maybe he didn't know," Daphna speculated, brainstorming as she spoke. "Maybe when God told them to get out, they stole it! Maybe he was worried about the other tree, the Tree of Life, or the Book of Life. Hey! Ruby told us that the one Word of Power not in the Book of Nonsense was the Word of Immortality! That was in the Book of Life! Maybe God got distracted protecting it."

"Maybe," Dex allowed, "but God is supposed to know everything. That's why he's God. He'd've known they were going to read it and steal it. And if he knew that ahead of time, why punish them? Why not just stop it from happening to begin with? The only thing that makes sense is that they killed him, probably before they ever read it, and then maybe they ran for it, and that's why they left the Garden, or the Library, I mean."

"But he'd've known they were going to do that, right? How does that make more sense?"

"Maybe he did know," Dex said. "Maybe he let them."

"Dexter, you seem to be suggesting that God basically committed suicide."

"Nothing else makes sense," Dex insisted, but he could tell his argument was pretty much smashed. He was trying to force the truth to be what he wanted it to be again. "Did Adam and Eve actually see God?" he asked. "Like, could they physically touch him?"

Daphna considered the question for a moment, then said, "We did a unit on creation stories last year, and one of the groups had a version of the Eden story. I think they said God was supposed to have actually walked through the Garden with Adam and Eve. So, if that's true, I guess they did have access to him."

"Then I still say they killed him," Dex decided. "The story's obviously been changed over the years, if it ever was accurate. Maybe it got changed so people wouldn't panic. People would freak if they thought God was murdered, wouldn't they?"

"I think most religions believe in a savior coming," Daphna mused. "I think they either want God to come or to come back. Either way, it seems like everyone agrees that—God's gone—"

"That's what I'm trying to tell you! He's dead!"

"If that's true," Daphna said, refusing to treat the idea as anything more than that, an idea, "where does Adem Tarik fit into the picture?"

"Maybe he knows everything we've figured out. Maybe he knows God is dead and wants to take his place!"

"Is that why he's trying to remake the Library? That's what he's doing, isn't it?" Daphna asked.

"He's setting up headquarters," Dex declared. "And he thinks he's going to get us to— What? What did you figure out?"

Daphna had gone white.

"What?" Dex repeated.

"Dexter," Daphna said, "he's wanted all along for us to read from the *Book of Nonsense*. He offered it to us, remember? And we bit. Oh, boy, we bit."

news travels fast

"He's the snake!" Dex cried. "Adem Tarik is the Snake!"

"He got rid of Adam and Eve," Daphna said, "so he could have Eden all to himself! Then he got rid of God!"

"But then why did he ever have to leave the Library?" Dex asked, despite the fact that Daphna had supported his general theory. "What was with the kids he taught the First Tongue to? What was with Fikret Cihan and all those copies? What's with us? What good does it do him to remake the Garden—or the Library?"

"Okay," Daphna said, "Adem Tarik, the Snake, who was obviously not really a snake, for whatever reason can't read the First Tongue. So, he talks Eve into reading the Book, who talks Adam into it. Then he trains them to use the Words of Power to take over the Garden for him. They were the first two kids he ever tried to train! Maybe he got them to kill God!"

Daphna paused, shaken by the increasing plausibility of this thought.

"So then," she continued, "maybe they realized he was evil, or maybe they just felt terribly, so they decided to run away from Eden. They were never banished! Or maybe they ran away because Tarik was going to somehow kill them! But anyway, they left Eden."

"And started having kids."

"And their kids had kids, and their kids had kids, and soon there was a whole world full of people—"

"Who weren't under Tarik's control. I'll bet his plan was to make the whole world his private Garden of Eden."

"And since he couldn't read the First Tongue, he had to find some more people to train—and he's been trying ever since to find someone who can give him his world back. Is—is he the Devil, Dex? Is that who the Snake is?"

Dexter, shocked by the suggestion, considered it awhile. He'd thought about the Devil even less than he'd ever thought about God. Was there such a thing? Did that explain all the horrid things that happened in the world? Was it the Devil that had it in for some people?

He wondered if Antin had ever considered the idea. If the Devil was real, then God, dead or alive, obviously couldn't stop him.

"Well," Dex concluded, "that would explain why God might not have known what was going on. Maybe the Devil's not under his—Wait a minute," Dex said, interrupting himself. He'd suddenly gone slightly green. "If he's the Devil, that would make us—"

"Yeah," Daphna agreed, going green herself. "Couldn't be."

"There must be another explanation, something we're missing."

"There must be."

A period of awful silence ensued. It reached up and around the twins, threatening to annihilate them, but the phone started ringing again, snapping them out of it.

"Maybe we should head out," Dex said.

"Where?"

"To school."

"Oh, right. Yeah. We should do that. We better hurry."

The twins walked toward school with their minds nearly shut down. The possibility they'd raised was simply too atrocious to contemplate. The sky was cloudless and the sun full and warm, but neither of them noticed.

In fact, they were so wrapped up in not thinking that they failed even to notice they were walking to school together for the first time in their lives. The pair just shuffled forward with their eyes on the ground. It was only when they merged with a crowd of fellow walkers that they gradually began to take notice of their surroundings.

The first thing Dex and Daphna noticed was the fogged look in most of the other kids' eyes, though that was no surprise after yesterday. The surprise was seeing the same look in the eyes of all the parents driving by. This was exactly what the twins needed to free them from their funk.

"Wow," said Daphna, turning to her brother after watching a string of SUVs go by. "Looks like every one—Do you think—?"

"Let's find out," Dex said, his voice tinged once again with excitement. Sitting in class this morning wasn't a good idea anyway. He spotted a taxi coming their direction, so he stepped off the curb and waved it over.

"Where to?" the driver asked. She had misty eyes.

"How about downtown?" Daphna suggested.

"Sure thing."

"But let's not go on the highway," said Dex.

"Sure thing."

As they drove down Barbur Boulevard, the twins pressed against the windows to get a good look at the people they passed. It was as they'd hoped: everyone had misty eyes. Downtown, Dex and Daphna got out and walked around for a while. It seemed their message had gotten out all over the city. In a bank, every customer and every teller had misty eyes. At the bus stops, everyone waiting had them, too. Only the eyes of small children with their mothers were clear.

"Let's go in here," Daphna said when they wandered by an electronics store. Dex saw that she was looking inside at a display of television sets all showing different stations. He understood what she was thinking, so they went inside to get a closer look.

A few morning news shows were on, which was perfect. Ann and Anthony were talking to the screen, fortunately not about them. Both had misty eyes, as did all the people captured by the camera when it swept the audience.

"Look!" Dex said. He'd turned to a national show. The hosts had the same misty eyes as Ann and Anthony. The camera swiveled away from them to capture a mob of people on the street peering at the set through a giant window. They were all jumping up and down and waving signs, and they all had misty eyes.

"And look!" Daphna cried. She'd moved down another few sets and found one with a cable news show on. A clip was being shown of the President shaking hands with a group of foreign dignitaries. They all had misty eyes. "Dexter," Daphna gasped, "that's the President!"

"It's everywhere!" Dex cried. Another clip was on, this one of a Western scientist shaking hands with the medicine man of a jungle tribe somewhere. Both had misty eyes.

"We've got nothing to worry about, Dex," Daphna sighed. "No one on earth is going to help Adem Tarik. He can just sit in his little Library of Eden and scheme until he rots."

"We just have to get Latty home now."

"Right. We need to go home and wait for

her to call. Dex, I feel badly. We're skipping school. We should go back. I'd like to talk to Mr. Guillermo again."

"I'd like to talk to him, too, but we shouldn't waste time. We need to talk to Latty."

"But—"

"Look," Dex said, "you'll go through one of your other lives without ever skipping school."

"Oh, all right, but that's a really low blow."

Back at home, the twins sat staring at the phone. Of course, now it wouldn't ring. They didn't know what to do with themselves while they waited, so they started to clean. The house had slowly become a mess, mostly because Dex didn't care and Daphna didn't have time to deal with it. They'd talked about hiring a maid but hadn't gotten around to it, which was fortunate because sweeping and spraying and dusting was the perfect way to make the time go by. Time did go by—the entire day went by—but that didn't make the phone ring.

"What do you think will happen when she gets back?" Daphna called out. She was setting the table for dinner.

Dex was carrying in Evelyn's evening delivery from the porch. It was chili, along with grapes and strawberries and chocolate.

"Don't know," he said, stepping into the kitchen. "Can Latty adopt us?"

"Wouldn't they need Dad's approval?"

"Well, he's not Dad anymore. We'll say he abandoned us. He did abandon us."

Dexter served up the chili, and the twins sat down to eat. As usual, it was delicious.

"First thing I want is to get our pictures back," Daphna said after a few forkfulls. "I want mom's face back on the walls."

"Yeah, I do to."

"And we need to start being a lot nicer to Latty, after all she's done—"

"You mean like letting us almost get killed two hundred times?"

"She's been doing the best she can, Dex. And she said she'd never let it happen again."

"I know," Dex conceded. Why did the negatives always come to mind first when he thought about anything?

The twins ate for a while, until Daphna finally said, "She might not call for days."

Just then, the phone rang.

Dexter lunged for the one on the wall. Daphna snatched up the cordless she'd set on the table.

"Latty!" the twins both cried. But it wasn't her.

A grinding voice came over the line. It belonged to Adem Tarik.

"Children," he said, "I have some wonderful news for you. I am sorry I was unable to share the truth with you when we last spoke. Now, I can. Your mother is alive. She is on her way to join me here in my Library, now, even as I speak.

"I apologize for letting you believe I did her harm. I had no choice but to mislead you. I'd like to prove to you once and for all that I am not a bad man. Come and see your mother. She will explain everything. I'm sure you can find me if you put your minds to it." There was the sound of a deep rumble in the background, then a click and the dial tone.

"M—Mom!" Daphna blurted. Tears had leapt to her eyes. "*Alive*?"

"He's lying," Dexter said, but his heart was throbbing every bit as hard as his sister's. "He's trying to lure us there. And if it's true, Latty will find out and tell us. We have to wait for her to call."

"But what if she doesn't? What if something happened to her? What if Mom really is there!"

"She's not, Daphna."

"Why not? No one ever found her body in the collapse! Everyone else keeps popping up that's involved in this mess! Why not?"

"Because she's dead, that's why. He's counting on us reacting like this and rushing in there. It's a trap! Whatever he's been setting up over there is ready."

"I don't care!" Daphna shrieked. She got up and paced around the kitchen like a rabid dog. "Dex, you're forgetting we know he can't use the First Tongue. That's our secret advantage! Let's just go there and see. You can be invisible if you want, but we don't even need that! We can just walk right in there and make him jump off a cliff or something. We should at least make him give up his stupid plan."

Dex saw the sense in this.

"I guess you're right," he admitted. "But, we shouldn't rush in without thinking everything out first." A strange feeling came over Dexter as he spoke these words. He realized what it was right away. He and his sister had switched roles.

"We'll be careful, Dexter!" Daphna promised. "I'm not really suggesting we just barge in there like a couple of idiots!"

"Okay, so what are we going to do?"

"Well," Daphna said, trying to calm down, "here, let me try something. Stand up a sec."

Dex stood up and stepped away from the table. Daphna approached him and took his hand. They hadn't held hands since their father first wound up in the hospital with his broken hip. Dex, uncomfortable this time, looked at his sister, but noticed at once they were no longer in the kitchen. They were in the living room.

"It does work," Daphna said. "I can take you with me."

"Okay," Dex said. "So we'll teleport to Turkey. Do you have to know exactly where they are?"

"I'm not sure. Here, I've got another idea. I'm going to close my eyes. You go somewhere in or outside the house, but don't tell me where."

Dex understood. "Okay," he said and then tiptoed back into the kitchen. He opened the back door and stepped outside, but then stepped back in and walked softly down the steps to his room. He'd only just reached the floor when Daphna suddenly appeared in front of him. She scared him, of course.

"I don't need to know," she concluded. "I just thought your name, and here I am."

"Great," said Dex, feeling a bit more confident about their hasty decision. "So, all right, let's go to where Latty is. We can tell her what's going on if she doesn't already know, and she can help us come up with a plan. But you better not really believe Mom is going to be there, too."

"I don't believe anything anymore," Daphna said, "except that it's time to end Adem Tarik's plans once and for all."

"Good. I'm with you on that one."

Daphna took up Dexter's hand again.

"Ready?" she asked.

"No," said Dexter, "but go ahead any—"

in the dark

The darkness was total. It was so dark, in fact, that the twins had the feeling they were nowhere. Only by squeezing each other's hand did they have any sense of their own bodies.

Once they realized they were somewhere, Dex and Daphna noticed it was cold, very cold, and this lead to an awareness that whatever they were standing on wasn't firm footing. It was uneven and sharp.

"Dex?" Daphna whispered. Her voice echoed all around.

"I think we're in a cave," Dex answered. "We must be in Turkey. This is incredible. I didn't feel a thing. I'm afraid to move, though. I can't even see my feet."

"But where's Latty? I teleported to her."

"Maybe it didn't work."

"It works, Dexter."

"So, where is she?"

"Latty?" Daphna tried. She didn't have to raise her voice much to send it what seemed a great distance. No one answered the call.

"Latty?" Dex repeated, but the results were the same.

"You know what this means, don't you, Dexter?" Daphna whispered, her voice shaking.

"What?"

"He killed her in here, just like Mom."

Dex refused to accept this. "No," he said. "There's another explanation. He didn't kill Mom, right?"

"I know he was lying, Dexter. Mom is dead. She's probably buried in here, too. I'm scared. This was a bad idea. Let's go back."

"No," Dex said again. He let go of Daphna's hand to make sure she wouldn't teleport them away. "Let's at least see what's going on," he insisted. "What's the worst that can happen? You can always take us right back if you have to. I can turn invisible, and we can both make Adem Tarik do whatever we want. Just like you said. Don't worry. We'll find Latty, and we'll find out if Mom really is alive, and we'll get out of here. Can you get us out of this cave?"

"I guess," Daphna said, "but to where? I could teleport to Mom, if she's really alive, but we might wind up right in front of Tarik.

There's probably some kind of trap. Maybe we're already in a trap."

"I don't think so," Dex said. "Let's try to find a way out of here on our own."

"Okay. You don't think there are any spiders in here, do you?"

"Maybe. I don't know. Daphna, this is no time for—Wait, I have an idea. If I can find a way out, you can teleport to me, right?"

"Yes!" Daphna said, grasping at the idea like a lifeline. The thought of crawling through the darkness with ten billion spiders lurking everywhere made her dizzy enough to fall right where she stood.

"All right then," said Dex. "That makes more sense anyway. It'll be hard enough for one of us to get anywhere in here. If we both go, that doubles the chances of a fall."

"Just be careful," Daphna urged. "But on the other hand, hurry. I feel like I'm in a black hole or something."

Dex squatted down to feel the ground. Jagged angles of rock face were all around. There was no way to tell if they were on a broad floor or the edge of a precipice, so Dex sat on his behind and felt forward with his heels, keeping his weight back. It was solid ahead. He slid his behind forward and felt ahead again with his feet. Still solid. It would be ridiculously slow to move this way, but it was the only way.

"Tell me when you're somewhere safe, and I'll catch up to you," Daphna called out after Dex had inched his way forward for about five minutes. He hadn't gone far.

"Okay," he replied, "but don't talk anymore. You scared me for a change." Dex closed his eyes, though that made no difference whatsoever. He told himself he was back on the loft of the ABC, spying on Rash, which seemed like child's play now.

"Okay!"

"What?" Dex cried. His heart had leapt to his throat.

"Okay, I won't say anything else."

"Good!" Dex pushed out a breath, then continued moving deliberately forward. The process was as painful as it was difficult because he kept scraping his palms and behind on sharp protrusions. He pressed on anyway, listening to Daphna's poorly controlled breathing behind him. After what seemed like well over fifteen minutes, he came to what felt like a wall.

Feeling blindly ahead revealed that it turned a corner.

"I couldn't wait anymore," Daphna said. She was suddenly there, standing immediately behind Dexter, who'd been sliding his heels forward to check the floor around the corner.

He jerked ahead in alarm when he felt her legs touch his back, and now his legs stretched into nothingness, pulling him down. Only a desperate, backwards grab at Daphna's ankles prevented him from going over, but it sent her off balance. She cried out as she tipped forward over his back. Dex shouted for her to get off. He was being bent painfully forward and pushed toward the edge.

Daphna, panicked, scraped her hand along the wall she hadn't known was there. She felt the skin on her fingertips tear on the stone, which made her cry out again, but her fingers found a hole. Her grip was weak, but she was able to pull herself up enough for Dex to force himself back, which pushed her all the way upright. Daphna stepped away, pressed her back into the wall and then slid down next to Dex.

The twins sat silently for a moment, breathing heavily.

After a minute, Daphna gasped, "I'm sorry! I'm sorry. I thought something was crawling up my leg back there."

Dex was too relieved to rebuke his sister. "Maybe you saved me," he said. "We're on some kind of ledge. It goes around a corner. I might have gone over on my own."

"It does," Daphna confirmed. "Go around a corner, I mean. I saw something when I almost fell. There was some light."

"Can you teleport us to it?"

"I guess, but I didn't see any ground," Daphna warned. "It might just be a hole in the side of a wall. If we go to the other side, Tarik might be sitting right there."

"Can you lean out again, if I hold you?"

"You're kidding me."

"I'd let you hold me, but a spider might—"

"All right. Let's do it quickly. Here, grab my belt loops."

Dex carefully got to his knees. The ledge they were on didn't seem all that narrow, but there was no way to be certain. He grabbed two of Daphna's rear belt loops.

"Okay," he said.

Daphna licked her suddenly dry lips and

felt around until she found the hole in the wall again. This time she got a good grip inside it with her abraded right fingers, and then, with her left hand, felt forward for the corner of the wall. Once she'd found that, she leaned forward slowly, trying only to let her head tip past the edge.

The entire process was disorienting. In the all-encompassing darkness, it was nearly impossible to keep her bearings. As her body moved, it felt like she might already be falling. It made her lightheaded, then dizzy.

Determined to fight through it, Daphna stretched out further past the corner, still unable to see the light she'd noticed. But the vertigo was too much. She lost her grip again. Daphna screamed and scrabbled at the wall, but her fingers felt like they'd been set on fire.

Dex screamed, too. He was being pulled forward, scraping his knees. Daphna was dragging them both over the edge. Forcing all his energy into his fingers, Dex yanked on the belt loops while heaving his weight back. Daphna stopped falling, but a ripping sound came as the loops began to tear.

Dex pulled again, this time hard enough to

lift Daphna's lower half right off the floor of the cave, causing her to fall flat. She kept screaming because now her head and torso were hanging over the edge.

Dexter kept his grip, but he had no leverage with which to haul Daphna up. "Help me!" he screamed.

Daphna waved her arms forward until she felt the wall of the drop-off beneath her. She dug at it, ignoring the pain in her right fingers and skinning the ones on her left. She pushed upward, and this gave Dex the support he needed to drag her up. All at once, Daphna was laying on her side with her face pressed into the wall.

The twins took several minutes to recover this time.

"Well," Dex finally wheezed, "if we try one more time, I'm sure we can manage to fall."

"That's so funny I forgot to laugh," Daphna said feebly, gingerly getting back into a sitting position next to her brother. But then she heard herself laughing. Dex was laughing, too. Somehow, it helped them settle their nerves.

"See anything?" Dex asked when they calmed down.

"Actually, yes," said Daphna. "It was definitely a light. It's coming from the top of a big pile of rubble. I can get us onto the pile, no problem. I just don't know what's around it. Dex, if we can't get through, we're going home."

"All right." Had Daphna insisted they go home right then, Dex would have agreed.

"Just give me a few more seconds," Daphna said. "I'll teleport over to make sure it's stable."

"Sure, okay."

Daphna needed more than a few seconds, but when she felt able, she spoke her Word and vanished. A minute later, she was back.

"It's fine," she said. "I think it's all sitting on a shelf, or ledge, but it didn't move when I was on it, and the rocks looked pretty loose near the top where the light is coming through. I think we can get through there, to what I don't know. I can't tell if the other side is outside or not. Ready?" Daphna asked, but she grabbed Dex's arm without waiting for an answer. She had to get out of that darkness.

"Ow!" Dex yelped. A sharp rock was suddenly jabbing into his thigh. But there was a dim light, just above him. They were on the pile. It was rubble, and it was apparently clogging a hole leading, perhaps, outside.

Painstakingly, the twins got to their knees and, leaning on their stomachs, started slowly pulling smaller stones away from the hole. The first stone Dex moved aside rolled down the pile and plummeted downward a great distance below. They couldn't hear it hit bottom.

"Don't think about it," Daphna warned as she continued moving stones. "Can you stick an invisible head through there?"

Dex spoke his Word, then put his head through the opening they'd made. He peered around tentatively, then pulled it back in.

"It's not outside," he said. "It's a huge cave full of—stalagmites, I think they're called. Some light's coming down from above, I think. Let's go through. I didn't see anyone in there."

Daphna eagerly agreed, so the twins began pulling more quickly at the rocks around the opening. Soon enough, the space was big enough to fit through. Dexter clambered into the cave first, relieved to find the ground smooth and flat inside. Daphna came through right behind him, and once she was in, she let out a long, shaky sigh.

The twins looked around. They were in a

monumentally large cavern, far bigger than Dex had imagined. It opened up around them like a fortress, reaching up hundreds of feet into the air. They could see the sky above through several large, jagged openings at the top.

Covering the ground all around the twins were not stalagmites but books, heaps and heaps of books. They were everywhere, reaching up to various heights like broken pillars. Around the walls of the cavern were dozens of darkened cave entrances. They all looked foreboding, like the thresholds of other, sinister worlds.

While the twins were still looking around, the sound of a match striking drew their attention across the cavern. A figure was standing in the shadows lighting a candle. Instinctively, Dex and Daphna grabbed hands.

"Welcome, children," said Adem Tarik, walking toward them. "Words cannot express how glad I am you came."

not a bad man ii

The twins stared at the strange, sputtering light coming toward them. It wasn't any kind of normal candle. Neither of them thought whether it would be best to run or attack. It was all happening too quickly.

Adem Tarik was walking swiftly, weaving around piles of books. When he was about ten yards away, Dex and Daphna saw that what he was carrying was no candle at all. It was a thin stick of dynamite. They cried out and raced away, but Tarik wasn't coming after them.

Instead, he walked to the hole in the wall they'd come through. Dex and Daphna stopped in the center of the cavern and watched him jam the dynamite somewhere into the pile of rubble on the other side. Then he straightened up and walked back in their direction.

The twins looked fearfully around at all the cave openings encircling them. They ran toward one, but before they reached it, the dynamite exploded. It was loud, but not nearly as powerful as they feared it would be. Some dirt and dust was shaken from the cavern walls, but the brunt of the blast was directed into the caves they'd come through. Dex and Daphna, who'd stopped and looked back, could hear the sound of rubble falling into the depths behind the hole.

Tarik was still walking toward them, and seeing this, the twins peered into the mouth of the cave they'd approached. Nothing whatsoever was visible more than two feet inside. They looked into the adjacent caves, but they all seemed to promise disaster.

"I wouldn't try any of them," Tarik warned, coming near. "Deathtraps, every one."

"If you think we can't get out of here, you're in for a serious surprise," Daphna snapped. Saying this reminded her, and Dex as well, that they were the ones with the upper hand. They were the ones who knew the First Tongue.

"Regardless," Tarik said, unimpressed, "may we talk first?" He was only a few feet away now. "All I ask is the chance to explain myself. I am not a bad man."

"Dynamite!" Daphna suddenly shrieked. "It was dynamite! The torch you lit when you were in the caves with Mom and Latty. Latty said you dropped it because of an earthquake, but you dropped the dynamite to fake an earthquake! Then you pushed Mom over! She's dead! They're both dead!"

Tarik nodded. He was right in front of them now. "Correct," he said. "Turkish authorities don't tax themselves much investigating tiny little accidents that happen to unwelcome foreigners attempting to loot their national treasures. But I don't see how—"

"Drop dead!" Daphna screamed. In her heart, she knew he'd been lying about their mother, but the confirmation made her want to kill. And having told her father to drop dead, Daphna realized she might very well be able to make him to do just that. She spat out her Word, then ordered him to drop dead again. The vengeance she was so badly craving was going to be hers. Right here and right now.

Adem Tarik did not drop dead. He only shrugged.

Daphna screamed her Word, fueled by all the rising venom in her being. She was saying it right, she knew it.

"Drop dead!" she demanded. "Drop dead!

Drop Dead!"

Adem Tarik shrugged again and shook his head. He looked like any father sympathizing with his daughter's frustrations.

"Dexter! Help me!"

Dex barked out his Word. Maybe it was too abstract to make someone just die. "Blow yourself up!" he shouted. "Go get some more dynamite, and blow yourself up!"

"It's no use," Tarik said. "Really."

"Jump off a cliff in one of these caves!" Daphna screamed.

"Children—"

"Hit yourself in the head with a rock!" roared Dexter.

"Children—"

"Dex! It's not working! The First Tongue isn't working!"

"And it won't work here, children. There's no use in trying."

The twins, both feverish with rage, looked at each other and went weak in the knees. If it was true, it was the worst of all possible news.

"But—but—" Daphna stuttered, trying to figure out a way it couldn't be true, "I teleported just over there—" she pointed weakly in the direction of the blast. "Oh, no—"

"That's the border," said Adem Tarik. "Here you stand in God's Library: Eden. That was the edge, beyond which the First Tongue holds sway, but I'm afraid that way is somewhat inaccessible just now. It's a shame the Garden that used to surround the Library is no more. You would have loved to see it. It was beautiful beyond words."

Dex and Daphna were in no condition to process this information. They turned and looked desperately into the cave behind them again, tensed, poised to run. But neither made a move to go in. It was too risky.

"You can't fool us," Dex declared, turning back to his father. The time had come at last to take a stand. If it killed him, he'd make Tarik back down. "We know you can't speak the First Tongue. We know the only thing you can do is lie."

"And you have no chance of ever carrying out your stupid plan," Daphna sneered, taking confidence from her brother. "We've made sure no one in the world will ever help you. We know you can't do it alone. We've outsmarted you. We've figured everything out. We know this is the Garden of Eden. We know the *Book of Nonsense* is the Tree of Knowledge. We know you stole it. We know you killed our Mom, and we know you killed God!"

Tarik had maintained a disturbingly good-natured, almost approving, air as Daphna ticked off these discoveries, but at this last point, his bushy brows lifted in alarm and his face drained itself of color. He looked appalled.

"How dare you suggest such a thing!" he cried. "Blasphemy!" He took a few steps backward, looking genuinely stricken.

"We know you're the Snake!" both twins railed. They were confused now, but determined to beat their father into submission with the truth.

"The Snake?" Tarik chuckled. "A loathsome creature, no doubt, not even allowed into Eden. Always sniffing about the Library, fearful and afraid should either of us come near! And it got what it deserved for meddling in God's affairs! Thrown into the abyss!'

"But—but—" Daphna stuttered. "You're not the snake?" How was it that she was engaging in conversation now?

"Of course not," said Adem Tarik, "but I applaud your powers of investigation. You are clearly two remarkably resourceful children, but I'm afraid you haven't quite got all the details exactly right."

"Sure," Dex snapped. He'd been working himself into the red-faced rage he thought would be necessary to fight. He didn't want to defuse it with words, but they came out anyway. "Like when you said you wanted 'Heaven on Earth', you really meant 'Hell on Earth', is that it? You may not be the Snake, but you're the Devil! And I don't care if you're our father, we're going to send you back to Hell!"

"I assure you, I'm not the Devil," Tarik replied. "No such thing I'm happy to say. My plan was never to make Heaven on Earth. My plan was, and is, to bring Heaven *to* Earth. I can't conceive of anything farther from what I seek than killing God."

Dex and Daphna looked at each other. What did this mean? Should they believe it?

"More lies," Dex said. It was going to come down to a physical fight, he could feel it in his bones, but confusion was overwhelming him again—Yes, again. Again and again and again.

"Please," Tarik said, "I understand your skepticism. It speaks well of you both. We're not going anywhere. Humor me?"

The twins nodded with profound resignation. They'd reached the point where understanding, once and for all, was more important than living through this final crisis.

"I am going to tell you a story," Tarik said. "It's a long one. You might want to sit down." The twins stayed where they were, lacing their father with steely, hateful gazes. They wouldn't do anything else he suggested, even to their own detriment.

"Suit yourselves," said Tarik. "My story begins when God was finished creating the world. You see, from the start, he intended it to be a gift. That is why he created Adam and Eve. It was a felicitous arrangement. Adam and Eve were grateful to be alive. With all their hearts, they loved their Creator, and they cherished every moment he spent with them in his Library and its surrounding Garden. He was their Light and their Life.

"Adam and Eve had the run of Eden," Tarik continued. "There was only one rule. They weren't to read from two Books in the Library:

the *Book of Knowledge* and the *Book of Life*. You must understand that they had no problem with this injunction. There were countless other books to discover and discuss. God was a generous teacher. He indulged his creatures' insatiable curiosity and entertained their questions on all fronts. He patiently explained everything they didn't understand about the world and its complexities. Adam and Eve loved to learn, and this pleased God more than anything else.

"And speaking of the Devil—what Adam liked best was hearing some of the stories God chose not to tell, stories from books not opened in his infinite Library. The story of the Devil was one of those. Adam went on, foolishly perhaps, to spread that tale in later days, along with many others—but I assure you, those particular pages God did not read into reality.

"For a while, the situation in Eden was ideal, but things slowly began to change. As you no doubt know, learning leads to deep thinking, and deep thinking leads to some difficult questions. Soon enough, Adam's and Eve's studies turned to matters philosophical.

"One day, they grew quite vexed about something. That something was the nature of free will. God had told them of himself, that he was all-knowing and all-powerful, that he was everywhere and nowhere, for all time. This was delightful at first to Adam and Eve because it made them feel safe and secure, but now they wondered what it meant that God knew everything about the past, the present and the future. It seemed to mean that everything they would ever do was already known, and that made them feel like puppets. They grew listless and sad to think that their destinies were already in some ways decided, that they had no real choices in life.

"God saw the melancholy change in his creatures, and he grew deeply troubled. Of course, he knew what they were thinking, but he let them share their concerns with him anyway. When they finished, he told them he'd consider the matter and would return to them the following day with a solution. He already knew what that solution would be, of course. He simply wanted to delay the inevitable.

"The next day, God returned with his countenance downcast. Adam and Eve expressed alarm, for they'd never seen God in any but the brightest moods. God told them that he'd thought long and hard about their problem, and he'd determined that there was only one way for them to live in the world as free agents. He would have to leave, and in his leaving he would deny himself ultimate knowledge of their future choices. God told Adam and Eve that limiting himself this way was the only way to remove the limits on them. It was to be his final gift.

"After hearing God out, Adam and Eve didn't want the gift. They tore their hair and fell on their faces and begged God to stay. They swore they didn't want free will, that he meant too much to them to lose. But God hardened his heart and ignored their pleas. Though he'd always known it would come to this, it pained him nevertheless. Without further discussion, God informed Adam and Eve that he would remove himself at the conclusion of the Sabbath. Then he withdrew to prepare.

"Adam and Eve were inconsolable. They sobbed into the night as they sought to discover something that would prevent God's departure. But though they wracked their brains and consulted every book they could, no answers were to be found. Just before falling asleep, Adam lamented that they didn't know enough yet to find a way on their own and that they didn't have enough time to search every book in the Library.

"The Snake did enter Eden, against God's will, and finding Eve, gave her an idea. Maybe they didn't need to search every book. As Adam slept fitfully, Eve snuck out of bed and made her way to the shelf on which sat the forbidden *Book of Knowledge.* She opened it, hoping to find a solution to their awful dilemma. Eve knew God had created the world with the Book. Perhaps she and Adam could create another one in which they had free will and God could stay.

"Of course God foresaw the Snake's actions—Eve's as well—and that is why he permitted Eve to learn what she did when she looked into the Book. This was knowledge of Good and Evil. It was knowledge God knew she and Adam would need when he was gone. That is also why he allowed Eve to take the Book, wake her companion and share with him what she had learned.

"This knowledge transformed Eve," said Adem Tarik. "She fell to her knees and gave thanks for the gift God had given, for she saw there was no other way. When Adam was done reading, she told him they were now to direct their love toward each other, and in so doing, they would never lose God.

"But Adam was unmoved. He could not accept God's gift. He grew furious at Eve for pressing him to see things her way, and when she would not give up, he finally chased her away from Eden altogether. But before she fled, Eve told him that she would always love him, that she would always wait for him to love her back, for that would be her way of repaying God for his gift.

"God saw what Adam had done and was deeply saddened. He came to Adam and told him that he and Eve must live together, but Adam would not listen.

"With tears streaming down his face, he desperately turned the pages of the Book until he discovered the First Tongue. God tried to be gentle, for he understood Adam's pain. But even so, he had to act.

"First, God made it so that the Words of Power had no effect in the Library, but this only made Adam determined to leave. God pleaded with him—for he loved him—but Adam only turned and fled with the Book, leaving countless other Sacred Books behind. The moment he crossed over the border of Eden, God altered his eyesight, making it impossible for him to read—and thus speak—the First Tongue forever."

Tarik paused and regarded the twins, who'd been riveted by the story. They'd stood listening like statues, unable to move as their minds scrambled one more time to readjust all they knew.

"That, children, is the truth," Adem Tarik concluded, "the absolute truth."

After a moment, Daphna said, simply, "Adem. You're Adam." There was no emotion in her voice, just the sound of final comprehension. "Milton Adam Wax."

"I am not a bad man," said Tarik. "I just want God to come back."

"That's your plan?" Dex asked. He felt battered and weak. His mind felt like an empty husk.

"It is," Tarik confirmed.

"But, why the kids?" Dex asked. "Why are you trying to teach people the First Tongue?"

"Don't you see?" Tarik asked. "God left in exchange for free will."

"He wanted someone to take over the world," Daphna explained, turning to her brother. "He wanted someone to use the First Tongue to enslave everyone. If no one has free will, then God might come back."

"He'd have no reason to stay in his Heaven," Tarik said with an almost childish hopefulness.

"When the world's population grew," he explained, "I left the Book laying by a well in a village not too far from here. I knew it would quickly find its way into the hands of someone who could use it."

"That's why all those great achievements happened in this region," Daphna said, "the first writing and laws and all that."

"Not my intention," Tarik said, "but there's a lot in that Book. I waited centuries, hiding here, but it didn't work out. Eventually, I decided to take a more active role, so I tracked down the Book and trained some child geniuses. I knew one of them would ultimately prove the master of the others, and I hoped that person would go on to master the world."

"You never cared about those kids," Dex

snarled. "You didn't care if Rash's side won and turned everyone on Earth into brainless drones!"

"On the contrary, that's exactly what I hoped for, though had the other faction proven victorious, they might have achieved similar, if more benevolent, ends. All along I've known there would have to be sacrifices. I know this is what God wants because he has kept me alive all these eons so that I can return us to his original plan."

"God's original plan?"

"Yes! He always wanted to live with Eve and me in the Library, alone. I believe he was testing us. We asked too many questions, and it ruined us. When God took my proper vision, he must have made me immortal in return. How else to explain my life? I never had the benefit of the First Tongue to stretch my days like your mother did. Nor did I ever touch the *Book of Life*."

"I don't believe you know the first thing about what God wants!" Daphna shouted. "Thank God Mom messed up your plans!"

"I'm sure you've observed that the best laid plans often go awry," Tarik replied. "It took me ages to track the Book down again, and then I found it had practically been ruined with all the changing. That was a serious setback, so I decided I had to get even more closely involved.

"I had to find a willing copyist and hope he got enough Words of Power written down before you came along to learn them. It wasn't easy finding just the right man. Then I had to get you, of course, and that took a dreadfully long time. But it all worked out didn't it? And better than I ever dared dream! The copies weren't even necessary! Though your mother interfered with my plans the first time, she was obviously instrumental in facilitating the new one—you. Of course, I never thought you'd be two. Fantastic luck, as it turned out."

"Well, you got more than you bargained for when you messed with our mother!" Daphna cried. "We'll never do anything you want. And we already told you, we made sure no one else in the entire world will ei—" Daphna stopped short, her voice swallowed in a gasp that nearly doubled her over.

Dex saw the profoundly satisfied smile that came to Tarik's face. It took a second for him to catch on, but catch on he did.

Daphna, clutching her stomach, looked up

at him in horror. "We—we—" was all she could manage to spit out.

"Yes, you've already done what I want," Tarik said, finishing the thought. "You've done exactly what I want." Then he looked from one twin to the other and winked.

"You two are amazing," he said. "We might very well be the only three people in the world with free will right now. I know, I know, you probably didn't get to everybody, but it won't take me long to—"

earth-shattering news

Tarik was interrupted by a dull hum emanating from somewhere underground. It grew louder as it rose, and the cavern floor began to sway. It was subtle enough that Dex and Daphna didn't realize what it was at first. They both thought they'd gone dizzy at the realization that everything they'd done was precisely what Adem Tarik wanted them to do, how they'd proved yet again to be pawns, pawns of pawns of pawns. But when the swaying ceased, they both realized what it was: a tremor.

"Don't worry," said Adem Tarik, "small quakes are quite frequent here. But that reminds me. Now that I've shared all I know with you, I wonder if you'd explain something to me."

Neither twin responded, so Tarik continued. "I did have dynamite on the little expedition with your mother and her assistant. But you said Latona told you I had a torch. I don't see how that's possible considering I—"

"You killed her! You killed her!" Daphna

screamed, snapping out of a stupor. "You killed everyone who ever loved us!"

"I know," Tarik replied. He sounded as if it was getting tedious to keep talking about it. "And I apologize," he said, "sincerely. But that's my point. I don't understand how Latona could have told you anything, seeing as how I killed her a few seconds after I killed your mother."

Dex and Daphna turned to each other, eyes suddenly wide with rekindled hope.

"He still thinks Latty fell!" Daphna cried. "She's still alive, Dex!"

As excited as Dex was, he was also angered. "Then where is she?" he demanded. "She said she'd never put us in danger again!"

"I don't know, Dex, but she's alive!"

Realizing this conversation might better have been kept to themselves, the twins went silent. They looked back at their father to find him regarding them with intense concern. For the first time since they'd climbed through the hole they'd made, he didn't seem overflowing with confidence.

Seeing this, Dex and Daphna turned and scanned the cavern. They both felt sure Latty would appear just then. It had to end that way.

Tarik began scanning as well, but he did so with suspicion and alarm.

When Latty failed to appear, the twins hopes sank as fast as they'd risen.

"But—where we teleported—" Dex said.

Daphna nodded. She'd forgotten about that. Tarik may not have killed her, but she had to be in there. She probably fell to her death trying to make her way to the cavern, just like they almost did. Tears filled Daphna's eyes. She couldn't take this.

"So my memory isn't as clear as I thought," Tarik grumbled. He didn't appear to have paid attention to the twins' last exchange, and he seemed suddenly in a hurry. "Our sharing session is at an end," he announced. "Latona is of no consequence right now. If she is alive, I'll deal with her and any others after I take care of you."

The moment these words left Tarik's mouth, he lunged at the twins. The speed and surety with which he grabbed them was shocking. Their father, as Dex and Daphna had always known him, wasn't remotely capable of such a thing. But Adem Tarik was someone else. By the time either twin knew what hit them, they were being dragged by the wrists toward the mouth of a cave.

Dexter dug his heels into the cavern floor, but he was sliding. Tarik was crushing his wrist and the pain made it difficult to think clearly.

Changing tactics, Dexter threw his weight forward and punched at his father with his free hand. The first swing missed wildly, but the second connected squarely with Tarik's ear.

Dex had never punched another human being before, and the impact of fist on flesh unleashed a torrent of wrath even more powerful than what he'd let loose on Antin's gang in the burned out ABC. It burst through his fist like bullets through a gun as he pummeled his father's face. He punched again and again and again.

Tarik turned his head to deflect the blows, but he made no move to let go of either twin's wrist to block the punches. Dex continued his assault, but he was already wearing himself out. Now the hand he was punching with hurt as much as his wrist. Dex managed one last feeble blow, then his arm went limp.

Tarik's face was bruised and bleeding, but he was still moving the twins toward the cave he'd chosen. Dexter had but one strategy left:

he collapsed. It only took a second to see this was useless, too.

While her brother was fighting like a wild animal, Daphna did all she could not to throw up. She pulled and pulled her arm trying to get free, but the only effect was to make her think it was going to rip right off. Tarik had a death-grip on her wrist.

"Please, Daddy!" she cried when Dex sagged to the cavern floor. "Please! I still love you!" she lied. She was trying to find a voice, not a flirting voice, but something similar, a voice like a promise. "We can help you with your plan!" she cried.

Tarik made no reply. He was staring straight ahead as he dragged the twins, focusing on the dark opening that was now only ten or fifteen yards away. He was muttering to himself, "Soon, soon, soon."

Daphna, abandoning her strategy, screamed for help, and when the only response was the echo of her plea, she let herself fall to the cavern floor next to her brother. Now they were both being dragged by their arms like corpses from a battlefield.

A few seconds later, everything went dark and cold. They'd left the cavern. Now they were being yanked to their feet like toddlers.

The twins knew full well they were about to be hurled to their deaths. Instinct alone renewed their will to struggle, and somehow they both hit on the same idea: they wrapped their free arms around their father and gripped him with all their strength.

Surprised by the double bear hug, Tarik let go of the twins' wrists. This let them lock all four arms around him.

The three, now one, teetered as Tarik shifted his weight, looking for the best way to shake the children off. He put his hand on Daphna's face to pry her back, but at the same moment, a voice, screaming, rang out in the cave.

"No!" it cried, "I can't let you do it! No matter what the cost!"

Latty!

She was invisible in the dark, but she was there, right there, in the cave.

The twins felt Tarik go rigid between them.

"It can't be," he said. "Sophia?"

There was a strange, silent pause, followed by a small voice that said, "Yes, Adem. It's me."

Dex and Daphna, still clutching their father between them, looked in the direction of Latty's voice. Long before she was called Shimona Wax, when she was one of thirty-six child geniuses recruited by Adem Tarik to bring Heaven to Earth, the twins' mother was called Sophia Logos. It was her original name.

"Latty?" they whispered, "are you our mom?"

The only response was laughter. Tarik was laughing, great rolling, deep-chested laughing.

Before the twins could gather themselves or mount an attempt to escape, the humming rose up into the cavern again. It was not a humming for long this time. Seconds after it started, the noise transformed into a thundering rumble, and it rushed up at them like some kind of monster from the deep. When it reached them, the ground jerked back and forth. Tarik and the twins lost their balance and fell.

The three interlocked bodies hit the ground and burst apart. Dex and Daphna, both winded, felt gentle hands helping them up in the dark. They managed to get to their feet and run.

Their mother was running with them.

The cavern itself lurched this way and that. Books were flung off their piles in every direction. Debris fell from the walls all around. The entire mountain seemed ready to collapse on the three figures staggering forward stubbornly, slipping on books, getting back up, falling as the ground tilted and rolled. They managed to stumble to the center of the cavern, and there they stopped, all equally indecisive about which way to go.

A cracking sound came then, the cracking of the earth itself, as a crevice in the cavern floor tore open just behind him. They heard a body make a leap. It hit the ground with a grunt. Tarik was there somewhere, trying to reach them.

The earth continued to jolt. The sound of rock ripping from all directions made the twins and their mother huddle together. Caves were collapsing along the outer walls.

"Look!" Daphna cried when a moment of calm allowed her to be heard. More light was coming in now through new gaps opened above. The wall they'd climbed through had disintegrated, revealing a vast and yawning pit. Daphna pointed at it desperately.

"There's nothing there!" Dex hollered, but then he understood.

"Run!" he screamed. He had Daphna by

the hand and pulled her along. She had her mother's.

The three sprinted for the hole, ducking every moment to avoid rocks falling from above. They pitched around the books sliding under their every step, refusing to give in to the ground that would not hold steady.

They were there, at the edge.

Latty, Shimona, Sophia looked into the infinite blackness below. "We'll fall!" she cried.

"Trust us!" the twins shouted together. There was enough light for them to see their mother's face. She looked terrified.

Daphna squeezed Sophia's hand. "We have to jump!" Daphna urged. "I can get us out of here. Just don't let go!"

Sophia looked at the twins, but as she did so, Tarik raged at them from somewhere close by. He was coming.

Sophia looked grim, but nodded. "I trust you," she said.

"On three!" Dex cried, pulling all three of them forward to the lip of the chasm. "One, two—three!"

Dexter, Daphna and their mother leapt into the abyss.

falling in love

Cold wind—freezing cold wind—rushed up at the twins' hurtling bodies. It was the only way they knew they were actually falling. The sensation was so astounding that neither Dex nor Daphna realized at first what they needed to do. They just fell. Had the fissure they'd jumped into not been unfathomably deep, they'd already be dead.

"What's happening?" Sophia finally cried, and her terrified voice brought Daphna back to her senses. She still had her mother by the hand, and her brother, too.

Daphna opened her mouth to teleport them home, but a gust of brutal wind punched into her throat. Then, before she could try again, something plummeting after them fell on Sophia.

Tarik.

Sophia would surely have been ripped away, but Tarik had somehow managed to grab Daphna's wrist again. All four bodies now fell together, lopsided, into the void. The only sound was the up-rushing wind and Tarik, who roared, "You will all die! All but me! I am immor—!"

Another sound came, swallowing his words, an awful, high-pitched wailing of some sort, echoing all around. Or was it—laughing?

But then the flapping started, a sound so large and looming it felt like a physical presence. Moments later it was, as the four figures fell through millions of surging, screeching bats.

Dexter screamed. Daphna screamed. Sophia screamed. They were battered and lacerated by a tide of whipping wings. None could tell if they were still holding on to each other.

Then, suddenly, the bats were gone, and they were falling again, enveloped now in a foul-smelling, sulfuric mist.

"*What should I do?*" Daphna managed to shriek. Tarik was still with them. Taking him home was something she couldn't bear. If there were any chance in the world he wasn't really immortal, it would be better just to wait for the bottom.

"Don't do anything!" Dex cried. He felt the

same way. Enough was enough.

"No!" Sophia cried. "I won't allow it!"

There then came the sound of a sickening crunch, followed by a howl from Adem Tarik. Daphna's hand, which had felt like it was being pulverized, suddenly felt light. The twins both felt light for a moment, almost as if they were floating up.

They both understood at once what had happened. Sophia had bitten Tarik's hand. He'd let go of Daphna, and so their mother had, too.

Daphna croaked out a Word.

An instant later, she and Dex fell onto their living room floor.

another mother

Dex and Daphna rolled onto their backs. Their hair was a mess. Their clothes were shredded. They seemed to be bleeding from a thousand cuts. Neither could lift their arms. The sickening mist they'd been falling through clung to them for a moment, then lifted and wafted away.

"It was Latty who fell when they went into the caves thirteen years ago," Daphna choked. She was looking up at the ceiling. "That's why I teleported us to those caves. She was down there somewhere."

"We've known Mom our whole lives," Dex said. He was looking up at the ceiling, too. He offered this like it was an observation no more significant than noting they'd lived in Portland all their lives.

"I'm so glad," was Daphna's answer. But then she said, "Very soon, I'm going to have a complete and total breakdown. And after that, I'm going to feel guilty for the rest of my life about the way we never appreciated—"

"Yes," Dex agreed. "Me, too. But not yet. Not yet, okay?"

Daphna and Dexter turned their heads to look at each other. Daphna nodded. Brother and sister sat up and hugged for an entire minute. Then they stood up.

"Why did she do it, Dex?" Daphna asked. "Why did she have to pretend she was Latty all these years? Why didn't she just get him arrested for attempted murder or something and divorce him?"

"What if she didn't win? No one in Turkey seemed to care what happened in the caves," said Dex. "Besides, people ask a lot of questions in court cases. She probably didn't want anyone to get suspicious of her identity. And I'm sure she probably worried that would make his memory come back. She saw a chance to stay with us and watch him, without having to be his wife. That must have seemed like a pretty good option."

"That must be why she never went back to Israel after the accident," said Daphna. "She told us she came here right from Turkey to find us a place to live, but it was also so no one back in Israel would see her. Here, no one would know who she was."

"Except Rash might have," Dex pointed out. "That's why she wouldn't go near him. That's why she had to leave it up to us. I'm going to get a fire started."

Daphna nodded. She ran to her room and then down to Dex's and came up with both the Ledger and the *Book of Nonsense*. Dexter had a treated log already burning, so she put them on top. It only took a few seconds for them to catch fire.

While they watched, Daphna asked, "Dex, did we stop God from coming back?"

"I don't know," Dex answered. "I don't know. For all we know, every single thing Tarik told us was a lie."

"Yes," was all Daphna could say.

"I don't know what the truth is, and I never did," Dex went on. "It was so much easier when I didn't wonder about these things. All I know is that we did what Mom wanted us to do.

"Daphna," he added, "I think the other reason she kept letting us get into danger was that she couldn't bring herself to interfere until she was sure it would stop Tarik once and for all.

I mean, we were her weakness. She had to realize that. No matter how much she loved us, stopping Tarik was more important than saving us."

"But why did she come out, then? In the cavern? She risked letting him win at the very last second."

"Because, Daphna, what I'm saying is she wanted stopping Tarik to be the most important thing. The truth is, in the end, she loved us too much."

"She loved us more than God?"

"I guess so."

"Maybe it's all the same."

For a long moment, neither twin spoke.

Then Dex, his voice quavering slightly, said, "We said we weren't having that breakdown yet."

"Right," said Daphna, trying to focus on something practical. "We better undo everything we've done. We need to erase our voicemail message and get those reporters back to put out a new message that unbends everyone, and I've got to take down the website!"

"You're right," Dex agreed. The books were nothing but ash now. "I'll change the voicemail."

"Maybe I'll teleport to the TV station and get that done right away."

"Good idea."

Daphna spoke her Word, but she didn't go anywhere. Concerned, she tried it again, with the same result.

Dex, also concerned, spoke the Word that made him invisible. It didn't work. The twins tried all the Words they'd learned. None of them worked.

"It's 'cause we burned the *Book of Nonsense*," Dex concluded.

Daphna hung her head. "We're doomed then, Dex. We're going to a foster home for sure."

Just then the doorbell rang.

Dex and Daphna looked around for a place to hide, but a voice came from behind the door. "Milton!" It was Evelyn. "Milton! I need to talk to you. It's urgent!"

Daphna shrugged. Dex shrugged. They went and opened the door.

"Dex! Daphna! It's so good to see you!" Evelyn cried, but she hadn't really gotten a look at them. When she had, she paled. "What happened?" Evelyn begged. "Did the gang come back? You're both bleeding! Is your father here?"

In the face of Evelyn's overwhelming concern, the twins had that breakdown. It was simultaneous and complete. They both folded into Evelyn and then clung to her long limbs for dear life. Evelyn guided them to the couch, and they all sat down. The twins wouldn't, couldn't let her go. They wept uncontrollably for nearly five minutes while Evelyn stroked their heads and inspected their wounds.

When, finally, they could cry no more, they spoke: the whole story tumbled out, all of it, from Milton's arrival home from the Middle East on that drizzly day to his fall into the bottomless hole in the mountains of Eastern Turkey. It took nearly thirty minutes, and Evelyn, silent as she listened, grew paler and paler with their every word.

The twins spared no thought to what it was surely making her think of them. If they wound up carted off to a mental institution instead of a foster home, so be it. They simply had to get it out. It was only when they'd finished that they noticed Evelyn was weeping harder than they were.

Daphna, despite her own sorrow and despair, put her hand on Evelyn's leg. "I know you loved him," she said of her father. "But he was—well, I guess he wasn't evil. I'm starting to think no one is really, truly evil—just wrong. I think, actually, he knew he was wrong. He kept trying to tell himself he wasn't a bad man. And he took the time to explain his whole plan to us when he was going to kill us anyway. I think he wanted us to tell him his plan was okay. He was Adam, like we told you—and lonely, and, I don't know—"

"Such a fool," Evelyn sobbed. She didn't appear to be listening anymore. Fat tears rolled down her face. "Such a hopeless, hopeless fool."

"Do—do you believe us?" Dex asked. He hadn't expected anything like this reaction. If she believed them, they might still have a chance at a life.

Evelyn couldn't answer. She was crying too hard, and all her shaking made her drop something. It was a gift, the same skinny little thing the twins had seen tucked into their father's file at the R & R.

"That was for him, huh?" Daphna asked.

Evelyn nodded and handed it to Daphna. She was nearly incapacitated by grief. Tears gushed.

Daphna looked at Dex as she pulled the wrapping off. Inside was the thinnest book she'd ever seen. And though it was well cared for, it was also obviously ancient. Dex came near as Daphna opened the book, and the twins peered inside. There was only one page, and it contained only one word. It was a blur to Dexter, but Daphna couldn't read it either.

Then it clicked.

The twins looked up at Evelyn, whose head was bowed. Her pointy shoulders jerked up and down with her every wracking sob.

"This is the *Book of Life*," Daphna gasped.

Dex swallowed hard and looked at Evelyn, who was now looking up at the twins with red-rimmed eyes. "And you're—" he said, "you're— *Eve*."

the difference a day makes

Evelyn, Eve, told Dexter and Daphna her story. She'd taken the other sacred Book after Adam forced her out of Eden. She never mastered the Word it contained but was able to use it well enough to prolong life. And that's exactly what she did, secretly stretching her days and the days of her beloved down through the millennia so that one day he would finally understand his duty to love and be loved by her. She hovered near him all that time to keep him safe as best she could, waiting. But he was not invulnerable. He could never have survived that fall.

Evelyn was a master of physical transformation, so Adam never realized he was constantly meeting the same woman all over the world up and down the years. It was terribly disappointing for her when he began meeting and marrying other women, but the marriages didn't seem to last long. Even when he married

Shimona—who of course he'd instructed as a child called Sophia Logos—she never gave up because she knew Time was on her side.

Evelyn did lie to Milton on the plane ride from New York by pretending to be moving from Brooklyn. The twins could only shake their heads at this information.

In all the time she'd followed Adam, Evelyn never once tried to discover what it was he was doing. She never questioned why he sought to have others read the *Book of Nonsense*, nor why he recruited those children, though she saw the consequences were disastrous. No matter what Adam did, her response was always the same: change how she looked, meet him again and try to make him love her.

But Evelyn had been preparing to let go. That's why the Book was wrapped and ready. She was going to give it to Adam and finish her days helping the old folks at the Home. She just hadn't quite worked up the courage until just that night.

When the story was over, the twins burned the Book. The moment it disintegrated, Evelyn said that it was so true that love can make you blind.

After that, they all went to bed.

In the morning, Evelyn fixed breakfast for Dex and Daphna and then left to file a missing persons report for Milton Wax and to look into the paperwork she'd need to start the adoption process when things settled down.

The twins cleaned up and headed out for school. As they walked, Dex and Daphna chatted about this and that. It was mostly nonsense—anything as long as it wasn't important. This kept them distracted until they'd just come in sight of the school. That's when a convertible full of Pops sped by. The driver was a high school boy. Wren and Teal were in the front seat smiling and laughing at whatever he was saying. Their skin was still blotchy, but Daphna clearly saw the old looks of entitlement plastered all over their faces anyway.

"I just realized something," Daphna said.

"What?"

"Flirting."

"What about it?"

"It's pretty much the same thing as using the First Tongue. It's trying to bend people."

"I guess you could look at it that way," Dex

replied. He was glad finally to have a reason to be so irritated with the idea, but he quickly lost his train of thought. A high school bus passed just then, and he could have sworn he saw Antin in the back seat. He could have sworn Antin nodded at him slightly, too. Intimidating people, Dex suddenly thought, trying to make them back down, it was pretty much like flirting—the other side of flirting, anyway—just one more way to bend people.

"You know this whole living trillions of lives thing you keep talking about?" he asked.

"I'm not so sure about that anymore," Daphna replied. She hadn't thought about it in a while, and it suddenly dawned on her that, though she thought she believed it, she hadn't really been acting like it. She wondered what that meant.

"You're not?" Dex questioned. "I was hoping you could explain it once and for all."

"I'm not sure it matters," Daphna replied, "but I'd love to talk about it some more."

"Good," said Dex, "'cause I've been thinking about revenge, you know?"

"What about it?"

"Well, I was thinking about how you nev-

444

er really know what people are thinking when they do bad stuff."

"Yeah?"

"And how, if you know that you don't know ahead of time—I mean, now that we know what Adem—what Adam—what Dad wanted—It's like Emmet, and Antin. Let me put it another way: if we all live a trillion lives and that means we do everything, good and bad, that also means one time *I'll be Adem Tarik*, and I'll do all that bad stuff, and so will you. So, what I'm saying is that, if you know that—all I'm saying is that the revenge doesn't feel that great. You know what I'm saying?"

"I know exactly what you're saying," Daphna assured. And she did. "Believe me, I wanted revenge worse than you," she added. "Like I said, I don't know what to think anymore. There's still something I don't get."

"What's that?"

"Why did God bother putting the Books in the Library to begin with? Just to test Adam and Eve? Why do that if, at that time, he knew how things would go?"

"I don't know."

"I mean, life is more complicated than

that. People fail tests for all kinds of reasons. I mean, look at you! I was thinking about how both Adam and Eve misunderstood what God wanted them to do, and they actually spoke with him!"

"Do you think it's true what Dad said about asking too many questions," Dex asked, "that everything was ruined because Adam and Eve wouldn't leave well enough alone? Maybe we're not supposed to know some things. Maybe Fikret Cihan was right: thinking is suffering."

"I was wondering about that, too," Daphna said. "And I don't think so."

"Why not?"

"When Adam and Eve were kicked out, Adam's punishment—mankind's punishment—was that it would have to work to make food grow. But it was a Library, not a garden, so I think it's not about food. I think it's about knowledge. I think mankind's punishment is that we have to work to get knowledge, and that's not really so awful if you think about it. So, no, I don't think we can ask too many questions."

"That's not bad," Dex said. "You're pretty smart."

"Maybe it's all beyond our understanding," Daphna replied, too embarrassed to acknowledge the compliment, "but I'm not going to give up thinking about it, even though I'm pretty sure I'm going to come to the same conclusion no matter what."

"What's that?"

"That the only thing to do is try to be the best person you can be here and now. That's hard enough for one lifetime."

The twins were climbing the front steps of the school now. Once inside, Dex veered toward the office.

"Isn't your homeroom that way?" Daphna asked.

"Yeah," Dex said, "but I'm gonna make a meeting with the Counselor. Maybe they can help with this syndrome thing you heard about, if that's really what I've got. I guess the answer isn't going to grow on a tree."

"I'm sorry I didn't find out more about it," Daphna said. "I've been meaning to."

"I guess you've been a bit busy."

Daphna smiled. "I'll help you if you want me to," she offered.

"Thanks," Dexter said, but then he smiled

back and said, "but not if I was Adam and you were Eve."

afterword

worth a thousand words (of power)

When Dex and Daphna got home from school, they found a package covered in strange stamps sitting on their porch. A closer look revealed the stamps to be Turkish. At once, they recoiled, regarding the box as if it contained all the world's horrors. But then they pushed their fears aside.

Neither Dex nor Daphna could explain why, but they both understood that the world's horrors were what they were, and when they arrive at your doorstep, they have to be faced.

Dex used his key to slice open the box. Then he folded the flaps out.

The twins peered inside.

Photo albums.

Their mother had taken them with her all the way to Turkey. She probably couldn't bear to throw them away, but she also had to make sure Adam, their father, never laid eyes on them. She must've felt safe sending them back when she was certain he was staying in Eden.

The twins turned to each other. Words failed—but the look they exchanged was magic.